IN THE GARDEN OF THE FUGITIVES

Ceridwen Dovey's debut novel, *Blood Kin*, was published around the world, shortlisted for the Dylan Thomas Prize, and selected for the US National Book Foundation's prestigious '5 Under 35' honours list. The *Wall Street Journal* has named her as one of their 'artists to watch'. Her collection of stories, *Only the Animals*, was described by the *Guardian* as a 'dazzling, imagined history of humans' relationship with animals'. She lives in Sydney, Australia.

ALSO BY CERIDWEN DOVEY

Blood Kin
Only the Animals

Ceridwen Dovey

IN THE GARDEN OF THE FUGITIVES

HAMISH HAMILTON
an imprint of
PENGUIN BOOKS

HAMISH HAMILTON

UK | USA | Canada | Ireland | Australia
India | New Zealand | South Africa

Hamish Hamilton is part of the Penguin Random House group of companies
whose addresses can be found at global.penguinrandomhouse.com.

First published in Australia by Penguin Random House Australia Pty Ltd, 2018
First published in Great Britain by Hamish Hamilton, 2018

001

A CIP catalogue record for this book is available from the British Library

TRADE PAPERBACK ISBN: 978–0–241–32517–9

www.greenpenguin.co.uk

'And, as lovers of volcanos know, radical change
is always worth watching.'

INGA CLENDINNEN
Tiger's Eye

Given our history, Vita, I'm aware you may decide not to read this. I turned seventy this past May, though I don't expect you to care. For me this long-anticipated leap year (MMXX, as the Romans would have written it) has brought unwelcome news. The rest of humankind advances bravely toward its future while I stew in sickness, and in my own nostalgia, as everybody warned would happen at this time of life. It's the craven need for absolution that has taken me by surprise. My thoughts are tuned ever more to Kitty, and to you. I am not a religious man, yet here I am, stuck in religious mode, coming to you as a supplicant.

I have something to propose, but I need to know you're still there, that you might be prepared to hear me out.

Yours,
Royce

Since I broke off contact, I've thought about you often. Mostly unkindly. But there – I have thought about you.

You've timed your latest entreaty well, which I'm sure is no coincidence. I'm crawling towards the abyss of early middle age myself. In a few months I will turn forty, as you would know. I read your email and was reminded that you're one of the strangest, most significant things that ever happened to me. I don't just mean the money. It was the quality of your attention. The generous yet questionable nature of it. Nobody has ever been so invested in me making good on whatever raw talent I once possessed – not even my parents, for their love was always unconditional. Yours came with strings attached.

Vita

My dear, your reply is more than I deserve. It made me light-headed, poised somewhere between apprehension and happiness.

I'll be clear about my proposal. Lately, I have begun excavating my memories of Kitty, a process that has been more than cathartic: it has been purgative, purifying. It has taken me a long time to look directly at all the images of her lodged in the undulations of my brain—for years I was stuck on a single, painful frame of her standing at the rim of Vesuvius, a fumarole within its core gently steaming behind her. That was the ending. In writing about her I am finally able to think instead of our beginning. All I need now is a receptive reader.

Perhaps you might like to do something similar for me and dig around in your own past, get rid of whatever it is that blocks you. Forgive me for saying it, but time is running out for you too. I have waited patiently until now for you to fulfill your early artistic promise. Under the right conditions, I believe it is still within your power to alchemize that potential into actual art. The rewards will be worth it; you know they always are with me. I am, if nothing else, an expert listener, something else we have in common.

Yours,
Royce

My last voluntary contact with you, seventeen years ago – you could not have forgotten – was a letter saying I never wanted to hear from you again. A request you chose to ignore. I could not afford to vanish entirely, and risk losing those bonus cheques with your spidery signature that arrived every two years like clockwork. So there was never a clean break, you always knew where to find me. Once the cheques stopped arriving, exactly ten years after my graduation, the birthday cards continued, asking if I was *flourishing*.

You're not of a generation to have these reminders automated. I imagine you still keep a paper diary, ordered from the alumni association of our alma mater, with a dark maroon cover and the crest discreetly embossed on the top right corner. Only those in the know would recognise it: three open books, the Latin for 'truth' split into syllables across their pages.

These things mattered to you a great deal, I mean the signifiers of a person's educational lineage. I recall your college class ring – class of '71? '72? – most clearly. I'd seen those clunky gold rings on the pinkies of my male classmates, markers of East Coast boarding schools, modern-day royal seals. They were useful as beacons of what kind of boy to avoid. On your hand the sight of the ring filled me with pity. Those boys were parading their power

in the present, but you were still clinging to old symbols, old asso-
ciations, to tell you who you were.

I understand what you're asking of me. Mutual confession, the
inside view.

I'm open to the idea, but for reasons of my own.

Vita

How wonderful to get you in stereo again, Vita. Rudely, I've not asked the basics. Are you well? Are your parents well? Are you still living in Mudgee, on the olive farm?

I write this from a very humid Boston. I have hardly left my air-conditioned townhouse this summer. Usually I escape to the house in Vermont, but the various commitments of dying—of what it does not matter—have kept me sweating it out here instead.

The only respite from the heat outside comes late in the evening. If my energy permits I go walking on the Common, past the illu-minated softball fields, all the way up to the spray pool at Frog Pond. A breeze comes off the river, or from the sea, it's hard to tell. Almost every night there's music drifting across the grass from the Bandstand.

Yesterday evening I felt so revived by my walk that I decided to treat myself to a late restaurant dinner. Since it's rare for me to have an appetite these days, I no longer mind dining out alone. The waitstaff were extra attentive. The sommelier spent time taking me through the cellar offerings. I couldn't manage dessert but I did have a glass of Sauternes, my favorite, as you know.

It made me think of our very first dinner together. Do you remember? I had ordered a bottle of Château d'Yquem to go with the warm pear sabayon. It was produced on Montaigne's family estate in Bordeaux, though in his day they amassed their fortune not from sweet wine but from salted fish, similar to the local delicacy Kitty and I used to eat in new Pompei.

You mentioned that you happened to be reading Montaigne's 'On Cannibals' in your social theory class, his reflections on a long-ago tribe's tradition of roasting and eating their enemies, even sending portions of the meal to absent friends and family members.

'Jungle takeout!' I laughed, and you looked uncomfortable. Montaigne, you told me, was the father of cultural relativism and recommended we suspend judgment of those cannibals. You paraphrased him: while we quite rightly judge their faults we are blind to our own.

Even then it gave me a little chill of recognition.

The sommelier arrived at our table, and poured a neat spiral of wine for you to taste. I must have bored you to tears, going on about the two types of *Botrytis cinerea* infection in the grapes of the Bordeaux region. Gray rot, which ruins the grapes, and noble rot, which partially raisins the grapes and gives the dessert wine its concentrated flavor. Yet you made me feel as if it were the most interesting thing you'd ever heard.

Partially raisined is an apt description of my own appearance these days. I would like to think that, as with all humans who have not been blessed with good looks, my own rot is noble rather than gray. I have had less to lose to old age.

I am indeed still in Mudgee. My parents have passed away (cancer, heartbreak). I see your old habits of surveillance die hard, but I am almost flattered by such conscientious snooping, for who else would care?

Our first dinner in old Boston. You ordered me the halibut, made a fuss of telling me that its name derived from being eaten on ancient holy days, and it arrived before me glistening with tarragon beurre blanc. I had to disguise how little I liked it.

You were bald, or at least balding, or maybe only going grey. Tall. A mild squint. Or am I remembering you as uglier than is reasonable? Back then I saw you as nothing but middle-aged: I was looking at the world as a 21-year-old does, in thrall to my own immortality.

Near the end of the meal, you recounted the story of your last visit to your father in Vermont before his death, when you were still at college yourself. How you'd known that he loved you because he left a glass of milk in the fridge for your midnight snack, as he had when you were younger.

I'd wondered why you couldn't pour it yourself, whether this was a tic peculiar to your relationship with him or some important clue to the entire culture. America and its traditions still mystified me, even in the fall of my senior year, when I could no longer claim to be a fresh transplant from other parts of the New World.

'Why do adults drink so much milk here?' I asked. In my dining hall, I'd watched grown men drink glass after glass of milk at dinner to wash down heaped plates of fried food.

But it was the wrong question, a rare slip-up for me. I was the queen of questions, unfailingly pitching them at the proper emotional register. Questions as presents to be opened.

You stirred in your seat, and a waiter appeared like a wraith to replace the linen napkin that had dropped to the floor. You would have preferred that I ask about your father. So I did.

I didn't have to fake my interest – I *was* interested, in your father, in you, in everything and everyone around me. Anything you can say about America is true, someone once said. You can never get to the bottom of the place, you can never pin the people down. Whatever it is you're up to here, Royce, you are still true to type in that regard. And so am I – an ever curious observer.

A touching detail, the glass of milk my father used to pour for me. I had forgotten it. There, you see, we can fill in each other's gaps and somewhere between us may lie the truth of ourselves.

Our memories are always imperfect, Kitty used to say. We have to leave ourselves clues—photos, scrapbooks, journals—or our very own pasts become inaccessible, though we lived through every moment. What hope, then, of deciphering somebody else's past, let alone the history of an ancient civilization? She didn't mean by this that we shouldn't try, but she did understand that in her work she would always be on the losing side of the battle against oblivion.

In the mail today was a save-the-date for my college class's fiftieth reunion next year. Fifty years. The received wisdom is that you should only attend a reunion if you've been a spectacular success or a spectacular failure, these being the states most attractive to others. The worst is to get stuck in the middling no-man's-land. That wisdom has held true in my experience, at least until my forty-fifth reunion a few years ago, when people seemed to have come full circle. They no longer cared what they had or hadn't made of their lives. Wealth was hardly mentioned—the sheen of it had worn off. Conversations were open, honest. Even those who had previously turned their backs on their college experience now felt wistful about those years.

At the Friday night barbecue several classmates, newly bereaved, asked my advice on how to live alone. We were being served lamb koftas by undergraduates working the reunions, just as you once did. In the courtyard lit with lanterns, I yearned for Kitty. Each time somebody tapped me on the shoulder I held my breath and hoped it might be her forever youthful ghost.

All I could recommend to my classmates as a tonic for loneliness was travel, but if you're not used to it, the vertigo of being in a strange place can make you feel as if you've paid for a seat in the boat on the River Styx and are heading toward the underworld's marshlands. Journeys need a point, a narrative arc. I was always traveling to be near Kitty, or to catch a glimpse of you.

I won't make it to my reunion next year. I've been agonizing over what to write as my personal entry for the yearbook. It will be my last message to my peers, yet when I think of what to say I keep lapsing into cliché. If I submit anything at all, perhaps it should be a sketch I once made of a mosaic skeleton on the wall of a villa outside Pompeii. The skeleton is reclining with a lurid, toothy grin as if at a feast, cup full. The Latin inscription reads *Enjoy your life*. Which made Kitty and me laugh at the time. How self-evident! But it is the only good advice the old have to give.

You've been waiting for me to respond to your prompt, haven't you? The bottle of Sauternes. The first of your unwanted gifts to me. It set off warning bells that the time I'd been spending with you was not quite kosher, not within the realm of normal interaction between an applicant to the Lushington Foundation and its founder.

It arrived near the end of my second-last semester of college. I'd cycled back from my final class of the week, following the salt trail along the path to avoid slick ice. The campus bus passed me and I glanced up at the resigned faces of my fellow Plaza residents, condemned to live in the ugly buildings far from the action of the main campus and the desirable dormitories along the river.

It was already dark, a December gloom, but as I flew along, the streetlights came on in unison and the snowbanks began to sparkle. Even on a bad day, in that world, at that age, everything meant something. I was at the centre of things.

I had been thinking about my seminar on narrative non-fiction cinema. Most of the other students wanted to be auteur filmmakers, inserting themselves into their documentaries as subject, character or guide, sometimes faux-heroic, sometimes as cheeky trickster figures. A confessional style of filmmaking was ascendant. It was the dawn of the age of baring it all.

I liked my classmates' work but I felt an ethical obligation to leave myself *out* of my films. No voice-over, no narration, no intrusion. Just observational footage. Film as an impersonal research instrument or an artist's scalpel making shapes from the world's putty.

'What about adding in some music?' someone in the class had suggested after I screened a montage of the wine farm footage I'd filmed the past summer in Paarl, near Cape Town. Close-ups of the vine stokkies in buckets of water, medium shots of them newly planted in the soil, wider panning shots of the vineyard land-scape. I had held these shots for a very long time. The class had practically fallen asleep. The professor praised the attentiveness of the footage, though he too seemed puzzled by my refusal to include any scrap of my own positioning. During the break, he asked me kindly, 'Are you getting what you hoped you would out of this class?'

The bottle was waiting for me at the front desk of my dormi-tory building. The store had sent it wrapped in clear cellophane. An ex-boyfriend with whom I remained friends was at the desk, examining the label with interest.

'From a secret admirer,' he said, handing it over.

I was aware that my eyes were watering from the cold. My mind was elsewhere, my stomach was empty, and there I was holding a thirty-year-old bottle of wine.

I knew immediately it was from you.

Did I take some pleasure in seeing that my ex-boyfriend was intimidated by this expensive gift, that it made him wonder if there were things about me he'd overlooked? I had broken up with him because he said I wasn't adventurous enough in bed. He kept asking me to kiss with my mouth open wider, which frankly was exhausting. You kiss how you kiss.

My two roommates and I drank the wine with a reckless abandon that I encouraged. One of them, who knew something about the vintage, suggested I save it for a special occasion. But my mood had turned savage. Was this gift meant to be a tribute to my fieldwork on the wine farm the previous summer, a taste of the high life to take the edge off spending time around the poor? Or a reminder that I was on campus by invitation only, my financial aid package made possible by donations from committed alumni like you?

I needed you to give me a Lushington fellowship. At the information evening earlier in the semester, the room packed with girls like me with hungry eyes, I watched you closely. The eunuch wizard in a coven of clever witches. I could live for two years off the initial grant, buy a video camera of my own. And, we were told, if Fellows kept delivering according to certain metrics of performance, they would keep being rewarded, every two years for a decade – bonuses for proven career gains, pure and simple.

Yet I wasn't always going to play Eliza to your Henry, hoping one day to pass as a proper lady. So in the living room of our coveted senior suite (our own bedrooms around a communal area, the recompense for enduring years of bunk beds and room-shares), we drank the Sauternes straight from the bottle, passing it around like the end of a keg hose.

It was a Friday evening. The wine was too rich. It began to snow again, and instead of going out we ended up going to bed early. In the morning we stumbled sleepy-eyed downstairs to the dining hall to fill our trays with bagels and pink grapefruits sliced in half, taking our everyday abundance for granted.

I meant to say in my last note how sorry I was to hear about your parents. Enough time has gone by since my own parents' dramatic deaths for me to be able to think of them only as having passed, without the precise pain of my loss. No matter how it happens, for only children like you and me it's more than usually destabilizing.

I have just returned from my final meeting as a board member of the Herreford Natural History Museum. I thought of you on the car journey to Salem. It was sleeting, I think, when we drove there during your winter break, near the start of your last semester at college. You had your glasses on, your first pair, and I sensed you still felt not quite yourself in them.

We stopped for a quick lunch in that coffeehouse where people looked askance at us. The way we spoke to each other must have seemed too intense for us to be related. I felt them wondering what about me was so fascinating that a young woman could listen so carefully, maintain eye contact for so long. In my work with the Foundation, I had always been surrounded by interesting young women, but most of them didn't ask much about my life beyond the bare outlines. Our conversations, though, yours and mine, felt like a dance, a fertile loop I had only previously experienced with Kitty. Like her, you hated to speak of things that were inessential.

Did you notice, at the museum, that things became awkward? The board's chairman had forgotten I'd asked him to set up a meeting for you with one of the curators. The secretary went searching for somebody to deal with us.

I knew you'd made applications for a postgraduation summer internship elsewhere, to a television production company most recently, and nothing had come of them. My suggestion that you apply for one at the museum was motivated not just by my connection there, but by Salem's proximity, only a forty-minute drive north of Boston. I would be able to visit often, take you to the Cabot Street Cinema, the lighthouse on Winter Island.

Eventually an assistant curator came out. She gave me a look of such contempt I thought it best to stay where I was. I knew you would win her over on the brief tour she gave you of the Native American potsherd collection.

I hoped the reason you were upbeat in the car on the way home was because you'd been stimulated by seeing the artifacts in storage, uninterpreted, rather than in an exhibition. But then you said they were remnants of a cultural tradition to which you felt no valid connection, and that you needed some personal history with a culture if you were going to engage with it, make films about it; it didn't feel right to pick a subject as if you were picking a book to read for your own diversion.

I dropped you outside your dormitory. In my rearview mirror, I saw an expression of weariness cross your face as I drove away. It had been an ordeal for you, not only the scene at the museum, the whole thing. The fellowships had not yet been announced— my power to change your life hung in the balance and you knew it, but you'd had to summon the courage to say no to something I wanted for you.

I drove from the farm into town this morning for my aerobics class, and became one among a legion of middle-aged women reflected in the mirror behind the instructor. The communal high hits halfway through and even the shy become uninhibited, counting down the kicks as we run towards our doppelgangers in the glass. We are proud of ourselves for still being so limber.

Something weird happens when a bunch of people come together to perform any kind of ritual, whether it's dancing, singing, painting one another's bodies or just jumping around. The participants begin to feel an ineffable energy hovering above them, separate from their own selves yet fed by their hearts and minds – and so religious feeling is born, then transferred to a totem or person, a god or gods. Collective effervescence, Durkheim called it. Don't you love that? All of us just bubbles caught up in the liquid flow of togetherness.

Yep, I've just used Durkheim to describe an aerobics class. (I had a lot of wine before starting this. My cottage on the farm is cold in winter, and alcohol is cheaper than electricity in Australia these days.)

In the gym, we are no doubt objects of ridicule to anybody looking through the partition. We are worshipping nothing more than ourselves, so it has no lasting meaning. The euphoria wears off fast. Afterwards we avoid eye contact, slink off to our cars. And yet going to the gym is one of the few ritualised experiences left in my life. That probably applies to many people. The good rituals are stacked towards true youth. It's all downhill after the teary high school farewells, the university orientations, the sports team initiations, the endless graduation liturgies. For the lucky, the weddings, the christenings.

This might be why I take some trouble over hosting the oil tastings on the olive farm, though it is difficult to get the tourists to look up from their phones, attached like biolimbs. The farm has long been owned by a family who made most of their money harvesting pearls up north, so they insist on displaying pearl jewellery in the tasting room. Visitors do a double take, the old purity and danger confusion, like being sold seafood in the desert. Diamonds would be a better fit than pearls; at least they've come from deep in the earth. But this family do not have stakes in a diamond mine. And so, pearls beside olives.

To me this gives the oil-tasting ceremony a touch of the votive: the long strings of pearls look like rosary beads to be counted off in prayer. I slow things down, ask visitors to hold their palms over the plastic cups to heat the oil to room temperature before swirling it around in their mouths, and tell them that an oil's pungency is measured according to how many times it makes you cough (a two-cough is medium-bodied, a three-cough more robust). I start with the grassier oils, move on to the infused ones – chilli, lemon – hand out half-moons of apple to cleanse the palate, end with a sip of verjuice. I like to hold up a ripe olive and say that each cell of the fruit contains a single droplet of oil.

Sometimes I think my four years of communal living at college set me up wrongly for adult life. I loved being part of a single listening organism in a hushed lecture hall, and feeling the body heat and breath of other students packed into the library in the middle of the night, and never having to eat a single meal on my own, not even breakfast. Nothing that comes afterwards ever fully reproduces that sense of belonging, of effortless community.

My present solitude is confusing. It makes me long for things I didn't properly value when I had them. When I first met you, I thought the fact that you'd never married could only have been a choice, especially for a man of your means, your background. Now I see that sometimes we have no say in the matter. If the person you want to be with can never be yours, what else is there to do but learn to be alone?

That dismal interview at the television production company, the one you mentioned – it felt like a warning that my years at college were a fairytale, a dream from which I would soon have to wake. I had cycled across the river, past the football stadium and soccer fields and into a place of blockish, Soviet-looking buildings. It was as if I'd crossed a line. One last turn of my pedals and I was beyond the university's magical reach.

The producer had rather generously suggested I show him a rough cut of my documentary about the wine farm. His caustic comment afterwards was that it was a film one had to commit to watching, that it didn't have enough narrative hooks to draw people along. Was this a failure on my part? Or were narrative hooks exactly what I wanted to avoid? I got defensive, told myself I didn't want the internship anyway.

Back in the hallowed safety of my room, I paged forward in my diary, picked a day at random in November, a date in my unimaginable post-college future, and wrote: *Are you happy?*

That young girl leaving questions for her future self was less self-assured than I was aware of at the time. She already had a premonition of what she would become, of what I am now. A person living out her life, no longer trying to do anything with it. A person who has accepted her insignificance.

Did you consciously model the Lushington's ethos on our university's rhetoric of individual excellence, of exceptionalism, etc.? It's meant to guarantee success, yet I wonder if it in fact nudges people towards failure, by planting the idea that you can maximise yourself outside of relation to others. Not one of the wise elders whose paths I was privileged to cross in my years there ever said to me: No human being should have to go through life alone; do everything you can to find your person, the one who makes it bearable, the one who will love you back. Or everything else will be for naught anyway.

At the coffee shop in town there's a blackboard where somebody writes pithy sayings. *Animals that lay eggs don't have bellybuttons.* This logic did my head in. I'm not sure why.

And yesterday: *Many animals cry. Only humans weep.*

I have been dwelling further on my parents since I last wrote. My mother, in particular. I would not have mentioned her to you in the times we spent together. You must have picked up on this, Vita, that it was a no-go area even for you.

It is hard to find the right words, the ones that won't reduce her to a tragic outlier. She died while trying to become the first woman to scale the Eiger. My father was so traumatized by her death that as a child I was forbidden to utter her name. I created a secret shrine to her memory, hiding the few items of hers I'd salvaged in a box under my bed. I used to kneel beside it at night. Worshipping her. She was the original idol for me.

I came to understand later why my father behaved as he did and I do not hold it against him. In my teens, I found news reports of the incident. One said my father, with his young son beside him, had watched helplessly through a window cut into the rock at the railway station on the Kleine Scheidegg as his wife froze on the rope on the face of the mountain, within sight but out of his reach. I must have repressed the memory (a small mercy).

Do not pity me. I have had other advantages, I am well aware. My family's great wealth, the power that comes with being of the establishment. My father made sure I had the best of everything, told me the night before I left for college that it was my birthright to be on that campus. I thought I knew exactly what to expect. But for the first time in my life, money could not buy me what I wanted, which was to belong. I made no friends, had no purpose. Until I met Kitty.

I used to wonder what it felt like for you, arriving on campus sight unseen, having never set foot in America before. It meant you could experience the place as possibility, perhaps, rather than pressure?

It interested me how unburdened you seemed by where you were. I don't mean you were naïve. Maybe I do.

Naïveté is a dying female art, I feel. In the half century since I established the Lushington Foundation, its reputation for jump-starting successful lives for women has grown. The young women who apply get younger every year—a trick of my own aging—and also more aggressively accomplished. Many of them, I have to admit, leave me cold. A breed of type-A automaton, claytronic creatures who know how to shape themselves into whatever is expected of them in any situation. They are nothing like Kitty was at twenty-one, like you were at twenty-one. There's no curiosity in their eyes, just knowledge that can be transacted for a reward.

But among them there will always be a few whom I think of as keepers of the light. These women have something burning in them, a zealotry. It doesn't matter exactly what they're zealous about. As you know, we do not categorize our Fellows according to their fields of inquiry. The project is all, the personal mission.

The announcement of the new batch of Fellows is slipped under each recipient's door early on the morning of March first, as it always was. I still insist on ceremonial paper, rather than the impersonal form of an email. *Welcome to the Fellowship of Extraordinary Women* on the envelope, and inside, their names on a dappled cream card, with the date, time, and venue for the banquet.

And I still do the maildrop myself, using the all-access card the alumni association has given me in recognition of the Lushington Foundation's services to the community—the digital key to the castle. I like the quietness of the lobbies and entryways, and knowing that upon waking, these young women will rejoice.

For this year's spring banquet I took a risk. I invited the first ever fellowship recipient, Rebecca Sogliano, to give the keynote address. She and her husband, Ettore, flew over from Italy for the occasion.

I had not seen them since the day before Kitty and Ettore were to be married, all those decades ago. Rebecca is now in her eighties, her youthful red-haired prettiness transformed by the lines on her face into dramatic gravitas, even beauty. Her mind is as sharp and clear as ever. She is one of the fortunate ones. As I leaned forward to kiss her cheek, she instead offered her hand. A note of caution.

For his part, Ettore, who had seemed ageless when I knew him in his mid-forties, is, in his nineties, the shell of a man. He seemed weighed down, his spine curled into a question mark. I could hardly believe he'd survived the plane trip over, let alone made it up the steps into the venue. I felt great satisfaction in being almost twice his height. My back is straight as a rod.

He shouldn't have been at the banquet, of course, and not only because of his advanced age. Perhaps I hadn't made the unspoken custom clear enough to Rebecca, that this is a night for women to come together in solidarity, leaving spouses and partners at home. It was her first banquet, after all. I only started the tradition several years after she was granted a fellowship, once I decided to award more than one a year, and she'd never attended any of the other gatherings.

A bizarre feeling came over me while I was listening to Rebecca's speech about her life's work, the study of skeletons in Pompeii and Herculaneum. I looked out from the podium at the rapt faces of the women before me in the audience, and instead of my usual pride in them, I had the sense of something fading.

This shift in my mood was not only due to the shadow cast by illness. I was rattled by the brief confrontation I'd had with Ettore, my old nemesis, just before his wife took the stage. He was still fueled by a desire for revenge that would never be satisfied, still wanting to accost me with the same delusional rant. I had thought enough time might have passed that we could meet, if not in friendship, then at least in mutual recognition of what we had lost. I was wrong.

I had brushed him off, but later felt growing anger at his comminations. It struck me with renewed force that I have no heir, nobody to speak for me when I am gone, no one to whom I can make good on a promise that they will inherit the earth. The Foundation will outlive me, of course, with its bountiful endowment, but within a few years of my passing nobody will remember I was its founder.

That was when I made up my mind to write you again, though it took a few months to decide exactly what to say. For while I was sitting up there, with Ettore's accusations about Kitty going through my head, I found myself casting my thoughts back to my first meeting with you. To my uncertainty about what happened between us. Meditation of a kind.

You wouldn't have known, but you were the last applicant the panel interviewed for that year's intake. I was tired, ready to go home, when you walked into the room.

Like Kitty, you were tall and slim but your face—unlike hers, which was strikingly beautiful—was so very plain that it had almost the same effect on me as extreme loveliness. Your dark hair in an untidy bun, dark eyes. Pale, unblemished skin, no makeup. You were in generic college uniform: jeans, sweater, sneakers. You had made no effort with your appearance. You were not ugly, far from it. Plainness like yours has its own appeal, as you must know.

You began to speak, telling us about your studies, your desire to be a filmmaker, your fascination with the country of your birth and early upbringing. You sounded just like Kitty. The details and accent were different but you had the same gentle conviction, the same steady voice. I was more than willing to overlook the fact that sincerity is another device for getting what you want.

Afraid to break the spell, I let the others ask you questions, and kept my shaking hands clasped beneath the table. All I could think about was the last time I had seen Kitty alive.

And now her spirit had found its way back to me, through you.

To my own banquet I wore a long-sleeved velvet dress, borrowed from one of my roommates, that made me feel like a character in an Austen novel. For the first time in my life, I had my hair done at a salon, in a loose chignon. Another roommate put make-up on me, eyeshadow and bronzer from her apothecary in our shared bathroom cabinet. They stood around smiling radiantly at me as I gathered my handbag to go, happy to see me putting my best foot forwards for once.

They didn't know there was a secret society out there of men like you. Men who congratulated themselves on seeing something in me that they believed nobody else could. My appearance unsettled them, or rather, my quiet confidence in spite of it. These men became fascinated by the disjuncture between my outward and inward worlds. They saw my face as a blankness onto which they could project whatever they wanted. They thought they alone had solved the enigma of it, that it was a disguise for something else, the more valuable for being hidden from view. They wanted to rip it off like a mask, make me show them who I really was. I used to let this happen, even encourage it.

The banquet that year was held in a meeting hall in the Masonic Grand Lodge, at the edge of the Common. There was still ice in the cracks of the cobbles outside the entrance, the sick joke of a

Boston spring. In the hall, there were glass bowls filled with glass pebbles reflecting the light from the chandeliers. The dead masons must have been revolving in their graves, for there were women everywhere, hardly a man in sight. Women of all ages, shapes, sizes, colours. Women in evening gowns and cocktail dresses, shiny pantsuits and long skirts. Years and years worth of Fellows, all there to celebrate the newest members of the cult.

I spotted you across the room. It was the first time I'd seen you since the night I spent in your townhouse. You were walking towards the bar like a king with a hundred daughters, but you were searching for somebody – Cordelia, the one who has not salted the meat. You stopped in your tracks, excused yourself from the little retinue around you, and made your way to me.

Your face fell as you studied mine. Wordlessly you handed me your handkerchief.

In the bathroom, I looked at my reflection. I considered wiping off the make-up and giving you back your handkerchief folded in half, the inside of it all black and blue – the spoils of war. Instead I binned it and went back out in my garish, made-up glory.

I told my backstory over and over that evening, as did the other new Fellows. Women kept stopping by our table to congratulate us. At a certain point, we had to get up onstage and describe the project we planned to work on during the following year. We were the usual suspects. A world-class ski jumper; a theologian studying the positive health effects of prayer; a musician who had invented a new instrument rapidly gaining in popularity somewhere in India; a social entrepreneur who planned to deliver free childcare in Detroit. And me. The ethnographic filmmaker about to return to my beloved homeland of South Africa (it was easier to leave out the Australian part of my history entirely) and give voice to the grateful voiceless, make documentaries of such emotional and artistic power they would change the world!

Am I ruining this with my cynicism? On that night, I meant every earnest word I said, regardless of my misgivings about you.

It has not escaped my notice, I should say, that the women you've cared most deeply about in your life – your mother, Kitty – were long dead by my age. No wonder you see it as your duty to remind your Fellows that the decade of our twenties is more precious than we know, that those years should never be wasted. And yet I ended up wasting them.

You say you have been writing about Kitty, whose beauty you do not need to describe to me. Thanks to you, I still receive the Foundation gazette each year, announcing yet another new batch of extraordinary Fellows about to be let loose upon the world, with Kitty gazing out from the cover. Her face is burned into my retina. Those piercing blue eyes offset by her black hair.

Have you been waiting all this time for me to ask? Tell me about the Kitty Lushington *you* knew.

I first set eyes on Katherine Margot Lushington through the doorway of the suite opposite mine in McEvoy House. It was the start of 1970, halfway through my third year of college. I'd returned from winter break ready for the slog of reading period before finals, but not much studying happened that week, anywhere in the university, for we had been thrust into an experiment in coeducational living. For the first time, a few students from the women's residences at the Plaza, your old dwelling place, had been allowed to move into the men's river houses.

It was very sudden, the change. We'd shared classes and extracurriculars for years, but living and eating arrangements had remained segregated. Male students were only allowed to visit female students in their rooms on Sundays—door open, three feet on the floor at all times. When a man brought along a girl to eat with him in the all-male Freshman Union, the practice was to chime our forks against the glasses if she was attractive. My own clinking was always melancholy. I had never asked a girl to join me there for a meal.

So I was flustered by the sight of Kitty smiling at me as she unpacked a box in her living room, her suite door propped open.

Looking back, she must have been nervous—not all the male students supported this experiment. There had been rumors that some of them were planning to urinate against the doors of suites harboring women. She may have left her door open as a pre-emptive measure.

'I can't believe how much space there is,' she said to me. 'You know how cramped our singles are at the Plaza.'

My expression must have revealed that I had not been into anybody's room at the Plaza. I think that's when Kitty decided to befriend me. And I knew I'd made a mistake, that she would never see me as a romantic prospect.

We began to play squash together once a week. Kitty was a natural athlete. She'd been a figure skater in her youth, and still sometimes spent time on the ice during the men's hockey off-season, when the rink was empty. Her squash technique wasn't great, but her graceful athleticism got her through.

The court was in the building's basement, cold in winter, cool in spring. The first time we played, she wore her tennis whites and leg-warmers, leaving a goose-bumped stretch of her thighs bare. She used to tap my back gently with her racket when I played a good point, a gesture of encouragement rather than flirtation. I think she was proud of herself for making a friend of the opposite sex—for what else was the coed living experiment about if not this, playing a game of squash before dinner with a guy from across the hall?

It was the same when she answered her suite door still in her bathrobe, or invited me to have coffee in the common room while she painted her toenails. At times it was physically painful for me to be around her. During the earliest phase of my infatuation, I would wake in the middle of the night and vomit into the trash can by my bed, as if my body could not cope with the constant need I felt for her.

My yearning wasn't only sexual in nature. It felt classical, ancient, as if I'd been waiting for Kitty my whole young life. As if she were my soul mate. An overused term, but still the only one that will do in some cases.

The frustration I felt at her friendly indifference to my passion is difficult to describe. Sometimes it made me want to kill myself, an internalization of her reflecting back to me what I'd always suspected I was: a placeholder, jinxed to be the one on whose shoulder she would cry but never the one about whom she would weep. Sometimes it made me want to kill her. Not because I wanted to cause her pain, that was the last thing I wanted, but because of the fanatic's false belief that no man deserved her, and therefore she would be safer dead, safe from suffering.

It was a politically turbulent time on campus, but I remember little of that. I had the immunity of the very rich; I was never in danger of being drafted. People forget that the student movements of those years were another kind of exclusive club, and even if I'd wanted to get involved, the gatekeepers didn't want people like me hanging around, ruining their fun. In that sense, Kitty and I were similar, disengaged from the politics of the day. Her roommate got into militant feminism that spring, based in part on her experience of coed life, but Kitty wasn't interested in joining a movement. Her desire to be an archaeologist meant her gaze was already turned away from the struggles of the present, back into the very distant past.

I knew from the beginning that she was hiding something. It drew me closer to her—after all, I had been trained by my father to conceal the circumstances of my mother's death. I invented a reason to see Kitty's student file at the registrar's office, saying I was considering her for an internship at my father's firm. In the fellowship biography I wrote for her much later, I stuck to the script she preferred, that the Lushingtons had been in Charleston a long while, a grand old Southern lineage.

In fact, as I learned from her college application essay in the file, her family lived in a hardscrabble part of that port city. She'd won an academic scholarship to a good junior high school and learned to skate at the only ice rink in the county, on breaks from her job working the till. There was no inherited wealth. She was at college on a scholarship of some kind.

Whenever I could after that, I found excuses to spend money on her—dinners out, flowers, jewelry, wine, silk scarves, things most women will accept if they're given as tributes, without expectations. I pretended I wanted nothing in return, and she must have believed me.

That spring, soon after we met, she invited me to study with her on weekends in the stacks of the oldest library on campus. She would roam between the bookshelves to stretch her legs, sometimes not coming back for hours. It was a sort of game for us; she always knew I would come to find her. Most often she would be sitting cross-legged on the floor in the ancient history section, fallen through a trapdoor to the past.

It consumed her, and the heat of her engagement threw some reflected light onto my own gray, bloodless major of economics, inspiring me to work harder and show I was serious. Yet it singed me too, left me blackened at the edges, for when she was lost in history she was also lost to me.

It's past midnight, I must go. I'd like to know a little more of your life in Mudgee when you next write. A charming place, or so I've been told.

Do you really think I didn't know that was you, in the baseball cap and sunglasses, sitting at the back of the tasting room and sipping oil from a paper cup? Of course you couldn't resist leaving a clue that you'd been to see me, a boast about your restraint in keeping your distance. The bracelet of poppy seed pearls in a felt bag (and the receipt, so nobody could claim I'd stolen it from the display case) on the doormat of my cottage. I started work very early that day – we were mid-harvest. I trod on the bag with my boots in the dawn dark and heard a crunch as the pearls popped off their strands. That was a long time ago now.

To people just passing through, Mudgee *is* charming. The town's quaint sandstone buildings and wide streets, and, further out, the wineries and orchards in perfect rows, the shaded paths along the Cudgegong River. The natural beauty of the surroundings blinds most casual visitors to the town's unexpected strangeness, its schizoid social self. Itinerant labourers, gentleman farmers, amateur winemakers, corporate wine overseers, fly-in-fly-out mine workers, tree-changers, bogans, all bumping up against one another. There's the cheap cafe serving pies next to a hipster cafe serving artisanal brews. The old shitty pub with greasy carpets and pokies beside an organic wine bar. The farmers' market displays vegetables with authentically soiled roots and handmade cheese, but the explosions from the coal mines ringing the valley regularly destroy the peace.

I fit in here because I, too, am caught between identities.

In winter I spend each workday on my feet, brushing the tops of the olive trees with a rake so the drupes fall to the plastic sheet beneath. The table olive varietals have to be picked by hand, then cured in rainwater and salt for a year.

When I first moved to Mudgee and found employment on the farm, my parents were baffled by my decision to do the manual work I had previously been motivated to capture on film. They couldn't understand why I wouldn't touch my video camera. They worried in their loving, protective way that my lack of intellectual or artistic productivity would mean that the Lushington bonus cheques would stop being sent. (They didn't know what I knew, that no matter how little I did in those years, the bonuses would still arrive right on time.)

They tried hard to pretend I hadn't become unknowable to them when they visited from Sydney, and seemed reassured to see other young people drifting around, some of them also overeducated, raised to live a life of the mind but now working seasonally on farms, attracted to the philosophy of life on the land.

'Is it because you no longer want to live at a remove from what you think of as real work, work done by people who are not in the game of self-actualisation?' my psychologist father asked me.

'Maybe this will make your powers of observation stronger when you pick up your camera again,' my mother, a musician, would say hopefully.

A while ago, after they had passed away, I spotted a flyer in the Mudgee library with the title 'Parents are People Too' – a resource for struggling new mums and dads. It almost made me cry, right there at the front desk. I had always prided myself on my ability to think of my parents as people, but had I really succeeded? At some level I preferred to keep them in place as archetypes – there to further my story, not their own.

This afternoon, once I'd finished work in the groves, I climbed into the loft of my cottage and went through the plastic tub containing the remnants of my four years of the best college education in the world. There were stacks and stacks of used MiniDV tapes, a format now so obsolete I'll never know what's on them. Notebooks, syllabi, photocopied articles from reading lists which no longer make much sense to me. I felt very stupid, struggling to understand the dense paragraphs of academic text and even my lecture notes, filled as they are with exclamation marks and asterisks, the symbols of my elation at grasping a thought and holding it for a moment in a fizzing, charged brain.

It strikes me now that thought is so much closer to image than to language. I wonder if that's what I once found attractive about film as a medium – that it suggested to me there might be a means of testing whether others were led by the physical evidence to the same mental picture of the universe. A way of saying: Here's what I think and see. Do you see it too?

You're right about it being difficult to attribute personhood to parents, perhaps to anybody but ourselves. We all secretly believe we are more real, in a material sense, than anyone else. It's a glitch in our species, how mysterious we remain to one another. I believe that love, or desire, if you want to call it that, is the fugue state in which we try to show someone: I am as real as you. For a while, in that state, we can trust in the possibility that they share with us true personhood. But not forever.

It had long been Kitty's plan to spend the summer at the end of her third year of college in Pompeii, where one of her archaeology professors was running a demonstration dig for international students, re-excavating a domestic residence. I had been dreading the separation, and when a classmate of Kitty's who was meant to be going with her suddenly dropped out, I seized the opportunity, making a case to the professor that I go instead, with Kitty's urging. Since I had no training, I wouldn't be allowed to help on the dig except with the most basic tasks, Professor Abbiati said, and I'd have to pay for my living expenses.

I wrote my father and asked for funding, which he gave along with a dry comment that he hoped my summer in Italy would be cooler than the previous autumn, his way of letting me know that he was not unaware of the factory strikes and bombings and student occupations, which in fact had entirely escaped my notice. Abbiati had assured his students things would be fine—much of Italy's turmoil was in the industrial north. And Pompeii was a microcosm, he said, with its own ways of doing things.

I had already bought Kitty's plane ticket, as an early birthday present. She hesitated when I gave it to her—my first gift of such magnitude—but she was smart enough to know that rich people don't kick up a fuss about having things paid for on their behalf.

On the flight over, I couldn't believe my luck. There beside me was Kitty, reading and smoking, every now and then gazing out the window. I could smell her perfume, a jasmine blend she loved; I had recently given her a vial. She was wearing a wide-necked shift that showed her collarbones. I was in a suit and tie: people still dressed up for flights back then, if you can believe it. At dinner, we shared a bottle of good wine, and over coffee we studied maps of Pompeii and discussed Abbiati's expedition notes, which I still have in my possession.

'Before it was accidentally rediscovered in the eighteenth century, Pompeii had for many centuries been a lost city, as fabled as Atlantis,' the professor had written. 'Its original location had been obscured by the changed coastline, which was pushed outward by almost a mile. The river port and shallow bay to the south had been filled in by volcanic deposits.

'When Pompeii was founded we do not know. The usual archaeological practice is to excavate a site in layers, down to virgin soil, which is the ground or bedrock on which the first human settlement was built. However, in Pompeii, excavations have been largely haphazard, and limited to clearing the volcanic deposits under which the town was buried in AD 79.'

I asked Kitty what the professor was implying with that comment.

'He doesn't like that the modern practice is mostly still about re-creating Pompeii as a Roman city frozen in time,' she said. 'Instead of digging down further to consider its place in history. It was only Roman for a small part of its existence.'

'Does that not have some merit?' I said. 'To be able to walk through the town and see that how people lived then is not so different to how we live now. The hands of time stopped.'

'But the people who lived then were nothing like us,' she said. 'It isn't fair to them, or to us, to pretend that nothing has changed. To say, Oh look, people back then also painted graffiti on the walls, and had election campaigns and slogans, and gambled, and ate takeout, and got drunk, and paid for sex. It encourages us to see only the most superficial similarities.'

I felt my hands go clammy—to a virgin, even the word 'sex' said casually is a taunt. I turned back to the notes and read in silence.

After a while Kitty fell asleep, and I watched her eyes move beneath her lids as she dreamed.

Naples was a shock to the system.

The traffic was terrifying, sometimes three cars across two lanes, and vehicles overtaking into oncoming traffic. The hotel was comfortable enough, but on our first day wandering about the city we were flashed twice, by two different men, and saw women young and old relieve themselves in the street, squatting in the gutter.

We passed a citrus store—bags and bags of oranges, and gigantic misshapen lemons—and two men came out and cupped their balls at Kitty, miming some kind of obscene slurping. It did not feel safe, and I felt powerless to protect her. She, on the other hand, was certain that nothing bad could befall her in a place so outside her normal reality.

I was thankful when we finally got to the little town of Pompei, south of the excavations, the night before the dig was due to begin.

We were boarding in a place called Paradise, a cluster of student dormitories in a quiet compound just outside the old city's walls. I slept well in the peaceful setting, and after an early breakfast we walked down the hill toward the ancient city, following Abbiati's directions.

From that height, we could see all the unexcavated areas around the site, the verdant overgrowth and cultivated farms. Farther out were several apartment blocks and a school with playing fields, signs that life was going on as usual.

The site itself, the dense stone heart, stood out starkly against the lushness of its surrounds. In the morning light the beige ruins glowed pink. Vesuvius looked close, unsettlingly so, its slopes a bright green. Against the horizon I could see the blue ridges of the Lattari Mountains, with clouds suspended low above them.

Already there were several women with trays hung from their necks outside the Porta Marina, selling individual cigarettes and tourist trinkets. We showed our student passes to the guard at the gate and passed beneath its cool archway, then out onto the cobbled Via dell'Abbondanza, wide and very straight, as Roman roads tend to be.

Our destination was the House of the Golden Peacock, named for a statue that had long since been whisked away to a museum in Naples. Professor Abbiati unlocked the gate and welcomed us inside, where a few other students were already gathered, mostly Europeans, a couple of Canadians. Only the walls and pillars of the House's peristyle garden remained, and the site was covered with a thick carpet of grass. Within its walls, I felt as if I were protected from cataclysm.

After introductions, Abbiati gave us the potted history of the House in which we were to work for the summer.

It had enjoyed a short period of fame after its initial excavation in the 1830s, in part due to the discovery of the gold statue in the atrium and the possibility that more gold might lie buried elsewhere on the site. But over time, the House had fallen back into obscurity. As fewer visitors came, the vegetation grew higher, denser, and gradually the ruins were concealed once more. The site was damaged by bombs during the Second World War, and afterward re-excavated as part of the feverish excavations carried out all over the city, then abandoned abruptly when funding ran out.

Most of this work had been done in a rushed and unscientific manner, with little documentation or thought for long-term preservation. Wall paintings that had been visible inside the House were now faded, the professor told us. The earth had covered its foundations yet again and plants once more ruled the rooms.

Listening to him speak, I registered that he wasn't a romantic threat to Kitty, and neither were any of the other male students. Abbiati was an elderly Italian scholar who had taught in America for decades, and was devoted to his research in a monkish way. As the days unfolded, Kitty's position as his protégée became clear, as did the fact that she was there to work, to learn as much as she could. She remained aloof from everybody except me, which gave me a minor, reflected status within the group.

Vita, I must retire to bed now. I have an early flight tomorrow morning. I've decided to go for the weekend to the Inn at Furnace Creek, insane as it might sound to subject myself to the late-summer temperatures of Death Valley in my condition.

Not to be too melodramatic, but this will be my final chance to travel. The last time I was in the Valley, years ago, it was early spring and the gravel ghost wildflowers were blooming near the alluvial fans. The desert had become briefly, riotously colorful. I watched the mass migration of horned caterpillars shredding every evening primrose in their path—a perfect metaphor for what time does to us all.

I've been thinking about how far back I need to go in order to understand how I ended up where I am, and have decided there might be some safety in chronology.

When I was given a place at our alma mater and a financial aid package, my parents were gobsmacked. An American teacher at my high school in Sydney had suggested I apply. I was an obedient immigrant daughter, after all; I'd done the work, had excellent grades, a fighting chance of getting accepted, she believed. I accepted the happy news blithely. Things went right for me all the time in those days. I didn't quite realise my great good fortune until much later, on freshman move-in day, when I saw the Americans around me arrive on that campus as if they'd been allowed to see the Holy Grail. Many had three generations of family there to witness the rapture. I turned up alone, with one suitcase, so unprepared for college life that I had to borrow sheets on my first night in the dormitory. My roommates were friendly, and curious at my being almost a year older than them. I'd had to bide my time in Sydney, waiting for the American school year to start in September.

Most of the time, when somebody asked where I was from, I said South Africa, though by then I'd spent exactly half my life, in non-consecutive stints, in Australia, and had flown to Boston after four years in Sydney. It was interesting to test what new mantle I could draw around myself in that enlivening novel context, to see what I could get away with. It was the start of my obsession with my African roots, a phase that I believed would last forever. I had come to think of myself as a child who'd had no say in taking leave of a certain place, who longed to return to the source as to a womb. At first cautiously, then with growing confidence, I spoke about my passion for South Africa to anybody who would listen, and found that my new American friends generally believed anything I said about it, though I had not lived there myself for years. They were the brightest of the bright but not always well travelled, and some of them were a little shaky on the geography and cultures of the Southern Hemisphere. I was sometimes complimented on my English.

A second strange certainty coinciding with my arrival in America was the realisation that I wanted to be an artist, though I wasn't yet sure what kind. I was in no rush. A liberal arts education, I'd learned from the glossy application brochure, allows the luxury of taking a nibble at a lot of different subjects over four brain-boosting years. I signed up for an introductory class on portrait photography, an abstract painting class, and a life-writing seminar; I would have a whole new roster of classes to choose from in the spring term, and every term thereafter.

Gradually, over the course of that fall semester, I was disabused of any notions of being a photographer or a painter or a life-writer. Each student in the photography class was loaned a stills camera and taught to develop black-and-white prints. I found I disliked taking portraits of people. It felt archival, like pinning something dead behind glass. I hated the darkroom, lit with a single red bulb like a brothel, and the chemicals, which burned the insides of my nostrils. Every time liquid splashed from the developing trays onto my skin, I imagined my flesh was sizzling.

In the painting class, I had no aptitude for making marks on paper. And it seemed to me an art form in which labour was irrelevant to outcome: the end result had no connection to the amount of time I'd spent on it. To another kind of person, that might feel like freedom. To me, it felt too unpredictable to pursue.

As for the writing seminar, in which a circle of eager first-years competed around a polished table for the professor's attention, I discovered I had very little to say about myself and my past. Or more accurately, I could not trust that the things I had to say should ever be said, or that anybody would care either way. When I talked about South Africa to friends, it was with very broad brushstrokes: apartheid, Mandela, elections, democracy, flags, rainbows. But my childhood there was like a speech bubble floating above my consciousness. An empty bubble, containing exactly nothing. For reasons I was not yet prepared to confront, whenever I sat down to write about my personal experience of that country I literally could not produce a single word. I almost failed the class.

So in the spring, I was forced to expand my focus. I enrolled in a social anthropology class because one of my roommates' mothers was an anthropologist. On a visit, she took us out for lunch and answered my many questions about her work by saying that anthropologists were professional outsiders, lurking at the fringes of other people's lives, slipping in and out of circles of belonging and exclusion. Fieldwork, she said, was scientifically endorsed hanging out, for an extended period of time, in a place you found strange. Until you could begin to pinpoint why it felt strange to you in the first place.

It hadn't been my first epiphany but it was still intense. The moving between two countries as a child, the strategies I had developed of wiggling my way into acceptance by a new group while still keeping a safe distance, the endless listening, the half-participating, my wait-and-watch approach. Maybe there was a way to turn who I was into what I did; maybe observing others could be an art form in itself.

Warily this time, I also signed up for a group filmmaking seminar, alert to the possibility of once again finding something about the medium that didn't suit me. In the first class, we were sent outside to handle the equipment. When it was my turn, I balanced the big celluloid-film camera on my shoulder, looked through the viewfinder, heard the film roll start to turn mechanically as I recorded my classmates moving about in the sunlight. I felt a jolt of power and joy. With this machine I had the magical ability to capture time, place, light, movement: life itself, streaming into the aperture and settling on the rotating spool of film. It was like meeting my medium soulmate.

And in one of those satisfying symmetries that seem to happen all the time when you're young, that same day – in the first meeting of the anthropology class – I discovered that film could be used as a research tool in ethnographic fieldwork, and that I could declare a double major in film and anthropology at the end of the year, hedging my bets between art and social science.

I hardly slept that night. I felt I had found it. The thing I was meant to do.

The film seminar was small, only ten students. Our collective assignment for the semester was to make a documentary. We brainstormed various topics and somehow settled on the BDSM scene in Boston, pleased with ourselves for our outré choice. We hung about in a local sex shop, asking permission to film people buying dildos and crotchless underwear and handcuffs. Most people, surprisingly, said yes. There were usually three of us filming – camera, sound-recordist, boom operator – a proper crew, which gave us some much-needed legitimacy, given how young we were. The staff at the shop began to pass on invitations to private BDSM parties and bondage events at clubs, and helped us negotiate permission to film, which was easier than we'd expected because people's faces were often covered by masks or blindfolds, and these parties and clubs were, after all, filled with exhibitionists.

At our first party, held in the basement of a large house somewhere in Boston's south, I was assigned camera. I was still learning how to operate the complicated instrument and had only a limited supply of canisters of very expensive film. They had to be loaded and unloaded inside a lightproof bag, making me feel like a clumsy magician.

The point of starting us out on celluloid, our professor had explained, was to give us an old-school training in frugality as a guiding artistic principle. You couldn't just let the camera run on and on as you could with video footage. Thought had to go into framing each shot so that no film was wasted. Capture the man climbing into the black leather cocoon strapped to the table. Cut. Follow the other man's hand as he zips him into the cocoon, all the way over his face. Cut. A long shot of the table, the black lump unmoving, waiting in anticipation for the other man to begin to flick at his body with a whip. Cut. The whipping man looking at a stopwatch religiously between flicks, making sure the man inside the cocoon will not suffocate. Cut. The unzipping, the first gasping breaths.

At the end of each shot, I had to remember to pan over to my boom operator, who would knock the mic twice with her hand in a chopping motion to make synching easier later, while behind her people continued going about their leather-clad business.

A man at one of these parties invited us to film him alone in his own house. The class decided it would be an important scene for the film, something more intimate than the bigger gatherings, but only two students were available on the day of the shoot: Kate, on camera, and Agatha, who would do sound and boom.

They showed the rushes in class the next week with no sign of being traumatised. As I watched, I could feel horror welling somewhere in the region of my heart. The man had warmed up by crawling around naked, then asked Agatha to use her free hand to unzip his gimp mask and feed him grapes, and to whip his bottom with chains. Eventually he told Kate to film him masturbating on his knees, mask still on, until he came in a spurt towards the camera. When Kate panned after this to Agatha, who with a deadpan expression hit the boom, everybody laughed, even the professor.

To hide how disturbed I was by the footage, I enthusiastically offered to synch the sound and image reels. That night, alone in the film department basement, I ran the footage repeatedly through the editing carousel, clipping frames out with the tiny guillotine, marking the film strip with an oil pencil. The cum shot turned out to be difficult to synch, and I had to listen to his high-pitched whine backwards and forwards many times to get it right. It later became a class joke to mimic the sound he made while ejaculating in reverse.

The last time we screened the entire film for ourselves, before the public screening at the end of the semester, the projector jumped and trapped a single frame in front of the lamp. It was from the final scene, of this man on his knees, hand around his small hard dick. The frame went bright white and then began to burn from the inside out, as if he were being roasted in the fires of hell.

I have never forgotten the shock of the public screening. In some ways I'm still recovering from it. It made me tentative, too conscious that all art is eventually viewed in cold and critical light. I became afraid of the hubris of creation, of how seductive the wrong artistic choices can be. For our film proved to be terrible. Not because of the subject matter, but because we were so enthralled by the idea of making the film that we failed to make it well. The shots themselves may have been shapely, but taken together the film was nothing more than a meaningless montage of people looking like freaks, doing freakish things. It was a vehicle for cheap voyeurism, the kind of filmmaking we were supposed to have been immunised against.

I wanted to leave the cinema but I couldn't, because Kate and I had thought it would be amusing to wear matching dog collars and handcuff ourselves together. So I remained beside her as the audience – other film students, professors, parents, room-mates – went rigidly quiet. It was a hostile silence, the silence of an audience watching bad art. And it magnified the sounds of the film itself, every single sound all the way up to the climactic scene: the jagged shriek of an older man getting off on his audacity at engineering the participation of two young women, by letting them believe *they* have played him.

Along with my crushing fear of artist's blindness, another insight came from that experience. I had initially assumed that people got into BDSM because they liked to break rules, push boundaries. In fact the opposite was true. The rules of engage-ment were precise, exhaustive, often set down in writing. Roles were strictly defined, pleasure and pain allowed only in prescribed amounts. Even the gimp-masked man had stuck to a script of sorts in his interaction with the girls filming him; he had not coloured outside the lines.

Until the night you locked me in your bedroom, Royce, I hadn't feared you or what you might do to me. I'd intuited that you too had set yourself certain rules of engagement, and must have done the same with Kitty. But now I know the discipline it takes to keep unrequited passion obedient, that it must be tied up if it gets out of hand. How hard it must have been for you to let me go untouched back out into the cold air of morning.

Well, that took a dark turn, didn't it? No matter. Bad behavior always needs an audience.

I write this suspended miles above earth, on the Boston-bound plane from California. I glanced up from my laptop a moment ago and noticed that not a single person around me was looking out the window at the quilt of land far below. Our respect for the thaumaturgy of modern flight died out fast. Now we close the blinds, eat the overpriced peanuts, stare at screens a foot from our faces. Beneath us are sights so astounding that humans just a few decades ago believed them impossible.

The Inn at Furnace Creek, within Death Valley National Park, the hottest, driest, lowest place in North America, is where my parents spent their honeymoon, in the summer of 1949.

The inn has changed so little that I feel I know how they spent their time there. They would have seen the same view of the Panamint Range from the spring-fed swimming pool, and played tennis in the middle of the night when the court was still hot to the touch. Perhaps they retrieved golf balls from behind the tamarisk trees on the course built hundreds of feet below sea level, and ate high tea in the sunroom where the cakes hover like mirages on silver stands. They would have been thrilled, as the young always are, by the many ways a person can die in Death Valley: from scorpion stings and rattlesnake bites, heatstroke or hantavirus. I do know they climbed nearby Telescope Peak, whose top is covered with snow even in summer.

After my mother's body was retrieved from Switzerland, my father had her buried in the cemetery outside the trading post at Furnace Creek. When his own time came, his will stipulated that he be laid to rest next to her. I used to think he wanted to be interred there because it was where their dreams had already died. Instead of making history later that year on the Eiger, they made me on their honeymoon, delaying my mother's climb for several years, so that when she finally began her ascent she was no longer in the fullest flush of youth and fitness. You might even say that I killed her.

Now, however, I prefer to believe that my father made his choice of burial site in the spirit of true love.

The first summer I spent with Kitty in Pompeii was like a chaste honeymoon. Our days together took on a shape. Early mornings were oppressively hot and still. It wasn't until midmorning that the sea breeze picked up, as if a switch had been flicked. At midday, Kitty and I would retreat to Paradise for lunch in the garden and a snooze. The primordial city was left empty then, except for a few tourists, dazed and desultory, stalking the boulevards.

In the early afternoon we would return to our House to continue working, and as the light slowly changed, the buildings became mysterious, their nooks and crannies no longer exposed to the glaring sun and the uncomprehending gaze of tourists, who were not allowed to visit the old city past four p.m. The evening stillness was welcome then, the stone still warm, the air fragrant.

Later I would hear the wind pick up again—this time blowing down from the mountains, it seemed—and the night would turn eerie, animated by an invisible force.

Kitty and I took meandering routes through the ancient city each morning to get to our House. Every address within the site had three numbers to guide visitors to it: one for the region, one for the block, and one for the individual entrance. Even so, it was more difficult to navigate than I'd expected. Often, after a digression through the main Forum, or after following the widest street of all, the Via di Mercurio, too far, we had to make our way back to the Via Stabiana, which we knew ran southeast to northwest, in order to get our bearings again. We learned to escape the early morning heat by walking under the umbrella pines along the north side of the Large Palaestra, planted in the nineteenth century to stabilize the soil disrupted by the digging.

We liked to buy fruit and vegetables, grown nearby, from stalls set up by locals under the shade of the pines; the same fruits for which ancient Pompeii had been famous were still sent each summer by train to other parts of Europe.

By eight a.m., whatever route we took, we would be cloistered in the ruins of the House, doing the repetitive restorative tasks assigned during our first days on-site. On a fresh dig in Pompeii, Professor Abbiati explained, part of the process was figuring out what to clear away of the ash and layers of lapilli—pumice stones the size of peach pits—but this had been done in the House's earlier excavations. A team of local men had also cut back the brambles and weeds that had regrown since the previous summer's demonstration dig. During those lean years in Italy, many inhabitants of the modern town of Pompei were unemployed except for the summer months, when foreigners arrived and paid them to dig. Often these laborers, from young boys to wiry old men, arrived at five a.m. and worked past dusk, putting us students to shame.

With my lack of relevant skills, I was given the menial task of cleaning a section of the floor of the lararium, the indoor domestic shrine that would once have contained statuettes of the gods who guarded the household. I didn't mind. I knew I was only allowed to participate at all because this wasn't a virgin excavation. The accumulated dirt was of recent origin, so I didn't need to be too careful about how I sieved and troweled, or how I marked out and measured the layers.

Kitty was given work of a different nature. Professor Abbiati's expertise was in the preservation and analysis of wall paintings in domestic residences in Pompeii, and he tasked her with a small piece of research on ancient pigments and methods of painting. He also wanted her to take a look at the wall at the back of the peristyle garden. After clearing weeds there, the workmen had uncovered a section of an outdoor mural not documented by the House's earlier excavators.

Kitty was aware, even then, that garden paintings like this one had never been considered important by scholars. Very few had been properly described or photographed in excavation reports. Though Abbiati admired her talents, he was still a traditionalist, and his implication in steering her toward the mural was clear: a young woman like Kitty might be able to do something with it as a sidenote to the serious scholarship.

Part of the reason why Pompeii's garden paintings had been ignored, Kitty told me, was that they were thought to be of poor quality, especially when compared to the mythology-heavy paintings on interior walls. They usually contained simple drawings of plants, birds, and fountains, done to make the garden look bigger than it was by extending the line of sight. Exposed as they were to the elements, they had been repainted often, and cheaply, by contractors who worked fast and charged for their work by the foot.

The low status of garden artworks did not deter Kitty. From the beginning, she could see why research on the House's outdoor mural—or indeed, on any aspect of Pompeiian gardens—might be of value. The ancient citizens had, after all, spent a large part of their domestic and social lives out of doors, as modern Pompeians still did. And the transience of these paintings meant that any still surviving would have been completed only a few months, or even days, before the volcano erupted.

I arrived back home from Death Valley to find that the first leaves have begun to turn, though the Boston weather is still mild. Fall will soon fall, and the slow, elemental parade will remind people that seasonal time is a severe but reliable metronome by which to live. Pumpkins will be put out on front porches to leer at passersby, and Christmas lights will be strung up in the solemn streets, and taken down again in the gray days of the new year, with or without me.

Vita, I have not heard from you in a while. Perhaps I might help you find your train of thought again ...

It seems to me that what you were trying to describe at the start of your last letter isn't an unusual phenomenon for immigrants, who often say they are forced to become caricatures of themselves, of their nationalities, in a new country.

I once watched you—without you being aware—perform in a fund-raiser for the African Students Association, a university event to which I was invited by one of the Foundation's board members, who prided himself on his charitable giving to Africa. It was soon after your Lushington interview, and I was startled to see you emerge with a gumboot-dancing troupe. I wondered if it would be construed as a form of blackface for you, a white South African, to take part in a dance created, the announcer said, by black miners in Johannesburg as a coded protest their white bosses wouldn't understand.

But the performance was fine, filled with energy. If anybody took offense, it wasn't obvious. The irony could not have been lost on you that it was thanks to the hiatus from the real world sanctioned by American college life that you were able to experiment with the degree to which you might still be considered South African. Seeing you perform that dance made me think of something you wrote in your Lushington application essay, that you did not yet deserve an African identity but hoped one day you would.

It might interest you to know that I have changed the format of the essay since your time. I no longer ask applicants to write about their interests (a form in which they are all far too proficient after years of coaching by college counselors), and instead ask them to confess to something. The abnormal nature of this assignment has the effect of ambushing these young women's stable notions of themselves. Some of them crumble completely. Others—the ones I immediately put on the promising pile—rise to the challenge and embrace the opportunity to parse themselves differently. I gorge on these essays, digesting them like a rich meal.

The sin to which the women most often confess, year after year, is that their ambitions are bigger than the culture around them says they should be. I am proud to be the one who says to them in return: Let your dreams for your life grow so big they burst the sky open at its seams.

I admit I was half expecting you to turn up in Mudgee again, though the long flight may well have killed you. And then the oil press broke and my laptop froze and I lost a letter or two.

I have been brooding over the idea of who should be able to say of another person that they have *potential*, which seems to be about having latent power, nothing in the here and now, only the uncertain promise of a future harvest. Being told as a young woman that you have potential can feel like a life sentence, as if an invisible scythe is hanging above you, ready to reap what you produce or chop off your head if you fail. The word ambitious troubles me for similar reasons. When used to describe an artwork of any kind it is the worst insult of all, implying that the artist's ambitions have been exposed for all to see, yet the work itself has fallen short.

During my second year at college, engrossed in putting together my arsenal of artistic-ethnographic skills, I managed to avoid the sophomore slump that dented the enthusiasm of some of my classmates. Things were falling nicely into place. I wanted to make films, I wanted them to be about South Africa, and I believed that an observational approach, endorsed by anthropology, would free me up to express something about my relationship to the country that I had been unable to capture in words.

But I still needed a specific subject for the film I planned to make at the end of that school year for extra academic credit, and for which I had a summer travel grant from the anthropology department and the loan of a video camera from the film department.

I knew there had recently been racial conflicts over land ownership in rural areas of South Africa. A farm, I decided – a relatively peaceful one – would be perfect for my purposes. The country's history and the renegotiation of the present playing out in a single, bounded community. My thinking was pretty hazy, but I thought I'd be able to work it out further on the ground.

A relative of my mother owned a sheep farm in the Eastern Cape; he agreed to let me visit, and at the start of the summer, heavily inspired but horribly unprepared, I set off to make my first solo film.

It was cheaper to split the flight to South Africa in two, and on the layover in London I stayed with a classmate, Wilson. It was a surprise to see where and how his family lived, and it made me realise that a modern college campus can be a deceptively homogeneous place, eliding real difference. The rich can slum it and the less well off can pretend that nothing much separates them from their wealthier peers. That illusion fell apart completely after college, when most of us moved en masse to New York, scattering like a handful of sand, each speck landing in a different pocket of the city. For a while it was fascinating to scrutinise each person's landing place and join the dots of their background, made visible for the first time.

Wilson's family had a large white house in the centre of London. Money virtually poured from the taps. His mother was very nice to me, but over afternoon tea she told a story about the day Wilson had his college application interview. Hours after he'd left, she still hadn't heard from him. She panicked, called the police, and turned up herself at the interview location, the university's club in London, to find Wilson sipping Scotch in front of the fireplace with a group of alumni. Her story helped me see why I was not attracted to Wilson – he had never been allowed to grow a backbone.

The night of my stopover was his birthday celebration, a coincidence. I was tired and jetlagged and had nothing very nice to wear. I felt judged by the set of friends who gathered at an exclusive nightclub to toast him. Men ordered champagne that came topped with sparklers so everybody could watch the bottle's glittering passage, and girls got on the tables to dance. One of Wilson's friends, on hearing how early my flight was in the morning, said, 'Why not change it? Surely you don't have a fixed ticket?'

It soon became apparent that I was going to sleep with Wilson. His friends seemed to have assumed as much, and I felt beholden for being allowed to stay in his family's immaculate home. We ended up on the bed in the guestroom where I had been installed by his mother earlier that day.

Wilson did not take off my clothes, or his. He lay on top of me grinding and grinding and grinding. Sweat began to fall from his face onto the pillow. I lay there and looked at the candy-striped wallpaper, the curtains in a matching shade of pink, and wondered who had glued the wallpaper sheet by sheet to the walls, who had carried the chaise longue into the room and laid the carpet, who had balanced the boxes of soap in a delicate pyramid on the bathroom shelf.

Eventually, after about an hour, when the grinding had still produced no effect, I asked Wilson to leave because I needed to sleep. He did, very politely, and in the morning I left before the household was awake, bumping my tripod bag and suitcase down the wide front steps and dragging them to the tube station. Back at college in the fall, we never spoke of the incident. We were civil if our paths crossed but the friendship was over. We had each shown ourselves to be as foreign to the other as a creature that makes its own light in the blackest depths of the ocean.

From Heathrow I flew across Africa to the southern tip of the continent. A connecting flight deposited me at a small regional airport, where Arthur, my mother's second cousin, was waiting for me. He had white hair and ruddy cheeks and a shy smile.

I'd visited the farm with my parents as a child, collected warm eggs, watched yellow-eyed goats licking a giant slab of salt. I had also almost died there, my mother said. The truck had a bucket seat screwed onto the bonnet, something to do with hunting apparently, and on one drive – me with the wind in my hair, mistress of the endless fields around me – the seat came loose and I tumbled down beneath the vehicle, just missing being crushed by the wheels. I had no memory of that, though I wondered if it explained the pull of destiny I now felt looking out at the landscape.

The farm was in aloe country, dry, hilly. I woke daily before dawn to go out on patrol with Arthur, to see if any stock had been stolen overnight. We drank coffee from a thermos as we bumped through his land, while a few of his workers sat on the flatbed in the cold. Back at the farmhouse Arthur, who lived alone, ate breakfast prepared by his maid: three kinds of meat – bacon, sausages, steak – and runny eggs from the henhouse.

I must have been a conundrum to Arthur, a girl used to city life turning up with a camera and showing such interest in the unremarkable routines of his life. But he tried hard to be a good guide. He would pick the fruit of the prickly pear and peel it carefully, giving me the watery pink flesh to eat. He took me to his beehives, smoked out the bees, sliced honeycomb before my camera lens. His pride and joy was a pomegranate bush his mother had planted as a young bride, outside the kitchen door. It was a strangely alien sight, the wonky crimson globes hanging low, almost vulgar, beside the other shrubs.

One morning at the end of the patrol drive, Arthur parked by the side of a dirt road and headed off into the bush, saying I should follow. He pointed out a cabbage tree with horns like a giraffe, a euphorbia that bled white sap, and a boerboon with a huge trunk. At a rocky overhang he gestured up at a series of Khoisan paintings on the rockface. Shamanic figures dancing and squatting, a gourd, lots of buck. One of the figures I recognised as a therianthrope – a mythical shape-shifter able to metamorphose from human to animal – with blood pouring out its nose, a sign that this was a trance ritual. I was glad to see these paintings but I knew they would not come alive for me on camera. I needed things in three dimensions.

'That's a hamerkop, flying north,' he said on the way back to the truck. 'There'll be rain tomorrow.' And I pointed my camera to the sky, following the bird's form against the blue.

Another day, so cold the grass was stiff with frost, Arthur's workers gutted a dozen gemsbok in the backyard, after neighbouring farmers had hunted for game. The dead buck were laid out in a row, their swollen bellies popping with the first incision.

I crouched beside a worker about the same age as Arthur, his dark hair stippled with grey. His clothes were threadbare but neatly pressed, a crease up the trouser legs. He puffed on a short pipe as he worked. When I asked in English if I could film him, he said nothing. I hung around, and after a while began to film his hands but not his face, telling myself this was respectful. I filmed him cutting away a buck's intestines, lifting them out of the stomach cavity and slapping them against a rock to work the dung from the casings. Then he removed the membrane holding the innards and organs, spun the translucent bag once and laid it on the step. Arthur later told me that the workers took these bags of offal home for dinner.

The people who worked on the farm – the women in the house, the men on the land – lived in basic huts down the road from Arthur's farmhouse, but I didn't once film there. I couldn't speak Xhosa, though of course Arthur was fluent, having grown up beside many of the workers. His father had been their fathers' boss, as he was now theirs. I sensed that his relationship with them, while close, was complex, filled with a lifetime of grievances, debts, obligations, tensions, responsibilities, which I had no idea how to capture on camera. And how could I know whether a worker had given consent to be filmed if the question was channelled through his boss? How could I ask anything worth knowing?

Arthur himself was not forthcoming on any of this. The one time I asked him about changes on the farm since the end of apartheid, he told me that a farmer in the region had been murdered in his bed, his entire family shot in cold blood by his own workers. When I asked why, he went silent.

Cowed by the human drama, and my own cluelessness as to how to depict it, I retreated into filming pure process. This is what it looks like to gut a buck, step by step, until it hangs upside down from a hook speared through the ankles, mouth dripping blood that the dogs lustily lick from the ground. This is what it looks like to shear a flock of sheep, the wool slipping off in waxy clumps, leaving the animals huddled nakedly together like embryos.

I knew I was avoiding the real issue, that what I was making wasn't exactly an ethnographic film, which puts human culture front and centre. My instinct to focus on animals and impassive vistas of the land was a precursor to the silences and blocks to come. I was still outside the country, looking in.

The temptation of any visitor to Pompeii is to look at the ruins as if they're trapped inside a snow globe, an illustration of ancient Roman life as it always was, the ur-illustration. It was only thanks to Kitty's guidance that I was able sometimes to grasp that Pompeii was not timeless but, like any city, always in flux, caught up in shifting currents of politics and style, opinion and preference.

An example of what I mean: at the time of its final destruction by Vesuvius, the city of Pompeii was still reeling from a devastating earthquake nearly two decades before, in AD 62. This earthquake had strongly influenced, of all things, home decoration in the years following. Some people tried to emulate the latest styles of Nero's Rome when rebuilding their houses; on interior walls they had theatrical paintings done in vivid colors with fantastical images, what Kitty described as 'illusionistic effects,' suddenly in vogue. Other families, unable to afford the new styles, or perhaps unaware of or unmoved by them, were left behind by the changing fashion. Little did they know that this minor failure of taste or economy would be documented forever.

There was something poignant to me in this detail; it seemed embarrassingly revealing. It was like me being caught today, if Boston were covered with lava, with my landline still in place— probably one of the few left in my neighborhood, a marker for all future observers of my antiquated ways. People would notice that I had not managed to keep up with the pace of change in the very culture in which I lived.

I hadn't known about the earthquake of AD 62 until Kitty took me to see an excavated public temple, rebuilt after the quake, which showed an artist's impression of what happened that day. Carved into the marble relief was a panorama of catastrophe: the Porta del Vesuvio collapsing, a cart pulled by two donkeys suspended in midair, the Temple of Jupiter already toppled. The inhabitants of the city who decided to stay and rebuild had created new shrines in penance for bringing the natural disaster upon themselves, and gave thanks for having survived it.

Seventeen years passed in peace. The people of Pompeii moved on with their lives. How could they have known what lay in store for them? They believed the very worst had already happened. Yet the earthquake held signs of the obliterating nightmare still to come. The ancients reported that a flock of six hundred sheep had perished on the slopes of Vesuvius, poisoned by the carbon dioxide emitted as the earth shifted, as the volcano slowly, slowly prepared for its next major eruption.

Clues to your own demise are more plentiful than you might think. The people who founded Pompeii had built their settlement on a prehistoric lava flow from the same volcano that was fated to bury the place forever. The city walls trace the edge of that lava stream, giving the hill town its oval shape and tilting aspect, starting high at the Porta del Vesuvio and sloping down to the Porta di Stabia. The founders chose to build their city as compactly as possible, so that it could be defended against human threats. Meanwhile, the real threat loomed above them, its reassuringly green slopes planted with vineyards in quincunx formation, pleasing to gaze upon.

Some years ago, there was a volcanic eruption in Iceland, which I watched on the news. No humans died, I don't believe, but there was a mass extinction of birds, poisoned by the layer of carbon dioxide that settled just above the ground. All except the seagulls, who were taller than the sparrows and the snow buntings and could keep their heads above that thin layer of gas.

It seemed an important message about how to survive in this world. Keep your head up or suffocate. How random the judgment between those who are spared and those whose time has come.

My third year of college, which my American peers called junior year, started out badly, even before the Twin Towers fell and knocked everybody briefly but violently out of their collective self-involvement.

I returned to campus a week before the fall semester started, to earn some pocket money as a member of the Clean-up Crew, scrubbing the dormitories before the students moved back in. I'd been on the Crew before and usually didn't mind the work. I liked seeing the rooms with their standard-issue furniture – single beds for the lucky, bunk beds for those less fortunate in each year's housing lottery, desks and chairs, chests of drawers – empty of all identity and decoration, and imagining who'd lived there before and who was about to, what constellation of emotions might be experienced in those narrow beds.

But that week, I was wrapped up in worry. I'd started to log my farm footage by hand in the evenings, noting down in as much detail as possible what each shot contained to make the editing process easier. Cataloguing my footage in that way, I could no longer ignore the very real possibility that I had got the filming all wrong. On their own the shots were technically sound, some even quite beautiful, but I could not see how I would stitch them together into something of meaning to anyone else. They spoke to me alone, a visual document of my time on the farm.

So during my Crew shifts, distracted and anxious, I did not find my usual satisfaction in sweeping the floors and polishing them with wax that smelled like the citrus of the future. I cut corners, stuck the mop head in the toilet bowl before using it on the bathroom floor, didn't bother with the shower tile mould. I wished upon the rooms' inhabitants woe and disappointment. I did not know then that this bitter wish would soon be granted.

After 9/11, like many of the students around me, I was unable to sleep. I watched them from my window, sitting in their pyjamas on the dormitory steps at midnight, talking and crying, fretting and processing. By morning the courtyard would be quiet again. Only a couple of weeks earlier it had been packed with tanned students and their proud parents unloading U-Hauls stuffed to the brim, everyone filled with the irrepressible energy of a new beginning.

I didn't join the students on the steps, and remained emotionally distant in those weeks, even from my roommates. By then they must have been used to me holding myself slightly apart, never quite a paid-up member of any social group though I desperately wanted to belong. My old survival mechanism. But this time it was more than that. I had no right to intrude on their grief as Americans at losing the country they thought they had, at being forced to watch it transformed into something else before their eyes. It was their country, their history, their loss of innocence, their long road to retaliation or forgiveness; some would even say their fault. It was their time to mourn.

When classes finally resumed, my shellshocked classmates found my first edited farm sequences irrelevant or perplexing, I couldn't tell which. The professor, a doe-eyed woman in her fifties, asked me to visit during office hours. She said that my communication skills, which seemed to her to be good, were perhaps wasted on plants and animals.

I felt I might cry, that familiar tightening of the throat.

'What I mean is,' she said, 'where are the humans? In person you appear empathetic, and I know you're also majoring in anthropology, which means you must be interested in people in general. But in your footage there's a . . .' She paused, considering me, and pushed on. 'A kind of dissociation, if you'll forgive me saying so. What are we learning from seeing twenty sheep sheared, one after the other? What does a row of cabbages in a field tell us, except that here is a row of cabbages in a field? Where are *you*? What are you so afraid of revealing?'

I was doing my usual thing, listening intently, giving signs that I was taking it all in. But my insides were shrinking into a tight black ball. This professor had lost her nephew on 9/11. Now I had forced upon her my images of sheep and winter cabbages, which in that moment seemed to me no better than stomping on her family member's fresh grave.

'And,' she continued, 'we can assume from throwaway shots of workers' hands and the occasional face that this is an African farm. Which makes it even more frustrating that you're focusing on the plants and animals and every now and then giving us a glimpse of the white farmer's life. But nothing of the people on whose backs this farm is built.'

In my mind I formed a response I knew I would not say out loud: If you want declarations and exposition about people and politics and history, then I have nothing to say, and no right to make any film at all. In order to confess, one must have sinned – but I am unsure which of that country's multiple sins are to be placed directly at my feet.

'Can I ask about your personal history?' the professor said.

'You're originally South African but your family moved to Australia, is that right? Why don't you tell *your* story, your family's story?'

I felt the old vortex of lethargy suck at my soul at being asked to account for myself, my life, with the meaningless markers of dates and geography. How to explain why my parents had moved between the two countries five times in seven years when I was a child? There were political reasons – oh yes, all the right ones – but there was also the conversation I once had with my father where he admitted that moving around like that had been a welcome distraction from his obsessive thoughts about mortality, a sleight of hand to delay existential crisis.

And how to explain that our final move back to Australia, made so that I could go to a good high school, happened just as South Africa was undergoing its miraculous transition? It was the usual immigrant story, education as deliverance, but marred by the year we left, 1995. How to tell this professor that my father would never forgive himself for leaving then? How to describe what I had discovered while filming in the Eastern Cape, that I had not yet worked up the courage to make images of anything more than the land and its creatures, that this felt like a blameless place to start?

I nodded, murmured my thanks, got out of there without crying.

It was cold outside. I went straight to the indoor pool at the gymnasium, changed into my bathing suit and jumped in. Underwater, I gazed at the very particular blue of the deep end to calm down.

Cycling back to my dormitory, my wet hair frozen into strands, I realised that the question I had to face was not: Where am I? It was more like: Whose fault am I?

The next day, I lied and told her I would take everything she'd said into account, that in my planning for the shooting of my honours thesis film the following summer I would make sure to put people first, and contemplate revealing something of myself.

Those who are considered to be good with people are also often depleted by people. Even a simple conversation can leave me feeling sucked out, bone-dry. Animals and plants ask for nothing in return, but humans take until you have nothing left to give.

Midway through the semester, one of the other students disappeared from my film seminar. The professor was vague about what had happened, but a rumour circulated that Vanessa, an African-American girl I'd become friendly with because we were the only two girls in a class of ten boys, had suffered a nervous breakdown and was in the psychiatric ward of a nearby hospital. She'd been making a film about her struggle with depression.

A few weeks later, I received a letter in my campus mailbox. The envelope was official hospital stationery. Inside was a photograph torn from a news magazine, the iconic image from the 1976 Soweto uprising showing twelve-year-old Hector Pieterson's dead body being carried by a man running from police, and beside him Hector's sister, her face contorted with grief. There was nothing else in the envelope.

I have kept that photograph, crenulated along its inside edge, to remind myself of the blow of being recognised for who I felt I really was, underneath my disguise as a good human being. Somebody who, though not yet born in 1976, was still in some way responsible for that boy's dead body.

Vanessa never returned to college, and I didn't tell anybody about what she'd sent me. It was our secret, a veiled accusation: I see you. I know where you come from, and what has been done in your name.

We touched on this over our dinners together, Vita, but I still cannot quite comprehend your compulsion to self-flagellate. As I see it, your parents' decisions were ethical—did they not move to Australia the first time because of a death threat from an apartheid operative who didn't like your father's activism? Did your mother not run a music program for kids in a nearby township?

But what do I know, I'm American. We are constitutionally bound to believe in clean slates, to worship the promised freedoms of the future rather than think too hard about the tyrannies of the past.

I do understand that you may be overstating matters to make your point. That's fine too. I'm happy for you to share anything you like with me, anything at all.

To return now, as before, to my memories of Kitty.

Within a week of our arrival in Pompeii, she had rescued me from the House's lararium and recruited me to work with her on the garden mural. The surviving section was very faint, so she'd hatched the idea of sponging water onto the plaster to bring out color and detail, something that wouldn't have been allowed on any of the internal paintings for fear of lasting damage. But Abbiati gave his permission.

Once wet, the slender tree with pointed leaves revealed red

blossoms, and the bird showed itself to be mustard-yellow. A water nymph appeared as if out of thin air, propping up a fountain in the foreground, and at the side of the panel another bird became visible, taunting a snake. Near the top we could see a garland painted to look as if it were hanging between the columns of the peristyle, as was the custom on festal days.

The rest of the painting was gone, the plaster long since sloughed off, yet there was enough there to guess how pleasant the scene must have been, giving the impression that the garden extended far beyond its actual dimensions.

The garden had by this stage become a subject of fascination for Kitty. It took me a little while to completely understand, beguiled as I was, like most people, by Pompeii's more dramatically public aspects, the violence and theatrics of political and social life played out in the Forum and temples, the Amphitheater and the Large Palaestra.

But Kitty saw the garden as a key to daily life. Residential gardens had been important to the Pompeiians, since the design of their homes celebrated outdoor living. It was in the garden that families ate the main meal of the day in summer, at the stone triclinium. It was there, too, that they often worshipped at the shrines of household gods, built into recesses in the walls. In other Roman settings, Kitty told me, only the extremely wealthy had gardens, but in Pompeii it seemed that anybody who wanted greenery in their life had managed to find a way to put it there, whether with actual plants or painted walls.

She also believed the garden paintings held clues, so far ignored, to the kinds of plants and birds common at the time the city was buried. Very little was known of what ancient Pompeiian gardens really looked like, how they had been planted and with which species of plants. The current vegetation did not necessarily reflect Pompeii's plant life before the eruption.

This was something else I had never paused to consider in my walks about the site. It is so easy to make the mistake of assuming that what is there now has always been there—the narcissism of the present.

All Professor Abbiati could offer when Kitty asked his opinion was that Pompeiian residential gardens may have included vine-yards or small market gardens—Pompeii had always mixed home and work life, with shops built beside or beneath homes—but nobody knew for sure.

Our sponge technique, Kitty was dismayed to see, did destroy the wall painting. The remaining plaster cracked and fell off over the course of a week. It felt as if we had stolen a piece of the past from the future. Before it was gone, though, she managed with my assistance to document how the painter had prepared the surface of the wall, using ochre to make sketches, and string to get the scale right. She also discovered the mark of a coin at the bottom of the wall, the most charming detail, for it seemed to have been pressed against the plaster while it was still soft. Child's play, she guessed, similar to writing initials in newly poured cement.

I believed that Kitty's consuming interest that summer was in the work we were doing together, and I dropped my guard. The work was paramount, of course, but even Kitty was susceptible to romance in that setting. And I was to be nothing, yet again, but a spectator to destruction.

I chose to remain in my dormitory over the winter break, which was allowed but discouraged, mainly because the central heating was turned off and the dining hall closed. My parents had offered to pay for me to return to Sydney but I said I needed to stay on campus to work on my film. They always supported my putting work first, putting my needs first. Is this why I have such a thin skin? Why I fell to pieces at the first evidence that it was possible for someone not to love me back? An only-child thing, people say, but I wonder if that's it.

There were no other students on my dormitory floor during the break. I didn't like waiting for the elevator to whirr into life in the stillness of the lobby, as if machines were my only company, and getting out on the darkened fourth floor, which was lit by the emergency exit signs as on a plane about to crash. Places that normally hum with life are doubly desolate when empty. The ghosts in school corridors at night, the fear of being the last one left in the cavern of a library at closing time.

When I turned out the light in my bedroom, I would watch the shadows closely, thinking that if I died overnight, nobody would find me until my roommates returned.

I'd taken on extra shifts waitressing at the Faculty Club, which was busy over the holidays (they served an excellent Christmas roast duck). I liked this job too, and with the dining hall closed it helped being able to bring home leftovers. But that fortnight, because of staff shortages in the restaurant's laundry, I was put on linen duty, ironing and folding heavily starched napkins and tablecloths. I think I was allergic to the starch, because the skin on my hands turned red and rough.

I didn't want to complain, since there was already an awkward class divide between the staff. Students were given nametags that also noted our graduating year, so faculty members and their guests could engage us in conversation. The permanent staff, the non-students, had no nametags, and nobody at the table spoke much to them. Tips for students were much higher, though it should have been the reverse. So the rest of the staff hated the student waiters, and we felt deserving of their hatred, and the two cohorts ate their staff meals at different tables.

One of the other students, a tall blond boy from Kansas, began to bring leftover crème brûlées to me in the laundry room at the end of his shift. He too was alone in his dormitory for the holidays.

One night he accompanied me to the film department basement to see my film about Arthur's farm, which was almost finished. In the warren of editing rooms, he sat through all forty minutes – patiently, I should say, as I had failed to render the footage engaging – before making his move. During the acrobatics (it was a small room) I sat on the keyboard, and the flesh of my arse somehow picked out the exact command to delete the film from the hard drive. I only figured this out a few days later, when I returned to export my final cut.

And do you know how I felt? In the face of the destruction of a creative work you've felt ambivalent towards, there is only relief. There is nothing as inspiring as an enforced fresh start.

The impulse to self-sabotage, which must be denied most of the time, is fulfilled. I still had the original footage on the tapes, and my mind spun with ideas for a new edit. But as it turned out, what I handed in was more of the same: sheep and cabbages, disembodied black hands.

The blond boy and I spent every night of the break together, in either his empty dormitory or mine, glad for the heat of another body.

I'd been so focused on my edit that I almost forgot about the short assignment my film seminar had been given for the holidays: to make a film about betrayal. The night before the students were to return, I set up the camera on a tripod beneath my desk, out of sight, before the Kansas boy came over. The captured image was unsullied – my sheet moving lower and lower and then dropping off the end of the mattress – and the finale was my words, spoken off-screen: 'I'm sorry, but this isn't working for me.'

Soon afterwards he quit his job at the Faculty Club, and in the way of university campuses, I never saw him again.

It was a Sunday, early evening, when I discovered Kitty with her lover, an Italian named Ettore Sogliano, Director of Excavations at Pompeii.

I had gone strolling, keeping an eye out for Kitty in the Theater complex beside the Triangular Forum, one of her favorite places. She liked to sit at the edge of the small reservoir, nestled in a grassy patch between the Large Theater and the Odeon. In ancient times, on the hottest days of summer, the water in the reservoir was dyed orange with saffron threads and sprayed onto spectators, making them part of the performance.

Sogliano was much older than us, in his mid-forties, unmarried. A handsome man, I have to concede, with his prominent cheek-bones and tousled hair. He had begun to visit our House regularly, usually in the dusk hour, as if he knew the golden light would be most flattering to him.

'How goes it, mortals?' he would say on arrival, a dumb joke the other students found funny; apparently it was the salutation some old, arrogant Roman scholar had used for his subordinates. I heard rumors circulating among our group that Sogliano had taken a bullet for the cause in Rome in '68, one of the few pro-fessors to support the student occupations. Whether or not that was true, it gave him a rebel's allure on the site. Everyone loved him, even—especially—Kitty, whose cigarettes he would light one after the other with perfect attention, cupping his hands around the glowing tip as if it held the spark of life itself.

I had begun to notice that there were two types of Italian men within the city's walls. The local Pompeians did all the physical labor and lived in the workers' village on-site, or in the nearby town. The academics and bureaucrats were usually from bigger cities elsewhere in the country, and it was they who governed the site, held the purse strings and the power.

Despite their differences, both sets of men would come to life like marionettes animated by wires whenever a woman appeared in their midst, and if that woman happened to be attractive, the perking up and lavishing of attention became farcical. Italian social life seemed to be fueled by a culture of permanent seduction. The worst part was that the women didn't seem to mind that it was over-the-top, a display rather than a declaration of true feeling. They were charmed by it, even Kitty, who was by no means a flirt.

On that particular Sunday evening, not finding her anywhere in the Theater district, I lay down on a stone bench high up in the Odeon and looked at the sky. After a while, I heard laughter coming from the portico connected to the Large Theater, where spectators used to stroll during intervals.

I peeped over the edge of the Odeon's upper terraces, the peanut gallery to which Pompeii's lower classes had been relegated. Sogliano (to myself I meanly called him Soggy) and Kitty were sitting on the lowest step of the portico and he was speaking to her in his mellifluous English. Then he paused and struck with a metal rod the piece of phonolite he had in his hand. A clear musical tone sounded in the air.

While it still hovered, he turned to embrace Kitty with a violent passion that at first turned me cold with fear, until I realized she was responding with intemperate passion of her own.

I lay back down, thinking I'd stay to protect her should his attentions become unwanted, and watched as the color leached from the sky and the moon rose slowly behind Vesuvius. Each groan and gasp felt like a sharp nail being knocked into me, pinning me to the bench. At its splendid peak, the Odeon had housed five thousand spectators, guffawing in unison at the sorry fates of the comic characters: the buffoon, the fool, the rogue, the deceived old man. Lying there, I felt as if I were all four rolled into one pathetic creature.

The scuffling and sighing finally subsided. But then, awfully, it started up again.

I peered over the terrace edge once more and found myself directly in Kitty's line of sight. She was sitting astride Sogliano, her summer dress hitched up around her hips, straps pulled down to expose a breast, which he was covering with his hand. Her eyes were closed but her face was turned upward. Then she opened her eyes. I ducked, certain she'd seen me.

In the morning, Kitty behaved as if everything were unchanged. Perhaps she had seen nothing in the moonlight except the promise of her own ecstasy.

She didn't tell me anything about her love affair with Sogliano. I allowed her space, and pretended not to notice when she snuck off somewhere or was unaccountably absent from the group meals. The only hint she gave as to what was on her mind was an anecdote she told over breakfast one day—that during the time of Augustus, women in Pompeii were fined if not married by the age of twenty.

Meanwhile, Sogliano began to take a special interest in me, most likely because Kitty had told him we were platonically close.

He suggested we go out drinking together in a tavern close to Paradise. It was clear that the purpose of these outings was to find me a woman of my own.

Had Kitty and he laughed together, lying nakedly entwined, about my hopelessness as a suitor? Had she asked him to help me, or had he cunningly taken it upon himself so I would no longer be a nuisance, perpetually hanging around and getting in the way?

He asked me sometimes to meet him in the morning outside his cottage in the workers' village, near the Amphitheater. It had been a tradition since the eighteenth century for all those with jobs on the site, from the superintendent down to the guards and the diggers, to live in this village. Many laborers' families had resided there for generations, refusing to move to the new town when it was developed, believing themselves to be the only ones capable of keeping the spirit of ancient Pompeii alive. From Sogliano's cottage we would walk together to the House.

This only made sense to me later, when I came across a description of the patronage system that had dominated life in Pompeii, and which still explained much of what I observed of Italian male behavior. Under that system, a less wealthy or influential man would gain the protection of a more prominent man, a patron, by accompanying him in public, joining a swarm of men to demonstrate his importance, and by voting for him in elections. The system also decreed that every morning, for two hours at dawn, the men of lower status—the clients—wait outside their patron's house, making a show of their loyalty. Sometimes they scratched notes onto the wall at the entrance: *Symphorus was here on April 2.* A visiting card of sorts, left by a client whose patron was not home that morning, a record that he had still done his duty. This practice was called the salutatio, or calling hour ritual.

Eventually, the clients would be invited into the atrium of the house, and one by one approach the great man, have a chat, be allowed to kiss his hand or cheek, and then be given money or food. After a patron had met his clients, he had to rush off to visit his own patron.

One night, after too much red wine at the tavern, I went home with a local woman Sogliano had introduced as his cousin, which was definitely a lie. She was very short and when she stood before me in the dark of my room her eyes were level with my chest, which made me wonder about the logistics of the act we were about to commit. I suffered through it, appalled by the smells and substances produced by our bodies. I asked her to leave immediately afterward.

In the morning, I didn't go to meet Sogliano at his cottage as I'd drunkenly promised, and went instead directly to the House of the Golden Peacock, where I spent all day on my knees, working in the garden beside Kitty.

When Sogliano arrived later, wanting to wink and backslap me to celebrate the loss of my virginity, I blanked him so completely that he left me alone.

My betrayal film was a small success when I showed it in my seminar. The boys, the ones who made ironic films mostly featuring themselves, looked at me with what I assumed was new respect. My professor was happy that her words of guidance had sunk in.

In the final cut, I had bookended the bedroom scene with extreme close-ups of me cutting my toenails, waxing an unidentified part of my body, spitting toothpaste with a tinge of blood into the sink, plucking my eyebrows. I hadn't really known what I was doing, but even I admired the expiatory tone of the result, suggestive of a woman punishing herself for her sins by cleansing her body.

In the discussion time, nobody questioned the ethics of what I had done. Hiding the camera, filming somebody in a vulnerable situation without his permission. I left the class on a high.

In the dining hall, I found my friends eating an early dinner. It was theme night, Tastes of the South, and there were steaming trays of fried chicken and collard greens, and it was easy to wash down a couple of plates of food with iced tea and join in the pointless banter at the table.

Upstairs in the common room, we started drinking beer bought using someone's fake ID, preparing for a Friday night out at the bars and clubs in town. The alcohol gradually roused me from my post-dinner stupor, and my thoughts began to percolate as I watched the others playing beer pong.

I was troubled by the success of my film. It had worked because I'd made my body both subject and object, and it had fooled the boys in the class into thinking I'd broken a taboo. To be fair, this was before social media existed – we were only on the cusp of the age of oversharing in which we're now entombed – but still, I knew that women artists who traded on the secrets of their bodies and sex lives very quickly ran out of material. If I followed this path, my work would become a monster that needed more and more saucy offerings in order to be placated. Art as titillation dressed up as empowerment.

On the other hand, the more ascetic traditions of ethnographic film could be just as confounding. Turning up uninvited with a camera to film people who might not have any choice in the matter was increasingly considered dubious practice in the anthropology department. 'The story we now want to hear is not ours to tell,' as one of the important articles of the time put it. The fly-on-the-wall approach was dead even for ethnography. The fly had to find a way to admit it was on the wall, manipulating the proceedings, muddying reality with its presence. The famous observer effect of physics applied also to documentary film.

I felt tongue-tied, unsure. I told myself that the next summer, on a new farm, making a new film, things would be different. I would find a way to train my camera on human beings while also acknowledging my complicity in the act. I would find my own style.

By August the days in Pompeii were slipping by quickly, with none of the slow, anticipatory ease of June. I was glad of this because it meant soon Kitty and I would be back at college, with an ocean separating her and Sogliano. It was a summer romance, nothing more. He did not seem like the long-suffering, persistent type but an opportunist in life and love.

Each day I waited for her to confide in me, but she remained silent on the topic of her lover. Her body seemed to radiate warmth and sexual energy all the time, as if she were thinking of him, of what they did together, even when she was doing the most technical tasks beside me. It became more difficult than ever for me to be around her without my own thoughts straying toward desire.

Under Kitty's direction, our work had taken a new tack. She wanted to identify the shrub and the bird in the garden painting, to see if they might have modern incarnations. Not by asking a paleobotanist, which would have been the sensible thing to do, but by making an appeal to the traditional knowledge of the locals. This meant, to my initial disgruntlement, that we no longer stayed hidden at the crumbling House, but had to go wandering around the site, into the garden plots in the workers' village and the surrounding cultivated land.

The first person to whom she showed her drawing of the wall painting, an old woman sitting in the sun outside her front door, identified the shrub as an oleander and the bird as a golden oriole and looked at us as if we were halfwits.

One after the other, elderly residents made the same identification, similarly confused as to why we couldn't figure it out for ourselves. One man took us to see oleanders growing in the cemetery in new Pompei, beside the highway to Naples. Colorful electric lights were strung above the tombs, on every single one of which was a bouquet of fresh flowers. These oleanders had light pink flowers, not red as they appeared in the painting, but the spiky leaves were unmistakable.

These small mysteries solved, Kitty kept doing the rounds, gathering information about other plants the locals claimed had always, in living memory, grown there. As the villagers got used to seeing us around the place, they began to invite us into their back gardens. Often the women would be sitting at an open hearth, cooking in quantity, or shelling beans or peas for the evening meal. There was always a dog or two in the garden, and frequently a tortoise sunning itself. An old man gave us ripe pears from his orchard and told Kitty a story about a Roman emperor's son once choking to death on a pear at Pompeii. A good death, he said, gesturing proudly to his fruit.

Laborers identified plants that grew only in the ruins and were prized for their medicinal value. One worker showed Kitty a weedy-looking plant that he'd dug up near the Amphitheater and which he said was used for liver ailments; another swore that hollyhock flowers boiled in water would get rid of a cough. Though Kitty's Italian was already strong, mine was less so, and some of the time I had no idea what people were talking about, except that they had great enthusiasm for steeping various roots and petals in hot water. Kitty would tell me the salient points afterward—an infusion of the flowers of the red valerian, for example, which grew everywhere on the walls and rocks of the ruins, was used as a sleep aid.

It did not seem a useful line of inquiry. I was afraid she would end up abandoning her scholarly research to compile a book of traditional remedies. She wasn't a botanist—how would she know if the modern plant and the ancient were indeed the same or only looked alike? And didn't this go against her approach of keeping the past foreign, not drawing an oversimplified line of comprehension between then and now?

She tried to reassure me that she knew what she was doing. 'It's immersion as inspiration, that's all,' she liked to say. 'A clue here or there as to what else I might look for in the gardens of Pompeii.'

Abbiati let Kitty pursue her new interest, though he probably would have preferred that she focus on the painting's pigments. Whether he knew of her romance with Sogliano I never quite figured out. He and Soggy remained on collegial terms, and Abbiati would have understood that it was to Kitty's advantage to have Sogliano onside, then and in the future. That, I think, is also why Abbiati made sure she met Rebecca that summer.

It was one of our last days on the site. Instead of returning to the House after lunch, our student group was to meet Abbiati at the Porta Nocera.

As we trailed him onto the Vicolo della Nave Europa, Kitty gripped my arm. 'I know where he's taking us. Ettore told me.'

So it was first names now.

All of us, by then, had heard the story of the dramatic discovery and plaster-casting only a few years earlier of a group of thirteen ancient bodies, and of the young British researcher, Rebecca

Birkin, who had found them on one of her first days at work on a dig.

It was due to her request that these body casts not yet be put on public view that nobody was allowed to see them without permission. Clearly, Rebecca had the ears of the Italian powers that be. In the swirl of student conjecture around her request, some thought she was being selfish, keeping the casts for her own research as long as possible. Others had heard that she felt it was disrespectful to put the bodies on display, especially given the poor condition and treatment of the few older body casts left scattered around the public areas of the site: tourists often posed standing on them for photographs.

I knew already that casts had first been made in Pompeii over a century before, during Fiorelli's tenure as Director of Excavations in the 1860s. Fiorelli instituted more systematic means of excavating Pompeii, and made the decision to clear buildings from above, removing the layers gradually from the top down, instead of cutting sideways into them as had been the norm. In the process, workers discovered cavities that held the shape of human bodies. This gave Fiorelli the idea of making casts by pouring plaster into the cavities, which had been created when the soft tissues of organic matter had decayed after being covered by a layer of fine-grained ash, leaving behind a bundle of bones within the hollows.

For a long time nobody had really known what to do with Fiorelli's body casts, Kitty had told me. Then came Rebecca's discovery of the thirteen fugitives. It was the only time a group of bodies had been preserved together exactly as they lay, where they had died. She had also, apparently, refined the casting process so that some of her bodies showed facial expressions, and occasionally finer details of clothing and jewelry, unlike Fiorelli's blunt, blocky approximations of the human form.

Abbiati, a mysterious smile on his face, led us through a gate in a high stone wall behind a row of cypress trees. Inside, the excavated area was mostly flat and barren, about the size of a basketball court. At one end, against the wall, was a windowless shed.

'Welcome,' Abbiati said, 'to the Garden of the Fugitives.' With some ceremony he unlocked the shed door and we filed into the space, our eyes slowly adjusting to the dark.

It was difficult to know how to respond to the sight of those thirteen bodies.

They looked naked at first. Only a few showed details of clothing. Some lay on their sides, legs pulled up, faces pressed to the ground. Two small bodies, children, lay beside an adult. At the edge of the group was a man trying to prop himself up on his right arm, his face a rictus of effort or pain.

The longer I looked, the more beautiful I found the casts. I could have stood there and gazed at them for hours. They seemed to me like sculptures arranged for maximum emotional effect, as if death had artistic designs of its own. Any one of the bodies would have been arresting, but together they formed a sublime work of art.

After some time, Abbiati guided us out of the shed and toward a patch of shade thrown by the cypresses on the other side of the wall. There, waiting for us in the breeze, was Sogliano, and beside him a woman in her early thirties with red hair down to her shoulder blades. Rebecca. She was dressed casually, in jeans and a T-shirt.

Sogliano introduced her with the obvious pride of a mentor. Not only had Rebecca discovered and made casts of these bodies, he told us, but she was doing some of the most interesting work on the site, the first detailed study of human skeletal remains in Pompeii.

Our small group applauded. A blush spread across Rebecca's face, but she seemed to gain control of her emotions as she stepped forward to speak.

'In the early afternoon of the twenty-fourth of August in the year AD 79, this city was plunged into darkness by a solid rain of pumice and lithics, and clouds of rock and ash,' she said in a soft British accent. 'The first few pyroclastic surges did not reach Pompeii, but on the second day of the eruption, the fourth surge did. Surge clouds move fast. They're hot, filled with rocks and toxic gas and everything they've picked up in their path. Anybody who had not yet escaped Pompeii by the time this surge arrived was killed, including the thirteen people who died together in this garden.'

I did a quick, grisly head count. There were thirteen of us alive in the shade, hanging on Rebecca's every word.

'Most of them died from asphyxiation, their upper respiratory tracts blocked by mucus mixed with ash,' she said. 'Some died of thermal shock. On average, they would have taken two minutes to die. It is tempting to interpret their flexed arms and legs and extended spines as evidence of pain, but in fact these are symptoms of exposure to extreme heat only after death.'

She tucked her hair behind her ear. 'I know it's not up to me to decide the fate of these casts,' she said.

The students fidgeted, feeling guilty like me for having gossiped about her.

'I was lucky to find them,' Rebecca continued. 'Luck, not skill, got me here. But once I *had* found them, I realized I must protect these people from having false histories forced on them.'

I glanced at Kitty. Her skin was drained of its usual healthy color. I knew it wasn't only the sight of the bodies that had thrown her. Sogliano probably hadn't told her quite how much he admired Rebecca, nor how close they were. He was enjoying listening to her tale, though he must have known it well.

'Let me give you an example,' Rebecca said. 'Soon after I discovered the bodies, an article about them was published in a magazine without my support. The superintendent of Pompeii at the time, who retired several years ago, was an enthusiastic man who believed it was his job to fascinate rather than educate the public, to keep the site funded. In the article, he spoke of the last moments of the figures you've just seen, in melodramatic yet authoritative language. How the slave's bag was stuffed with food. How the two little boys died hand in hand beside their distraught parents. He claimed the owner of the plot was the last to die, forced to watch helplessly as his family members perished around him.'

She paused. 'All very moving. But none of it is based on fact. We can never know the truth about these thirteen fugitives. I cannot access their bones without destroying the plaster casts. This is why I no longer agree with the practice of making casts like these. And it's why I decided to focus on the skeletons of Pompeii instead, most of which have been stored without classification or care. Thankfully, Signor Sogliano is now in charge of excavations, and in favor of my more forensic approach.'

She smiled, and I saw in an instant that she was in love with him. My heart raced; this I could use.

'The skeletons can give us proof of such things as gender, age, state of health, nutrition, injuries, and illnesses,' Rebecca said. 'They can help us figure out whether there is any support for the theory that many of the city's richest inhabitants had already left their summer residences in Pompeii to return to Rome before the eruption. Without the bones, it's guesswork.'

Some of the other students asked questions at this point but Kitty remained silent. In solidarity, so did I.

One of the Canadians asked Rebecca which skeleton had so far made the strongest impression on her.

'Earlier this year, the skeleton of a young woman, about sixteen, was discovered inside a house being excavated for the first time,' Rebecca said solemnly. 'She was pregnant when she died. About seven months along, according to the fetal skeleton. This was her first pregnancy—keep in mind that Roman girls usually married at the age of twelve. She hadn't done much physical work, so she was most likely not a slave. She'd had one bad childhood illness, which had prevented her from eating for several weeks, the proof of which were some lines of hypoplasia in her teeth.

'But the most affecting discovery was that her pelvis had not sufficiently matured for her to be able to give birth to a baby at full term. Which means that if she hadn't died on the day of the eruption, she would have died two months later during a long, painful labor. The baby would have died too, unless her birth attendants had tried to save it with a caesarean section, after giving up on saving the mother. Back then, women rarely survived such a procedure.'

The group was quiet after this. Until Kitty, her voice unusually hard-edged, said, 'What kind of garden was it?'

Rebecca tilted her head. 'I don't know.'

'You didn't excavate further?' Kitty asked.

'The small house at the north of the site, yes, but it didn't tell us anything interesting. The garden was basic, is all I can say. No peristyle or fountains. The house and parts of the garden had been excavated in the nineteenth century and covered over again. Most of the notes are missing, so we don't know what, if anything, was found.'

I watched Kitty afterward as we walked the perimeter of the enclosed site and peeked into the ruins of the house Rebecca had mentioned, which seemed to have two discrete sections with interlocking rooms. Sogliano tried to say something to her in passing but she ignored him, using me as her shield, and later dragged me along with her at a rapid pace back to the compound at Paradise.

That night, we stayed up late drinking the local wine, which was still potent even when mixed with water, as it was served in ancient times. (Pliny had observed, 'Pompeiian wines are rather dangerous as they may cause a headache which lasts till noon on the following day.')

One of the students suggested we project Rossellini's *Viaggio in Italia* onto a wall of the garden behind the dormitories. The story was that Rossellini himself had given this rare copy of his film, and the projector, to the family who owned Paradise, in thanks for hosting him and his actors and crew during their shoot in the ruins. Kitty and I lay next to each other on a blanket to watch. My head was already spinning from the wine, and the film's plot was vague to me then and even vaguer now. The only scene I remember is one in which the main couple, whose marriage is on the rocks, watch as some archaeologists tap on the ground, listening for an echo suggesting a cavity in the volcanic ash below. They pour liquid plaster into a small hole and wait for it to harden. Eventually a single body cast of two entwined lovers is revealed, and the wife is overwhelmed with sadness.

Kitty sighed as the cast emerged. I began to think I might kiss her.

The stars above me had gone green, swirling around and around like the northern lights. I thought of my visit earlier in the week to the House of the Lovers, and the inscription still visible above its doorway: *Lovers, like bees, wish life to be as sweet as honey.* I turned to face Kitty. But she had fallen asleep.

With my renewed commitment to making another film in South Africa over the summer, this time to submit as part of my honours thesis, I sent email inquiries to a few farms in the winelands region of the Western Cape. My parents had mailed me a newspaper report about some of the wine farms there starting cooperatives, sharing profits with the workers, a first step in atoning for the region's notoriously pro-apartheid history.

One of these cooperatives, Seeds of Hope, sounded promising. A Swiss company had recently bought the property from the white farmer whose family had owned it for over a century. To my surprise, the farm manager wrote back right away, saying I could rent the guesthouse and spend several months there filming.

During the remainder of the semester, I tried not to think too much about the things to do with the project that frightened me. The manager, not knowing I was South African, had asked how I planned to communicate with the workers. 'The workforce is mostly Coloured, which is considered a separate ethnic group in this country,' he wrote. 'They're a mix of many races, white, black, Bushmen and Malay slaves. They speak Afrikaans.'

I wrote back that I could speak basic Afrikaans, a language I'd been forced to learn at primary school but hadn't spoken for many years. At least I'd have some way of communicating though, unlike on the sheep farm.

I took a primer class on practical fieldwork methods, hoping it might help me feel more prepared. The professor quickly undermined any assumptions of heroism on the part of the solitary ethnographer venturing into foreign lands and enduring hardships (hostile subjects, bad food, lack of creature comforts), but she believed fervently in the anthropological principle of participant observation – waiting, watching, listening, learning. It was a messy process, she said, but nothing could beat the feeling of getting to peek at another culture in all its mysterious workings, to glimpse (and here she paraphrased a line from a Wharton novel) the huge cloudy meanings behind the daily face of things.

I had a vivid mental picture of her as a youthful ethnographer, hiking up through mist until she was high enough to look back down and see a solid-seeming layer of cloud beneath her.

Deep down I feared I would never be good at fieldwork – my self-consciousness would block some essential human connection, so that my images did not capture a culture but glanced past it. The responsibility seemed onerous: to capture a *culture* on film? I could only hope to apprehend the crumbs of one, or worse, the crumbs I had myself dropped along the way, mistaking them for something of wider significance. Of course, I did not mention any of these doubts in my Lushington application.

The university's anthropology department at that time housed, somewhat uncomfortably, all three strands of the discipline – biological anthropology, archaeology, and social anthropology. I was required that semester to take a class in each of the other fields, to have a grasp of their approaches for the sake of disciplinary unity.

In the bio anthro class, I was intrigued by what was done in the sterile top-floor laboratory. Monkey DNA was studied under microscopes, and simian skeletons were picked free of flesh by dermestid beetles in the bone chamber, a vacuum-sealed glass box. The carcass went into the box stinking and hairy, the beetles had their meal, and out came a clean skeleton. But I was no hard scientist. When the biological anthropologists turned up for their obligatory social anthro class and listened to us discussing kinship and cosmological worldviews, I saw on their faces the same unease I'd felt in their lab.

The archaeologists, for their part, didn't have to pretend to be interested in the lives of living people. I envied them this, though I wasn't exactly riveted by the dry, slow methods by which they pieced together the past from fragments of material culture. I noticed that many of my archaeologist peers were estranged from their families, just as it seems Kitty was from hers. Perhaps it's true, whoever first said it, that we dig to fill the void.

At the start of that summer, my friends and I scattered across the globe on our various adventures. One went to Hungary to study medieval manuscripts, another to Hollywood to write about the history of actors' strikes, several went to New York for internships at banks or law firms. Nobody really got what I was planning to do in South Africa, but that was reassuring to me. Whatever happened on the farm, in the fall I would return to the same dormitory, live with the same roommates, eat in the same dining hall, for one more year.

I arrived in Cape Town on a chilly winter's day, an entire season changed overnight. At the airport I rented a car, studied the map, and nervously took the N2 away from Table Mountain, out towards the winelands.

Taxi minibuses kept stopping without warning on the side of the highway to collect passengers. The shantytown shacks were built right up to the edge of the asphalt, but I couldn't pay close attention to the poverty – I hadn't driven a car in a while and was dangerously rusty. I gave up trying to look at the map. There was an exit sign for Stellenbosch, which I took, though in fact the farm was closer to Paarl, and then I got lost as it was getting dark.

Eventually I found the road to Paarl and followed the signs towards something called the Afrikaans Language Monument, a set of strange phallic obelisks on a hill. A dirt road signposted 'Seeds of Hope' finally came into view. In my headlights I could see rows of bare vines, their intertwined branches like skinny gnomes holding hands. I rounded the corner and there was the cluster of cottages where the workers lived, and further up the road the big house that had previously been the farmer's residence but was now, I learned later, the renovated tasting rooms.

I parked and wandered around, looking for the guesthouse, past a pond filled with sleeping ducks. From the fields came the chirping of frogs. I found the house, located the key under the mat, got myself and my bags inside, and immediately – a little sheepishly – locked all the doors and windows.

A few days later, needing a break from the intensity of trying to form relationships on the farm, I drove up to the language monument. There was not a soul there, and very little to explain its existence. Etched into the concrete leading up to the obelisks was a phrase in Afrikaans, which I could translate only as *This is our earnestness.*

I was overtaken then by a foreboding that I was on the wrong path, in life and in art. What if my own earnestness were a cover for something else, something left unexamined, something putrid?

I was delighted that fall to have Kitty out of Sogliano's clutches and safely back on campus. The fact that she'd fallen for an older man proved to be briefly to my advantage, for I could see her freezing out any college boy who dared approach her.

We spent whole days in each other's company, eating our meals side by side in the dining hall, studying in the stacks, going for walks along the river through piles of leaves, playing squash, drinking hot chocolate in her suite.

During all that time together, though we spoke often of the previous summer, she did not say anything about her relationship with Sogliano. We did not share the type of confessional intimacy that seems to come so easily to young people these days.

At Thanksgiving we both stayed on campus—Kitty, I suspect, because she didn't want to go home to her mother, and me because Kitty was there, and my father no longer celebrated holidays of any kind. We took a walk around Walden Pond, and had turkey sandwiches and mulled wine for dinner in my room. At the end of the evening, as she was leaving, she invited me to a charity performance she was taking part in the following week at the ice rink.

I thought of nothing else for days. It felt for some reason like a date.

On the night, I wore my father's tuxedo, which, given later events, was an act of grim prescience. I collected the corsage I'd ordered for Kitty, a yellow rose flanked by baby's breath, and wound my scarf around my face to brave the wind coming off the water as I crossed the bridge.

Inside the rink it was even colder. My tuxedo was wasted, unseen beneath my bulky coat. A team of hockey players took to the ice to do a badly synchronized routine, to the audience's great amusement. I drank two cups of coffee to get warm. The crowd, by that stage, was getting rowdy. They were used to seeing blood on the ice. When Kitty glided out into the center of the rink, they went berserk. Her hair was in a bun and she was wearing sparkling earrings I'd not seen before. I was suddenly certain that Sogliano had given them to her.

Her skating partner joined her in the circle of light and the music started, a classical theme loud enough to drown out the noise of the crowd. The two of them started by doing big figures of eight with arms extended, and a few delicate jumps. As the music built to a crescendo I held my breath, knowing they were about to attempt a more difficult move, but somebody distracted me, tapping on my shoulder.

I turned in irritation to see my roommate, whom I did not consider a friend, standing in the aisle. I knew immediately, in the way you know these things, that something had happened to my father, and my roommate had been dispatched by a university administrator to find me.

I turned back to the rink just as Kitty leapt into the air, throwing her limbs wide, ready for her partner to catch her. He fumbled.

Kitty's head struck the ice and somebody in the audience screamed. I could see blood coming from her mouth or nose. She wasn't moving.

My roommate took the opportunity to drag me out of the stands toward an exit. He was stronger than me and overcame my attempts to break away, to get back to Kitty. Outside the rink a car was waiting. My roommate bundled me into it and left.

The dean of the college was in the backseat. He nodded to his driver and the car began to move, taking me across the river and further away from Kitty.

'I'll be direct,' the dean said. 'I think it's the best way. Your father is dead. Suicide. I'm sorry.'

I felt as if I had been put atop a funeral pyre and set aflame.

My father had donated money to the university's endowment fund, enough that the dean clearly felt he needed to look after me personally. It dawned on me at some stage that he was going to drive me all the way to Vermont, that we were already on I-90 heading west.

I could not stop thinking of Kitty bleeding motionless on the ice. I considered asking the driver to turn back, but knew this was impossible. To manage my anguish, I mentally compiled a list of tasks I would need to carry out in the coming hours and days, all the paperwork and preparations that death entails.

The dean turned on the car's ceiling light and spread a newspaper. I looked out the window at the silhouettes of ash and hemlock trees lining the highway. I had been planning to bring Kitty to Vermont that winter, to introduce her to my father.

When we finally arrived at the house, my father's longtime housekeeper, Dorothy, was freakishly composed, her way of warning me to keep myself together too. My father's body had already been delivered to the morgue, and the bathroom where he had taken his life was spotless, emptied of all evidence that he'd ever used it. No toothbrush, no half cake of soap, no crumpled hand towel.

Dorothy served tea. The dean escaped as soon as he could. While she was seeing him out, I called the student health clinic, asking for information about Kitty, but since I wasn't family they refused to tell me anything.

I survived the week by walking for hours every day, through the farmland and the maple woods around the town. One morning I walked along the edge of a farm where a barn-raising ceremony was taking place. Everybody in the community was there, helping with the wooden frame. They all turned and stared at me. The news had spread. In those days, in certain places, suicide was still unforgivable.

Several times a day I called my roommate, Kitty's roommate, her skating partner, and the university's teaching hospital for news about Kitty, but nobody knew anything, or if they did they wouldn't say, which further compounded my anxiety. Did this mean she was dead, or that my place in her inner circle was not as secure as I'd thought it was?

I made arrangements for Dorothy to accompany my father's body to Furnace Creek, to be buried beside my mother. I organized the memorial service for my father, though I couldn't bring myself to speak, leaving a distant relative to drone on about a man he'd hardly known.

On the Saturday afternoon, as soon as the service was over, I took one of my father's cars and set off to Boston, filled with dread.

We seem to be on parallel narrative tracks, like the nocturnal journey of predator and prey. Each creature leaving a set of prints in the sand, each experiencing the wind and the moonlight, the two bound together by a mutual awareness of death. I will remark only that your parents' story is so tragic it seems to me invented. I would not put this past you.

I could not stick to my pledge to focus on humans that winter in the Western Cape. I spent my days making images of every step in the wine's production, from the planting and grafting of the vine stock to the pruning of the shoots and branches, and the fermenting of the wine in metal vats so huge that men in masks had to climb inside to clean them after each batch. I was seduced again into trying to capture the quality of the sunlight; it was nothing like winter sunlight in the Northern Hemisphere. In the tasting rooms, I left my camera off as I watched the mostly white visitors swirl and sniff and gurgle the wine.

Over the course of those weeks I began to wonder if suppressed guilt could be extreme enough to stunt a person's emotional growth.

I tried to think of my most lucid childhood memory, and found that it was of grief and guilt bound together. My parents and I had returned home one day to find we'd been burgled. The burglars had placed our kitchen knives all over the house, to use if they were disturbed. A baby bird that my mother and I had rescued and installed in a shoebox had been decapitated.

I knew, even then, when I could not have been older than five, that there was something right and fair in the bird having been killed. I understood the insult of my sentimental care of an animal when all around us human beings were suffering because of people who looked like me. For a while after the burglary I secretly hit our next-door neighbour's cat, as hard as I could, anytime it came within reach of my little hand. (I can see now, with sudden clarity, why I was so fascinated by Luis Buñuel's films in my first film class; why I used to wait with bated breath for his signature mad dog to appear and wreak havoc, a symbol deployed, as Ernest Becker wrote, to mess with the security of repressed living.)

One day on the farm, I spent a morning in the vineyard filming the hands of an elderly worker as he pruned the rosebushes planted at the end of each row. He had the pickled face of a heavy drinker and his hands shook as he clipped the stems. I zoomed out, stepped in. I didn't ask him any questions, but at one stage he volunteered something about the rosebushes and why they had been planted there.

'The thorns made the donkeys do a bigger turn at the end of the row,' he said in Afrikaans.

'The donkeys?' I said.

'Before the machines, we used donkey carts for the harvest.'

So the rosebushes now had no practical purpose, only an aesthetic one, but in the past their thorns had forced the donkeys to make a clean, wide turn as they trudged around the end of one row and into the next, leaving the vines undamaged.

'With that thing,' he motioned to my camera, 'can you see through people?'

Maybe I had misunderstood his Afrikaans. I was alarmed that he thought the camera might be like a portable X-ray machine. Or did he mean that I could see the truth with it? Was he afraid I would show the footage to the farm manager, who might find fault with his work?

I stopped recording, pulled out the display screen, rewound, and showed him the footage I'd just taken.

'It's not safe,' he said – I don't know if he meant for me or for him – and he turned back to the rosebushes.

We didn't exchange words again.

A month into my stay, the big wine boss from Switzerland visited the farm. He was a confident, paunchy man in his late forties. One afternoon he offered to drive me to the company's bottling plant in Worcester.

He drove too fast through the Huguenot Tunnel, talking about what a bastard the man who previously owned the farm was, how he hadn't paid the workers a wage in decades, but kept them dependent on him by meting out alcohol on the weekends. He told me the first thing the company did was install flush toilets in the workers' houses.

To pierce his self-satisfaction, I asked what the company charged for a bottle of Seeds of Hope wine in European supermarkets, where I knew they were sold at a high price to consumers wanting to make an enlightened choice. He raised an eyebrow, retook my measure. The subcurrent of air in the car shifted.

At the plant, I was happy to film the bottles being filled with wine from rotating spouts, the corks being pushed into necks one after the next with a hiss and a thud, the labels being smoothed on at the end of the line before the bottles were plunked by a machine into a partitioned box. Each image felt more satisfying than the last, but it occurred to me that I had stooped even lower in my artistic dissociation, that I wasn't even filming live creatures anymore. I consoled myself by thinking that maybe machines could say things I didn't yet dare. A metaphor, after all, is only a vehicle to transfer meaning from one thing to another.

On the way back to the farm, the Swiss boss wanted to know what it felt like, making a film. I thought he was asking about the ethics of it, and launched into a speech about implied consent, afraid he was going to revoke my permission to roam about the farm with my camera.

'No, what does it feel like physically?' he said, his eyes on the road.

Nobody had asked me something like this before, not even you.

It turned out to be a question I'd been waiting to answer, for the details poured out of me. I told him about the ache in my right arm as I held up the camera, how the muscles around my left eye sometimes went into spasm from all the squinting in order to see more clearly with my right eye through the viewfinder. How smooth the rubber of the eyepiece felt against my skin.

I described trying to get the bubble into the circle of the spirit level at the base of the tripod, and how the name made me think that if I could get it perfectly level, my own spirits would lift, or the spirits of the filmmaking gods might be appeased and grant me good footage. The coin I used to clip the camera into and out of the tripod's head, and how it felt to slide the hairy boom cover onto the microphone protruding from the camera – as if I were preparing it for hibernation – to help dim the sounds of nature, of weather. What it was like later, in the editing suite, being able to erase wind noise from footage, elastic-band the audio track to fix accidental pops.

I told him of the challenge of knowing what raw material I had, since it was trapped on multitudes of tapes that I could only watch in real time, or skip forwards and backwards in, inevitably losing my bearings. That the only way of taking stock of my footage was to describe it in words, shot by shot, timecode by timecode, in language that was by necessity flat, reductive.

Sometimes, I said to him, when I watched my footage after the fact, it looked dead, as if the images had been murdered by being sucked through the lens. But on rare occasions it was more alive than I could have imagined, like real life on steroids, and I felt I could not take the credit, that some vital force must have streamed into my lens while I was filming. I described the first, impossible day of any edit, confronting the flabby footage spread across storage devices. How difficult it was to know where to start, which piece of flesh to pinch and cut off in the butchery of editing.

While I talked, he drove to an expensive French restaurant above the valley in Franschhoek and said he was buying me dinner.

I realised at some point during the meal that he believed me to be American, and I didn't correct him. Many of the workers on the farm had assumed this too, maybe because my Afrikaans was stilted. I'd felt mildly offended, and then relieved to have cast off a burdensome identity. It allowed me to avoid answering questions about when I'd left South Africa and why, and what had brought me back. I felt liberated inhabiting the skin of an idealistic young American, who could be held to account for many, many things but not for this particular disaster, not for *this* country's decades of trauma.

The Swiss boss and I drank a lot of wine and I knew exactly where he thought the night was headed.

He told me about the small organic farm he'd bought nearby as a passion project. His workers were planting oats and clover between the rows of vines to provide nitrate and phosphate. He'd bought ducks to eat the snails but the ducks had disappeared – onto the dinner tables of the workers, he believed. Now he had a woman come and pick the snails off the leaves individually before they were shipped to Switzerland as a delicacy.

Freed by the wine, he began to tell me other things. That he was an animalist, that he based his sexual attraction on smell alone, and had been intoxicated when he greeted me – with three weirdly formal Swiss cheek kisses – by my natural musky scent.

I excused myself. In the bathroom, I caught my reflection – lips stained red by the wine, hair dirty, eyebrows needing attention. My deodorant had worn off and my armpits were ripe with the aftermath of the heavy lifting of camera and tripod. And there was a sharper odour, of anxiety or excitement, which seemed to have attracted the attention of an older man who did not see a woman who should by that age have learned to look after herself better. The Swiss boss could see only my youth, which was invisible to me, and would remain so until I turned thirty-five and suddenly grasped what I had, only to lose it overnight.

In a class on feminism my second year at college, the teaching assistant, a woman in her mid-forties, had asked all us peachy-faced girls in her study section if we'd ever felt discriminated against as women. Not a single one of us put up a hand, and we refrained defiantly, with a hint of swagger: things had changed, the world belonged to us, we had always been treated as equals.

The assistant, who had been raised in a commune set up in permanent protest outside a weapons factory somewhere in Sweden, looked at us sadly. 'Mark my words,' she said, 'the doors will start to slam shut in your faces the day you are no longer considered youthful. Only then will you see how misguided you were to equate being young and female with being empowered. You may turn your back on feminism now, think you don't need it, but by God you'll need it once you start to age. The opportunities you thought were based on merit will dry up just as you do.'

I'd looked around the classroom and seen on the faces of my fellow female students no alarm, nothing but the pity I too was feeling for her. We all believed that her prediction was the product of personal disappointment, and we felt safe in the conviction that for us it would be different.

Men could only harm us if we let them, and, just like me, most of the women in that room had already armoured themselves against the need for a man. We slept around at college, making sure it wasn't about anything other than answering for ourselves the interesting question, Am I fuckable? None of us believed in searching for a Grand Romantic Passion, unless it was the grand passion for the self, for realising the self. I had seen my female roommates, and they had seen me, return from one-night stands and efficiently set about the process of readying themselves for the real work of the day: getting to class on time, diligently handing in assignments, volunteering for campus organisations related to our choice of career, feeding our CVs as if they were ravenous beasts that would die without fodder.

Nothing happened with the Swiss boss that night, or any other night – I made sure of it. Before he left for Switzerland, he offered to do an interview for my film, to explain the history of winemaking in the region, all the way back to the Dutch who had planted the first vines and enslaved the first workers to tend them, and the community of Huguenots who had fled religious persecution in France, secretly bringing with them to Africa their treasured vine stocks, sometimes tucked into the folds of their babies' nappies. I refused politely, saying I wasn't doing any talking heads for my film.

'But you surely have to provide some background for your footage?' he said.

I stood firm, he left me alone.

In fact, during my time at that farm I had come to change my thinking a little, and was beginning to see the differences between artistic and ethnographic filmmaking. The latter owed something to people other than the filmmaker, but art could stew in its eccentricities, owing nothing to anybody but its creator. If I made an ethnographic film it would need to be shepherded out into the world. It would need to seem principled, both in the conditions of its making and those of its circulation, and would be judged according to what it added or took away from the ethnographic canon.

If, on the other hand, it was put forward as art, I could ignore the human subjects as much as I wished, indulge my visual interest in processes, not bother with contextual explanation. I could revel in being an unreliable witness. Even if the film I produced was a hybrid mess, so long as I could demonstrate in the accompanying written reflection, required for my joint thesis, that I had made it in good faith – with an inquiring mind – I hoped it would be enough to please my professors and let me pass.

It is somewhat difficult for me to read of your interactions with the Swiss boss, indeed with any man. For two reasons. One is concern for you and your well-being (though you won't believe me when I say that). The other is that you're right about me priding myself on seeing in certain young women things to which others might be blind. Not in terms of physical attractiveness, which is irrelevant. I am an angel investor of a kind; the product I buy into is the person, the mind. The bragging rights come later, when the chosen ones mention me in their origin stories. So no, I do not like to contemplate the possibility that other men have looked into your eyes and seen what I did. Which must also be why I missed all the signs during my first summer in Pompeii that Sogliano had decided to make Kitty his forever.

When I arrived at the university's teaching hospital in Boston, he was the first person I saw.

He was smoking outside the main entrance, and as he greeted me I smelled his bad breath, tones of stale coffee and nicotine, and noticed that his shirt was rumpled. Clearly he had been at the hospital for days. For once I was happy to see him—it meant she was alive.

'No permanent damage, the doctors say. They're keeping her in for observation,' he said. 'Where have you been? She asked for you.'

'Is she taking visitors now?' I looked at my watch. It was already dark.

'Only family this time of day. They say she must rest. But for you,' he winked, 'we will break the rules.'

I digested this information. Soggy wasn't family. Why was he at the hospital outside visiting hours?

He made a show of first getting another cup of coffee from the all-hours canteen, rubbing in how long he'd sat sleepless beside Kitty. He navigated the hospital with ease, up this lift, through this doorway, waving at the nurses as if they were old friends. At the door to Kitty's room he stepped back to let me enter, secure in his place in her life.

She was sitting up in bed wearing a mint-green nightdress I knew well from our evenings together in her suite. Her head was bandaged. The bruising on one side of her face had a yellowish tinge, signs of healing.

'Hello, stranger,' she said.

I felt the reproach in all four chambers of my heart. 'Katherine,' I said, a name I never used for her.

'Did you hear our news?' she said, smiling at Sogliano, who had eased himself into the chair next to her bed.

She held up her hand to show me the diamond and laughed at the look of shock on my face. 'Oh Royce, you knew about us, didn't you? It must have been obvious all summer. I thought you were being discreet about it, never asking me a thing.'

'A good friend,' Sogliano said, cementing my place as loyal third wheel.

'Though *this* was a shock even to me,' she said, gazing down at the ring.

The rest of the room was starting to come into focus. A dozen vases filled with flowers, cards propped on every surface, balloons that had been there long enough to wrinkle and sink to the floor. I didn't know Kitty had so many friends, so many people who cared about her. Was I just one among countless others to whom she gave her time and friendly attention? And was I now at the bottom of the heap, the one friend who had not yet visited or shown signs of concern at her injury?

I had a single card to play and I played it. 'My father killed himself,' I blurted out. 'I was told the night of your fall on the ice.'

In the back corner of the room someone coughed. I turned to see a middle-aged woman slouched in an armchair. She had beautiful features but the telltale red nose of a heavy drinker, and was painfully thin. I knew she must be Kitty's mother, come from Charleston.

Kitty was trying to get out of bed but Sogliano stopped her, putting his hand over her legs. 'You have to rest,' he said.

'Ettore,' Kitty's mother said, 'let the girl get out of bed for Chrissakes.'

He responded to her with a familiarity apparently earned through sharing that small space for days. 'Zelda, you heard the doctor. Bed rest for another week.'

Kitty surrendered, sinking back against the pillows. 'That's awful, Royce. Are you . . . are you okay?'

'I don't know,' I said.

A nurse stopped at the door. 'Visitors out,' she said sternly.

'Will you come tomorrow?' Kitty said to me. 'Ettore has to go back to work, and Mother's flying home too.'

'Of course,' I said, brightening to think of having her to myself again. 'Can I bring anything?'

'The books I've requested from the library. I'm lagging behind on my thesis.'

'Katarina, you are not meant to do any reading,' Sogliano said.

'Well, Royce can read to me,' she said.

I watched as her mother patted the lump of Kitty's blanketed feet. 'Take care,' she said. 'See you when I see you.'

'Thanks for the visit,' Kitty said with coolness in her voice.

As Kitty's mother passed me to leave, I smelled alcohol on her breath. 'Goodbye, whoever you are,' she said breezily, with a bully's instinct for intuiting a stranger's weakness.

I closed the door to the room on my way out a bit later, and through the small window saw Sogliano climb onto the bed beside Kitty in his socks.

At the end of my time on the wine farm I flew to Sydney to see my parents. During the day, while they were at work, I mostly slept and cooked, happy to stay home in their flat. In the evenings they insisted I hook up the camera to the TV and show them some of my footage.

My mother, who hated mawkishness in all things, tried to put a positive spin on my peopleless imagery. 'I like that you're not taking any position on the past,' she said, her glasses slipping down her nose. Her hair was streaked with grey that she refused to colour.

My father, I could sense, would have liked me to be more expansive in my attempts to portray the lives of the workers – his passion was always people – but he seemed content that I was focused on South Africa, that I'd inherited some of his ardent feelings about the place. He gave me a lot of hugs, his tall, thin frame matching my own.

Yet I could see they sometimes thought my self-scourging was overblown. In their eyes I had been too young to know what was happening under apartheid, let alone be responsible for it. Any time I brought up the strange feelings I'd had on the farm, my inability to move beyond guilt, they kindly but firmly shut down the conversation.

They, at least, had had their agency. As adults they'd been fully aware, able to make informed choices about their ethical obligations and act on them. I, on the other hand, had soaked up all the feelings of wrongness, had intuited that my privileges depended on others' suffering but was powerless to act on such knowledge, as all children are, and it had festered.

By chance my father's Australian citizenship ceremony was scheduled for the week I was in Sydney, and he asked me to go with him. My mother and I had been citizens since our first stints here in the early '80s, but my father always felt it would be disloyal to take on dual citizenship. He still lived under the belief that he would one day return to South Africa, that his time in Australia was an interlude – one that kept happening every few years.

So he was unhappy that morning about having capitulated on the citizenship issue, while I was glad he was making his long relationship with Australia official. When my parents had first turned up here they'd been welcomed in the warmest possible way, with pathways to citizenship, a PhD scholarship for my mother to study musicology, free preschool for me, free medical care.

And then the cherry on top. A few months into our second stint in Sydney, my parents picked six of the seven winning numbers in a lotto competition and won five thousand dollars: we had found the way to utopia! The three of us danced around the sprinkler at the local park in celebration. The irony, of course, was that we had just fled another utopia designed for whites alone. And this was the point I kept getting caught on while trying to think it all through, trying to determine exactly where my complicities began and ended.

Take this, for example. At around the same time that my father was persuading a renegade group of his graduate students to give free tutoring and counselling on campus to black high school students, my mother was in an excellent hospital, recovering after giving birth to me, all expenses paid by the apartheid state. Or this: at some point in their early married life they bought a plot of land, which they later sold at a profit. It turned out to be land seized from an Indian community, who were removed to a shittier part of Durban.

Then there were my grandparents, and their conferred and complicated privileges: on my father's side, poor and working-class but without much sympathy for the plight of the poor blacks all around them; and on my mother's, educated and gentle churchgoing people who nonetheless did not lift a finger to oppose apartheid.

And before them? Every human on earth has inherited privilege and inherited pain, I knew. But I seemed to have something wrong with me. I wasn't proud of the guilt-wallowing, I didn't want to be fixated on the ledger of rights and wrongs chalked up by my family, by previous generations. I didn't like the way I sometimes felt as if I had some sixth sense, as if I could see the ghosts around an individual, a degenerate halo of wrongdoing. That was arrogance, exceptionalism. I had read Primo Levi on Kafka and recognised an aspect of myself in Kafka's simultaneous fear of and desire for punishment, which Levi characterised as a sickness.

At the citizenship ceremony, my father and I took our seats in the town hall among other family groups, as diverse as could be, everybody in their best clothes.

The mayor gave a surprisingly moving speech, tuned exactly to my father's state of mind. 'We're not asking you to give up your previous identity, or your feelings about the country from which you came,' she said. 'Think of your new Australian citizenship as an augmentation of who you are, not an obliteration of what you have been. It will add value to your life, just as you, by choosing to become part of our community, will add value to the lives of those around you.'

My father shook her hand stiffly as he went up to collect his certificate, forced a smile as he posed for the photograph. After the ceremony, tea and lamingtons were served, Slim Dusty was played over the sound system, and the atmosphere was festive. I went to the loo, and returned to find my father in discussion with the mayor.

'But why would this country want me as a citizen?' he was saying. 'When the shit hits the fan, I run away. If that happens here, chances are I'll do the same. What use am I to you? I've demonstrated I have no loyalty.'

The mayor was young and smart, unruffled. 'Nations aren't that loyal to their people either, so don't worry so much about being loyal to a nation,' she said. 'A passport isn't one thing to all people, it's anything you want it to be. An insurance policy, an escape plan, a new beginning, a passage out of hell. Put it in your bedside drawer and forget all about it.'

She smiled, welcoming me into the circle. 'Let me tell you a story,' she said. 'A few years ago, I went to Lord Howe Island on holiday. I happened to be there for what the locals call Discovery Day. I braced myself for it, sort of like I do each Australia Day, cringing at what it symbolises for Indigenous Australians while secretly wishing I could participate wholeheartedly in showing my love for the things I value about this country.'

An aide said something in the mayor's ear and she paused to listen. I found myself thinking of the white balloon I'd held in my hand as a child on the school oval in Sydney. We had just moved yet again, for the second or third time, from South Africa. It was the Australian bicentenary year, two centuries since the First Fleet arrived, and the school was hosting a week-long festival to celebrate. My parents had told me to opt out of as much of it as I could, without satisfactorily explaining to me why. And I wanted to hold a balloon, so I stood there with hundreds of other students, all of us holding white balloons on strings, and when the band struck up the national anthem we released them in a bubbling mass. It was an amazing sight. But once they were nothing but specks, I felt ashamed that I hadn't been strong enough to resist the ceremony, and wondered if my parents had disapproved because birds might eat the balloons and choke to death.

The mayor apologised for the interruption. 'Discovery Day commemorates the same year, 1788, as Australia Day,' she continued, 'and it's the same story of white settlement. But the difference is that Lord Howe was uninhabited when whites claimed it for Britain. Nobody was dispossessed of their land, nobody was massacred. It was such a relief to learn that, and be able to celebrate without feeling a drop of guilt.'

My father was quiet once the mayor had taken her leave. I could see he was processing her words, incorporating what she'd said into the weave of his self. He pushed sugar grains around on the table with a finger. I looked at his hands, as familiar to me as my own.

Eventually he said, 'For decades of my life as an adult, from when I became aware of what was happening, I had an identity I was ashamed of. To be a white South African during those years was to be evil incarnate, no matter what your own politics were. Though really, my Australian colleagues had no cause to feel superior, they'd just been more successful at hiding their shameful history from the rest of the world.'

He slurped the dregs of his tea. 'Then the miracle of 1994 happened and I had an identity I could be proud of, for the first time in my life. And what did we do? We left again, a year later. And became instantly suspect once more in the eyes of certain

Australians, who thought we didn't want to live under a black government.'

'Why *did* we leave that time?' I asked. 'Just so I could go to a good school?'

'In part,' he said, his dark eyes weary. 'I got offered another job in Sydney. I thought it would only be for a few years, until you finished high school.' He looked down at his citizenship certificate, with its red wax seal. 'But now we seem to be stuck here. I don't know if I've got the energy for another move. And what if the new South Africa doesn't need me? Or even want me? It would be too much to bear.'

A person's pattern of ethical thinking is similar to muscle memory, and seems natural only because it's so often reiterated. My father's circular self-blame scared me. In it I heard echoes of my own guilt, but whereas his had been earned through long experience, mine felt like insincere parroting of beliefs I'd picked up from him and my mother, in the same way I'd picked up certain facial expressions, table manners, ways of walking or speaking. I remembered sitting between them on the couch in Sydney as they wept with longing when Mandela waved to the crowd at the 1995 Rugby World Cup on the other side of the world. I had cried too, mimicking their emotion, wanting it for myself.

I knew I had to find a way to release myself from those fantasy bonds to the country of my birth, to make my feelings personal, not familial. The night after the citizenship ceremony, lying in my old bedroom listening to the roar of trucks passing on the Pacific Highway, I decided I would move to South Africa after graduation. It was too easy to flit in and out, spend a winter filming here and there, and fool myself into thinking I was engaging with the place. Living there with no prospect of leaving? That would be something entirely different.

Is it presumptuous of me, Vita, to suspect you're starting to enjoy this process? You may not see our project in the same light as I do, but once you let yourself delve into it, I believe there's nothing quite so fascinating as your own past, whether it's a story of enlightenment or downfall.

As soon as she was out of hospital, I helped Kitty burrow back into her studies. Before our summer trip, she'd been focusing on the archaeology of Rome, but now she had an entirely new purpose. As Sogliano's future wife, she would be living with him on-site in Pompeii. He'd promised to try to arrange an unpaid research position for her with the Naples Archaeological Superintendency, though it was known to be hostile to foreign researchers.

The doctors had said Kitty would make a full recovery but that it could take some time for her vision to return to normal. Reading left her exhausted, and this gave me the idea of offering to become her research assistant. I knew my own studies would suffer and I gave up any possibility of doing a thesis myself, but this was no loss to me at all. It was of concern to Kitty, though, and I had to wear her down with my insistence that through her I would be able to experience real intellectual immersion for the first time.

Mindful of her injury, Abbiati had suggested that in place of a thesis, Kitty write a paper on aspects of the discovery and historical reception of Pompeii's interior wall art, drawing on the extensive scholarship on the topic. She agreed; the garden research could wait until her return to the site after graduation.

During the previous year, I'd seen Kitty lowering herself into her studies as if into a literal cavern of wonders. Sitting opposite her at the library, I'd been able to pinpoint the moment she became unaware of anything in her immediate surroundings, as the words took her somewhere else. I'd felt jealous then, not of that feeling, but of losing the possibility of her attention.

Now, locating and reading aloud to her every source Abbiati recommended and noting down Kitty's responses, I was able to lower myself into that cavern alongside her, to see how the ruins and their artistic treasures were rediscovered and interpreted differently in each century leading up to our own.

In the sixteenth century, a royal architect directing his men to build a channel close to the Sarno River had discovered Pompeii's ruins. Finding ruins was nothing new to him. He had long worked in Rome and knew that to the powerful men—popes and viceroys—who employed him, ancient ruins were considered a nuisance, structures to be cleared to make way for large-scale public works. This architect discovered Pompeii at a time when its location had been erased from history, though rumors had long circulated of a lost city beneath the fields in which his men were digging. To us it would seem to be the discovery of a lifetime, yet neither he nor anybody else was the slightest bit interested. The city was allowed to keep its secrets for another two hundred years.

By the eighteenth century things had changed. Antiquarian studies were very much in vogue. Herculaneum was rediscovered, celebrated. The well of Resina, long known to yield ancient colored marble from monuments buried deep below it, was plundered, the marble sold to wealthy locals or visiting foreigners. Grand tourists from all over Europe came to visit. The bravest were lowered down the well's shaft to follow the network of tunnels carved underground, winding through the remains of Herculaneum's theaters and temples, marking the walls with chalk so they could find their way out again.

Those in power then, unlike their predecessors, were no longer indifferent to the riches of the ruins. Charles VII, new King of Naples, made archaeological excavations in the Bay a royal priority. He bought the Resina well, and sent chain gangs of captured pirates down to dig in the tunnels, where some were asphyxiated by pockets of poisonous gas. Whispers of a curse began. The king's aim was not to make the excavation of Herculaneum accessible to the public, but to strip whatever was there for the royal collection: statues, jewelry, precious artifacts. Any wall art that the king did not consider worthy was destroyed.

When Herculaneum's yield of treasures began to dwindle, one of the king's engineers, recalling the rumors of another lost city, decided to start digging beneath the hilly village of Civita. And Pompeii was found once more.

At first the engineer tried to make underground tunnels, as in Herculaneum, but they kept collapsing. Gradually he realized that the conditions of Pompeii's burial were different. The ash and lapilli on that site were easier to remove than the rock-hard lava covering Herculaneum, and the workers could dig in the open instead of trying to excavate deep underground. This meant they could follow the actual layout of the city, instead of digging down at random as they had in Herculaneum.

As a consequence, Pompeii soon became the more popular place to visit. Who would choose to descend into the bowels of the earth when you could wander about the streets in the sunshine, admiring the view of Vesuvius? By the late eighteenth century, Pompeii was a regular stop for Naples tour guides. Visitors were allowed to take away with them anything they found on the site—gold ornaments, coins, even a skeleton. The cost of a session of antiquities collection was not much more than they paid for a meal.

I liked reading to Kitty the stories of well-known visitors' reactions to Pompeii. The fifteen-year-old Mozart walked the site with his father in 1770, ate eggs and broccoli for lunch, and gazed with trepidation at the plume above Vesuvius, which at the time was in an active phase. On their way back to Naples they visited the Grotta del Cane, where the guide dangled a dog in the cave and timed how long it took to die from the poisonous gas (a minute and a half).

Or Goethe, still trying to decide whether to be a painter or a writer, who climbed to the summit of Vesuvius in early 1787. He stood on the glowing rubble at the edge of the abyss, hardly able to see through the smoke, and used his own pulse to time the pauses between each shower of rocks the volcano hurled at him. Walking the streets of the city below, he struggled to imagine how it had been buried—Vesuvius looked so very far away—until he formed a picture in his mind of a mountain village buried beneath a layer of snow.

And Charles Dickens, exploring Pompeii in 1845, who had seen, just as we had, 'at every turn, the little familiar tokens of human habitation and every-day pursuits; the chafing of the bucket-rope in the stone rim of the exhausted well; the track of carriage-wheels in the pavement of the street; the marks of drinking-vessels on the stone counter of the wine-shop . . .'

Kitty, for her part, was more intrigued by evidence that

eighteenth- and even some nineteenth-century visitors had looked at Pompeii's wall art (most of it now destroyed), and not been impressed. In fact they'd found it quite off-putting. To them, it seemed disordered, the scenes and images much coarser than the Renaissance artists' reinterpretations of ancient Roman art with which these visitors were familiar.

I read to her about the painter Raphael crawling down into the grottoes near the Colosseum in Rome, to see the underground ruins of Nero's Golden House—really a sprawling palace—in the early sixteenth century. He and his followers found the ancient wall paintings very beautiful and named the style grottesco. Renaissance painters used this style as inspiration for their own work, but they realized it needed sanitizing to be accepted by their culture. They took elements of it and transformed them into a celebration of Christianity, while erasing all evidence that the ancients had enjoyed rich erotic lives.

This was why, I began to see, only a few centuries later, the real art of antiquity looked uncouth to viewers, accustomed as they were to the Renaissance versions. The dominant style of wall art in Pompeii's homes at the time of their destruction was thought to be too busy, too cluttered, too wild, and the celebration of sex of all kinds in art displayed in public places unthinkably crude. The term grotesque came to mean something closer to its modern sense: shocking, unsightly.

Notions of significance, taste, value, worth, have always been unstable, Kitty wrote in her paper, an idea that, at the time, nobody was much considering.

Did I ever tell you I once considered writing a book on Pompeii myself? This was years after Kitty's death, when my grief had eased just enough that I could look back through the detritus of our shared past, the reading notes, my transcriptions of her thoughts. Fortunately, I recognized early in the endeavor that I was nothing but a flimflammer, an impostor who wrongly believes that because he has brushed up against a body of knowledge he has understood it. Contact should never be confused with comprehension.

On the evening before she was to submit her paper, I gave Kitty a bottle of wine produced from grapes grown on the slopes of Vesuvius itself. It was called Lacryma Christi—Christ's Tears. I'd visited the vineyard the summer before to taste the wine, and it was pretty awful but the symbolism was perfect. We drank it that same night, joking that what had brought Christ to tears was this terrible swill.

On the plane back to Boston from Sydney, I read a chapter of Primo Levi's *The Periodic Table*, the one about vanadium and Dr Müller, and then I fell in love. Not with the living, breathing man sitting beside me eating his dinner, but with a man who appeared on the screen in front of me, a presenter for a show called *Global Encounters* featuring documentaries from around the world.

He looked to be in his late twenties, had a Californian accent and long brown hair, and wore the rugged documentarian's uniform of cargo pants and flak jacket. His name was Timothy Doring. He introduced a film he'd shot himself while climbing in the Himalayas, slightly too fast-paced for my taste, but I understood the requirements of the genre. It was the kind of film I needed to learn to make if I was ever going to attract an audience.

Strong feelings washed over me while I watched Timothy on the screen. Did I want to love him or *be* him? Whichever, it was energising, and I scribbled detailed notes on his film in my journal. I tended in those days to have epiphanies on long plane trips, though more often than not they turned out to be closer to delusions, inspired by sleeplessness and the unreality of flying.

This rush of industry was followed by creeping dullness as the hours accumulated and the human dross encroached – food spilled on blankets, other people's piss on the toilet seat. By the end of the flight I was capable of doing nothing but staring in a fug at the screen, my ankles swelling.

In Boston I took a taxi, and as the driver approached the familiar streets around the university, I felt as if I were coming home. I loved everything about the campus by then, even the Plaza and the ugly block of my dormitory. Students were out throwing frisbees on the grass, lining up outside storerooms to retrieve boxes of possessions hastily packed at the start of summer. Each year, we were assigned different rooms according to the pecking order, and finally my friends and I would be seniors, with a top-floor suite, and a bathroom shared only between us, not the whole floor.

In our suite, one of my roommates was singing in the shower, the scent of her shampoo instantly recognisable. Music was blasting down the hall, probably the football boys openly sharing a beer keg, now that they were twenty-one. On my way through the lobby I'd smelt something good coming from the kitchens. The dining hall usually did a comfort meal like sloppy joes to welcome everyone back the first day of term.

It was all so quintessentially American that I had to pinch myself. There I was, ensconced in the perfect dream of what I'd imagined college life to be like. In my earlier years there, that wonderment had been mitigated by uncertainty about what was expected of me, but not anymore.

My roommates and I didn't exchange many details about our summers; it was enough just to be back together. We traipsed downstairs to the dining hall as soon as it opened, and were still there when it closed hours later. I fell asleep that night listening to the reassuring sounds of people living all around me.

This happiness at the start of my senior fall was tinged with an awareness of time running out. I think we all felt it. We had one more year in that magnificent twilight between youth and responsibility, and then we would be pushed out to survive on our own. That joyful return to campus is one of my few recurring dreams, even now. In my sleep, I get to experience that feeling again – a gift of a kind – but it always ends in sadness, with the realisation just before waking that something is wrong, and my years at college are gone forever.

My euphoria persisted for the first few weeks of term. I walked to the film department basement one September evening as the bells of the church were ringing and the giant trees were shedding red leaves. Around me, students were gathered in twos and threes on the paths, on the steps of the library. I could see fairy lights framing a window in one of the freshman dormitories, roommates bent together over a screen. It was a moment of grace. I felt as if I had gathered the threads of my existence together in one fist.

I took that godlike energy into the editing suite, and that night cut two hours of life as I'd filmed it on the wine farm down to ten minutes.

In the morning, I woke feeling low. Whatever happy drugs my brain had been producing had worn off and I was mortal again. I needed a better career plan. Or maybe what I needed was a man.

At my computer, I found Timothy Doring's email address, and wrote asking if he might be willing to meet with me so I could find out more about his work in documentary film. Within a day he'd written back; he was happy to meet if I could get to DC. I booked a train ticket, and spent the rest of the week fantasising about what might happen: he'd offer to screen my thesis film on his show, he'd make me his co-presenter, we'd soon be shooting films all over the world together.

I arrived early and was buzzed in to his office. He was even better looking than he'd been on screen, wearing a blue fleece that matched the colour of his eyes. He didn't have much time to give me right then, he said, but I could watch a film in the screening room, and afterwards we could talk over a meal.

I felt my insignificance in his busy day. I'd worn my only pair of heels but I felt young and foolish, and sensed the gaping divide of eight years of professional work out in the real world. What did I know of any of that?

The film he put on for me was a documentary by a young photojournalist who left his comfortable life in middle America to cover the crisis in Somalia. There was a lot of shaky, grainy footage of journalists running for cover under fire. By the end of it I had a headache, and was starving. I ventured into the corridor and managed to find Timothy's office again.

He was sitting at his desk eating sushi from a plastic container. My face must have betrayed my disappointment, for he said, 'This is just a snack. I missed lunch today. Dinner's on me.'

It was cold outside, and getting dark. We walked along an alley between buildings, a wind tunnel. He ducked down a set of steps into an unmarked restaurant. The place was empty.

'Have you tried Ethiopian food?' he said.

In fact I had, in Sydney, but I pretended I hadn't. I sensed he liked to give people new experiences.

He studied the menu and when the waiter came over requested the banquet for two. My spirits lifted: that would take a while to eat. He ordered a beer and asked if I was old enough to drink.

'The same,' I said to the waiter, though I felt too cold to drink beer.

His take on documentary filmmaking was straightforward, I soon discovered. His interest was in showcasing different people of the world, going where few had previously gone (with a video camera at least), and celebrating the triumph of the human spirit.

When I asked if he ever had any doubts about turning up in a community whose language he didn't speak, where people might not understand how the footage of their lives would be used, he gave me a knowing look. 'So you're one of those,' he said.

I backtracked. 'I admire that you don't let yourself get put off by all that.'

'I'm no anthropologist,' he said. 'I'm a filmmaker. All I want to do is tell stories. If somebody speaks to me while I'm holding a video camera on my shoulder, I'm going to assume they're okay with being filmed.'

By the end of the meal, the restaurant was crowded, I was sitting beside him on the banquette, and we were all over each other. It was wordlessly decided that instead of taking the late train back to Boston, I would spend the night with him.

On the way to his apartment in Adams Morgan, he asked the cab driver to stop near the White House and leave the meter running while we had a quick look (I'd told him I'd never seen it). The colonnaded building seemed unassuming, exposed to its surroundings. The gaps in the fence surrounding it were nearly big enough to climb through, and the building so close you could see people moving around inside. Of course I knew there were unseen snipers all over the place, policing its borders, but still, it felt open, as if to signal to the public that it belonged to them.

Later, in his overheated apartment, we took a polaroid of ourselves standing naked, side by side, which was rather too brave on a first night together.

He called every day after my return to Boston, and said he wanted to visit me. I thought of how my roommates, without even realising, would exclude him from our richly woven verbal codes and jokes, the shorthand way of communicating we'd developed. So instead I offered to return to DC. He paid for my train ticket.

On the morning I arrived, he'd organised brunch with some of his work colleagues. 'For you to make contacts,' he said.

I kept to myself, ate my eggs, didn't pretend to be older than I was. Timothy told the table about my thesis project in hyperbolic terms, saying things like, 'She's investigating race relations in the new South Africa.'

When he urged me to describe my experience on the farm, I undermined him, and myself. 'It's just a student film,' I said, shrugging.

Afterwards, he took me for a walk around the Vietnam Veterans Memorial and stopped to trace his finger over the names of the dead engraved in the wall of black stone. He closed his eyes. 'You can sense something about the person by feeling their name,' he said.

I laughed, then apologised.

'Try it,' he said.

I closed my eyes and put my finger against the stone. I didn't feel anything except embarrassment at his presumption that he could sense his way into the life of a man who'd died in such circumstances. But then, as my finger reached the end of the name and the grooves gave way to the smooth surface, I felt a sudden sadness, and moved my hand away as if I'd received an electric shock.

'See?' Timothy said. It was a misty day, overcast, and his eyes were very blue. 'Can I give you a piece of advice, Vita? If you want to make it in this business, you've got to talk about yourself and your work with more enthusiasm. It's a myth that art speaks for itself.'

That night, he cooked prawns in coconut cream in his apartment filled with photographs he'd taken on his travels, about which he talked incessantly. I began to miss my roommates. It took me by surprise when he suggested after dinner that we smoke hash together; it seemed an activity more suited to a college dorm than his Northwest residence. I said yes, hoping it would dispel the feeling of distance between us.

We sat facing each other on his couch. It must have been too strong, or laced with something, for soon I began to hallucinate wildly. My brain felt as if it were about to fall out the back of my head like a watermelon out of a window.

Our laughter became manic and I could hardly breathe. I kept staring at his incisors, which looked like fangs, convinced he was going to kill me. He was going to smash the window and use a piece of the glass to slit my throat. When he went to the bathroom I was too terrified to move, thinking he'd gone to get razor blades with which to slice me open. His laughter when he returned was more maniacal than ever; his body twisted from side to side.

Eventually we ended up in his bed but my hallucinations kept going for hours, until the light showed beneath the blinds. Over breakfast he apologised and said that had never happened to him before. He too had hallucinated – that *I* was going to kill him. He'd also thought his brain was going to drop out of his head, had formed the same mental picture of a watermelon falling out the window. This calmed me somewhat, the fact that the substance had activated the same pathways in our brains. It didn't have to mean anything more ominous.

But when I left for the station, I couldn't forget the image of his sharp incisors, and of a vein popping out of the skin beneath one eye. I knew I had to end it, and called him from a payphone to say I had to focus on my studies. He was relieved, I think.

It was on the Monday after this weekend that I was scheduled to have my interview with the Lushington Foundation. I'd not prepared properly, and I recall the effort of moving my face into an approximation of brio when I was summoned into the room.

I didn't pay you much attention during the interview. The other three trustees were much more talkative, more engaged. You seemed preoccupied and hardly asked me a thing. I now know why.

When you emailed two weeks later to ask me to the first of our dinners in a stately part of Boston, I assumed this was another round of the judging process, that the other trustees would be there too.

I arrived in the lobby of the restaurant and gave your name to the host standing as still as a statue. It acted on him like a magic password. He parted the velvet curtains keeping out the cold air and led me through the low-lit dining room to a corner where you were seated at a table for two.

If Kitty had agreed to have me—in any way she wanted, as a life helper or a life mate—I would gladly have served her forever. I wanted to protect her from making the wrong choice, from choosing domestic comfort or romantic intrigue over the stimulation of her work, her ideas. She rejected me in the end, just as you did, but that was my fault. I could never rid myself of some deep desire for reciprocity, of the conviction that my loyalty would eventually win me love. I wasn't slavish enough.

As Kitty and I made our postgraduation plans, I tried to come to terms with the role I was to play in her life, though I still liked to imagine a violent, often ridiculous end for Soggy, a collapsing wall on-site, or an attack by the black bumblebees that swarmed within Pompeii.

He, on the other hand, remained unthreatened by me, though he'd had limited time with Kitty since their engagement; she spent Christmas with him in Rome, he visited her over spring break. He was not that keen, however, when she first broached the idea of me accompanying her to Pompeii again for the summer, at least until she was sure she could handle the demands of her work alone. She had recovered well but was still sometimes debilitated by headaches, which left her vision spotty. She had to be careful how she spent her energy.

I worked hard to convince her to keep me on as a research assistant. Kitty would probably also have preferred to be alone with her fiancé after their long period apart, but Sogliano eventually conceded that he would be too busy to give the close assistance she might need.

It was to my advantage that the family fortune was now in my name; Kitty wouldn't have to pay me for my services. I even offered to cover her costs, but she'd received a modest fellowship from the National Endowment for the Humanities, which she said was sufficient for the time being. Together we designed a program of research on aspects of garden wall art to keep her busy for several months. My Italian was good enough, if still patchy (I'd worked on it with Kitty over the year). Hers was by then close to fluent. Love is a potent motivator.

Neither of us had any family members attend our graduation. We sat together at the ceremony beneath the whispering trees and skipped the lunch at our residence. The benefit of my unhappy college career was being spared the nostalgia that seems to afflict those who fear that everything following it will be a letdown. You, Vita, seem to count yourself among them, though I wish you wouldn't.

We left for Italy the day after we graduated, in the early summer of 1971.

It's not often in life we are given the chance to return to a faraway place that has moved us. And that summer, I was amazed by how little I had really noticed about Pompeii the year before. Perhaps it was thanks to Kitty's interest in the gardens of the city that I was charmed afresh by its natural beauty. I inhaled the mingled scents of the rosemary, laurel, and Spanish broom that grew everywhere in the ruins, and admired the masses of poppies and acanthus, and the chamomile flowers spread like a living carpet over the floors of the ancient houses.

I was drawn back to the wilder places of the town. The green, unexcavated regions around the Amphitheater, and the rows of umbrella pines whose canopies mimicked the shape of the cloud that had risen above Vesuvius when it exploded. Sicily's ever-active Mount Etna had erupted once again that spring, and tourists who'd worked their way up the peninsula to Pompeii told us there was a low plume hanging above Etna's crater, formed by clouds of vapor and lithic ash. A reminder of the violence skulking within Vesuvius's quiet cone.

Soon after our arrival, I discovered a walking trail around the old city wall. To follow it was to travel backward and forward in time. The wall and its traces took me past farmhouses surrounded by snapdragons, unused railway tracks, and half-built factories so ghastly the locals called them *un pugno nell'occhio*, a punch in the eye. On one of my walks, a kaleidoscope of butterflies alighted on my shoulders, their wings pulsing open and closed. The ancients, Kitty later told me, believed butterflies carried the souls of the dead.

Professor Abbiati was not in Pompeii that summer, and there weren't many student groups on-site. Sogliano introduced Kitty to his superiors, the big men with the authority to make decisions about who could do what, and to mid-career researchers who might have an opening for a junior member on their teams. But Soggy, while powerful, turned out to be not quite powerful enough. I saw the men, young and old, learned scholars and low-level functionaries, look at Kitty with appreciation for nothing but her American beauty, and turn the conversation Sogliano was trying to have with them about a position for her into a sly game of congratulating him on his catch.

It soon became clear to me that foreign researchers were

tolerated on the site only if they came with substantial funding of their own, or, even better, co-funding agreements whereby some of the money could be controlled by the Italian archaeological authorities (who were often suspected of giving favorable on-site contracts to the local Mafia). Rebecca had come with abundant funding, which had bought her their compliance. Kitty had come with too little. I had a plan to change this, but I knew I had to wait patiently until she was ready to agree to it.

To make matters worse, Sogliano was caught up in a political battle for survival of his own. Trouble had been brewing for some time over disagreements about how deep excavations in Pompeii should go. Soggy shared Abbiati's view that they should go below the ground level that had existed in AD 79, down into the subsoil of the site's earlier history, but many of his superiors did not. He was also opposed to a younger, more revolutionary faction who believed that large-scale, open-air excavation on the site should be halted altogether, because exposure to the elements spelled doom for the buildings and everything precious within them. Pompeii's structures had been preserved thus far because they'd been held together by the volcanic lapilli packed tightly around them. Once that supporting material was removed, they were on their way to collapse. Sogliano, however, argued that archaeological knowledge had always come from destruction, that to dig was in a sense to destroy, and nothing new could be learned without taking that risk.

The country was still in some upheaval at the time, and funding for further excavation was drying up. Sogliano was trying to make the case that tourists, and their money, were attracted to the site by the promise of exploring newly excavated parts, but the younger archaeologists felt that what scant funding there was should be spent on conserving what had already been uncovered. Parts of the site had fallen into disrepair, but maintenance was done on an emergency basis only.

I had given Kitty a gift of her own set of tools and equipment, and paid to ship boxes of her books over express, so that she might be somewhat independent. Yet when she told Sogliano about her plan to continue her work of the past summer, examining the pigments used in the garden painting in the House of the Golden Peacock, as well as the plants growing within the ruins, he said it held no interest for him, no relevance.

He urged her to choose something with more sex appeal than birds and flowers. What about the painting of the well-endowed Priapus in the vestibule of the House of the Vettii? He went so far as to offer to bribe the guard stationed permanently beside the screen clamped on the wall, covering Priapus and his giant offending member, to unlock it for Kitty whenever she liked. She said no.

Next, he suggested she use his connections to gain access to the collection of Pompeii erotica held in the Naples National Archaeological Museum. Again, Kitty refused. She told him she didn't want to fall into the same trap as other female scholars trying to make a name for themselves in the field, by offering up the ancient world's risqué material—scenes of sex, dead bodies. Arousal and horror, she claimed, were overused as methods for engaging people in the past. Rebecca's name was not mentioned, but it was obvious who Kitty was referring to.

I remember clearly that it was after lunch on the first riposo of the summer, the weekly rest period during which the site was closed to tourists, when Kitty and Sogliano had this argument.

I had eaten too much pasta and was looking forward to a nap, but in support of Kitty I stayed at the table. She had moved into Sogliano's cottage in the workers' village and I had rented a nearby cottage from an archaeologist who was away for the summer. It was hot in the dining room even with the windows open; we should have been eating outside.

'Did you not read my paper?' Kitty was saying to him. She was upset and had abandoned her Italian.

'Of course I did,' he replied.

'And did my research on the historical reception of wall paintings also bore you?'

Sogliano shrugged. 'Let me say this. A young Italian would not have picked that topic, not in these times.'

'*These times?*' Kitty repeated.

'You know what I mean. Americans have the luxury to come here and pull off a small piece of history and chew away on it for years, but meanwhile we are fighting for survival. The place falls to pieces around us. We must keep making offerings to the public or they will forget Pompeii is here. It has happened before, and it can happen again.'

By that point I was desperate to escape the stuffy room and I excused myself. In my cottage I couldn't fall asleep. I gave up and went for a walk, the only person within the city walls. I felt spooked. Ghosts sensed in daytime can be the most terrifying, for having the pluck to venture into the light.

I half knew where I would end up. But I didn't expect the gate, and the shed too, to be unlocked.

This time, on seeing the thirteen bodies, I felt repulsed. They were not beautiful. They formed not an artwork but a mass grave.

Fiorelli's decision to pour plaster into cavities to create human shapes was not made entirely in the name of science. I knew from Kitty's research that the people of his time and place, a hundred years before, had worshipped the dead, leaving offerings to the thousands of skulls in the catacombs beneath Naples. They believed that the bodies of the saints could stop Vesuvius from erupting again. An ancient body in its death throes meant something very different to them than to me.

I remembered Rebecca saying that the bodies in the Garden were twisted into their poses from muscle contractions post-mortem, but I looked at those casts now and could not help but see agony.

I felt a growing sympathy with her approach. Suffering like this should remain private. Nobody should have to endure the humiliation of a cast of their corpse being stared at by millions of strangers. Let the casts made from other organic bubbles in the ash layer—the hunting dog, the pig, the loaves of bread—be put on display. But not those of humans.

I was beginning to feel delirious. I wondered if I'd eaten something at lunch that hadn't agreed with me, and sat with my back against the cool stone wall beside the casts, waiting for the feeling to pass.

After a while I became aware of a low buzzing from one of the bodies. I thought I was imagining it, but as I watched, a bee emerged from a hole bored into the cast. What would I find if I hacked it open, a body-shaped golden comb of wax, dripping with honey?

Pompeii seemed to me then like one big, unendurable tease, taunting me with the possibility that I might be let into its secrets, throwing up paradoxes if I got too confident. Too much death? Here are some signs of pulsing life. Too familiar, too close to what you think you know? Let us retreat into the inscrutable, cover our tracks. Shall we whet your erotic imagination? Now we shall throw you to the gods of disgust.

It is impossible to experience a place like Pompeii outside the prism of your own desires.

In the course of our research the previous year I had read aloud to Kitty Freud's essay on Wilhelm Jensen's *Gradiva*. Published in 1902, the novel concerns an archaeologist who becomes convinced that a woman from Pompeii's ancient past has appeared to him in the ruins, as the ghostly double of his childhood love. He stalks her ghost through the quiet city, slowly going mad. In writing about the novel, Freud made his claim that 'there is no better analogy for repression, which at the same time makes inaccessible and conserves something psychic, than the burial which was the fate of Pompeii, and from which the city was able to rise again, through work with the spade'.

He believed that the human psyche could be excavated like an archaeological site, made to throw up fragments which, once rinsed of dirt, might seem tantalizingly important. But in that moment beside the casts, the thought came to me that not everything from the past is precious. A lot of it is just other people's baggage, discarded for good reason.

My skull was heavy, wet with sweat, as if soaked in blood. The poor of Naples, Abbiati had told us, still ventured into the underground vaults of the Fontanelle cemetery to pick a skull to name, decorate, even caress. All this in the hope that its dead owner might, from its place in purgatory, negotiate with God a place in heaven for the carer. If the skull grew moist, it was taken as proof that the prayer had been heard.

That night I ran a fever. I dreamed I was in the Garden of the Fugitives with Kitty's honeycombed body beside me, sometimes dead, sometimes alive. In the morning, I woke feeling deterged.

The dinner invitations from you kept coming. I kept accepting. I turned down only one, to Thanksgiving dinner at your townhouse, which you quickly modified to a restaurant.

When you dropped me back home, there was a moment when I thought you were going to ask if you could come inside, into the mostly empty dormitory. You asked which room was mine and I pointed it out, the lamp I'd left on colouring the interior yellow. In the middle of the night I woke startled by a noise, but it was just wind in the branches.

I knew what was happening, to a degree. I hadn't told my parents about you, a sign I was discomfited by our intimacy, and my reasons for encouraging it. I worried, of course, that if I offended you I would ruin my chances of being given a fellowship. But I must also admit that you were good company.

It was soon after Thanksgiving that you sent me the bottle of Sauternes.

I didn't return your calls for a few days. When I did finally call you back, I lied and said I was going to Miami with a roommate for the winter break. I spent those days and nights mostly in the film department basement, editing. On the last day of the break, you called to ask if I wanted to go with you to Salem. I relented: a potential internship was another opportunity too good to refuse.

When the rest of the campus returned for reading period before exams, I was glad to be surrounded by people again. The libraries were full through the night, and our dining hall was transformed into a makeshift study hall. I was stressed and giddy, like everybody else, which must be why I agreed to run Primal Scream with a roommate in one of the coldest winters on record.

It was our last chance to participate in this campus ritual, designed for students to let off steam the night before exams began. That naked lap of the campus at midnight with the rest of the student population watching was generally the province of the jockiest of the jocks, or the drunkest of the Final Club boys, pretending they didn't care if they failed their exams. Not many women took part, and those who did tended to be on college sports teams, at home in a pack of fit bodies.

It was all fun and games at first, and easy to take off my clothes in the waiting throng beside the naked brass band. Safety and warmth in numbers. The gong sounded at the stroke of midnight and my roommate and I jostled forward with the crowd, hardly moving at first as runners took off in waves.

But my adrenaline wore off at the first corner and soon I was gasping for breath. My roommate, caught up in a faster group, was out of sight. By the second corner, a gap had opened up between me and the group running in front of me, which meant the students watching from the sidelines had an unimpeded view as I struggled on. I slowed down even further, until I was right at the back of the pack.

'There goes something,' a boy said unenthusiastically as I passed.

By the third corner, I didn't care anymore that I was literally coming last. All I wanted was for it to be over. The air was searing the inside of my lungs, and my limbs felt like iron.

That was when I thought I saw your face in the crowd.

When I finally made it back to where I'd started I was so far behind that most of the other runners and spectators had already left. I wandered around exposed, looking for the plastic bag containing my clothes.

Somebody took pity on me and offered me a coat, but I no longer felt cold. A rage at you had begun to burn in me. The dinners, the expensive presents were one thing. But this was a step too far.

In the morning, over breakfast, I told my friends the story of you watching me, embellishing it, enjoying the frisson of group disgust. They knew vaguely who you were, that I'd had interest from an older admirer. It felt good to have my experience made relative. A stalker wasn't so unusual among the young women in my dormitory, nor the men for that matter.

Nobody asked if I was sure of what I'd seen, or suggested I report you to the other Foundation trustees or the university administration. It didn't occur to any of us to do that. We ended up laughing about the interminable naked run and the places where my roommate and I had frostbite, and that was the end of it.

I didn't hear from you for a while after that, six weeks or more – not until I received the letter under my door informing me I'd been selected as a Lushington Fellow, unaware that you had delivered it yourself while I slept. On the following day, when you called to ask me out to dinner to celebrate, I thought about saying no but once again my mercenary instincts stopped me. Your decision could still be reversed.

You took me to my first opera, explained the rites of a class to which I did not belong: Italian lyrics translated on small screens, dainty binoculars, champagne at intermission.

At dinner afterwards, you asked in detail about my plan to spend the summer in New York before moving to Cape Town, and in spite of myself I told you everything. The internship I'd finally secured at a documentary production company in Manhattan, the ideas I had for embedding myself in the filmmaking community in Cape Town, a city in which I'd never lived and where I knew almost no one.

You suggested we have a nightcap at your house, and I'd had enough wine by then to go along with it. You left me in your grand living room while you fixed drinks in the kitchen.

I went looking for a bathroom and found myself in your bedroom. I'm not sure why I used your en suite. Some impulse towards desecration? Back in the bedroom, I discovered the door was closed, and it would not open. Tipsy as I was, I did not feel alarmed at first; I thought it was stuck. But then I realised it was locked from the other side.

When banging on the door had no effect, the gravity of the situation began to dawn on me. The double-glazed windows were also locked. There was no phone by the bed. I dragged a chest of drawers across the door and armed myself with the heavy metal toilet brush from the en suite. Then, drunk and exhausted (and fear is exhausting), I simply fell asleep on your bed.

I woke to early morning light streaming through the window. The chest of drawers was still in place in front of the door. I moved it as quietly as possible, tried the door handle. It resisted, then opened. You were asleep on the sofa in the living room, the TV remote in your hand, volume on low.

My memories of the night before were blurry. Maybe you'd passed out before realising I'd managed to lock myself in your room. On the train home, I indulged some darker interpretations. You'd locked me in there to protect me from your own worst instincts. Or you wanted me to sleep just for one night in your bed, to lay my head on your pillow – closeness at a remove.

Back in my dormitory, my roommates at class, I curled up in bed and opened my laptop. An email from you was waiting for me, asking if I was okay. Nothing else.

I composed a chilly reply that still came out frustratingly courteous, saying you should never contact me again except on official fellowship matters. A fortnight later I attended the spring banquet.

I took refuge in my film. It was almost finished and I needed a title. I'd considered naming it *An Artful Ethnography*, but decided on *Fragments of a Wine Farm*. This now strikes me as uninspired but at the time I was pleased with its acknowledgement of what the film would *not* be doing: presenting a full, layered profile of a community of people.

Boston turned warm overnight, which was jarring. I felt like a grub that had been buried underground for too long, and found myself laid low by the good weather rather than uplifted. Every green spot on campus was soon covered with bodies desperate for sunlight. Very, very far away, the invasion of Iraq had begun. Blossoms exploded from branches outside our dormitory and gave everybody hayfever, and the parties lasted longer, encouraged by the mildness of the nights. Then it got abruptly cold again, the sky even briefly threatening snow just for a day.

I tried to ignore the evidence of our impending May graduation, the manicuring of the grounds, the fresh painting of buildings. I went with my roommates to hire a cap and gown, and to pose for our senior portraits, and afterwards cried alone in my room.

My parents arrived the day of the film department's final screening event. We had a happy reunion over dinner, and I warned them not to expect too much of my film. In the theatre I sat beside them in the dark, sick with nerves. As the title card faded to black before the first image – the farm at dawn, a long shot with no movement on the screen, only the sound of frogs beating out a heartbeat – I once again had the out-of-body sensation I'd felt three years previously, handcuffed to my classmate.

But this time, the distancing felt fabulous.

I watched the film with new eyes, no longer its maker. I sensed the audience accepting my invitation to follow the long journey from grapes on a vine to bottles in a box. The few markers of location, of context, did not seem as evasive as I'd believed them to be.

At the end of the screening there was energetic clapping. The professor who had told me to focus on humans came up to apologise for not understanding what I'd been trying to do. I didn't tell her that the final film felt like a lucky accident, like something that had happened in spite of my own confusions. An anthropology professor who had kindly come along was less enthusiastic, but I already knew from her comments on the version of the film which had been used to grade me (a pass only, no distinction) that it fell short by ethnographic standards.

You were far from my thoughts that evening, and during my graduation the next day. But later that night I received your email congratulating me, and noting that my mother had borrowed my red shoes for the ceremony.

You're really quite determined to paint me in a bad light, aren't you? That is your right, of course. And anyway, my word against yours is a fight I cannot win.

I've been meaning to tell you something since you mentioned the rosebushes growing in the vineyards. Virgil, in the time of Augustus, wrote that grapes should grow with roses, and his advice was duly followed. Many of the vineyards around Pompeii are still planted with rosebushes, just as you describe. I too like the idea of the roses signifying something about the past that's no longer transparent to us.

This links to Kitty's interest in letting the past remain peculiar, rather than forcing it to become relatable. She thought it right that the people of ancient times seem fathomless to us. Over the centuries, she claimed, the key that might unlock the truth of how they lived had been lost. Artifacts dug up by archaeologists are often treated as clues to the missing code, but in Kitty's mind this was the wrong way to look at it. To her, those artifacts were more like pieces of alien matter dropped from outer space.

I had always liked to follow this train of her thought, but I was beginning to worry that it would get in the way of her future success as a scholar of Pompeii. As Sogliano had tried to impress on her, that future depended not only on the quality of her thinking, but on maintaining good relationships on-site. I wished she would sometimes be more open to shaping for the rest of us a cogent narrative about the past—to encourage us to exploit our imaginative abilities instead of shutting them down.

She and Sogliano reconciled after their argument, but I had the impression he didn't feel quite as responsible for her. He didn't invite her to meetings at the directorate anymore, or offer to make introductions. This troubled me. I didn't want their relationship to endure, but I wanted *her* to endure in that place. While he was right in pushing Kitty to extend herself, Soggy was wrong in thinking her work on gardens would prove to be of no value or interest to others. She was in it, or would have been had she not died so young, for the long haul.

We set up our workspace that summer in the House of the Golden Peacock once more. Abbiati had given Kitty permission to keep testing the pigments in the sloughed-off plaster we'd collected the previous year, and to use the House as our base. Kitty's stamina had improved greatly, but on certain days, when it was hotter than usual or she hadn't slept well, she still fatigued easily. To prevent her headaches from returning, I read to her while she worked on the pigments, and sometimes she spoke her thoughts out loud to a Dictaphone and I later transcribed them. I used to listen often to those tapes after I lost her, just to hear her voice, until the ribbons stretched and her voice became distorted—it sounded as if she were speaking from the afterlife—and I could no longer endure it.

I remember one particular early summer day with her. I had a cold, which she hadn't seemed to notice, so I was listening to her musings that morning in a small sulk.

She was speaking about how the House of the Golden Peacock was pulling itself apart along the fault lines between the ancient Roman concrete and the concrete that had been patchily applied in the twentieth century to prolong the building's life. The Roman concrete—seasoned for two years before use, extremely durable—was deteriorating less quickly than the modern concrete, seasoned for only two weeks. The latter was alkaline, which made it react with the ancient stone. Instead of holding the house together, the two substances were eroding each other, hastening its collapse.

Kitty had started wearing a bandanna, I suspect to cover the scar at her hairline, and when she was thinking hard about something she pulled it off unconsciously. 'You see?' she said, rubbing her temples. 'We look at the Romans and think they're not so different from us. They too seasoned concrete. They used it in similar ways. But the two materials are so different they shouldn't even share a name.'

I considered saying something to rebut this. I knew Abbiati had often challenged her on this point in his feedback on drafts of her senior paper. Why, he'd asked, did she get so worked up about our natural desire to connect with humans of the past *as* humans, no matter when or how they lived—was it not a good thing to look for common ground, common practices? Had we not learned by now, he wrote, the dangers of distancing other cultures, other places, other civilizations, of believing them to be less human than we are?

Kitty responded to his criticism with a kind of manifesto in the final paragraph of her paper. 'Relativism is essential for people who have to share time and space,' I had typed out for her. 'We are all one, all essentially the same. Yet for people who do not have to share the earth in the same timeframe—ourselves and the people of Pompeii, for example—relativism is no longer useful. It disrespects them and us, and all the generations in between who may have given their lives to change what humans are and can be, and how life is expected to be led. The more we dig, the more we think we understand of the past. In fact, the more we uncover through excavating, the more we potentially obscure. One way of seeing can be mistaken for the *only* way of seeing. Freud said, "The stones speak!" But they don't. They keep a dignified silence.'

In the House's grassy peristyle, I watched as Kitty retied her bandanna over her black hair, having worked through in her mind the little detail about the concrete.

I found myself thinking about a red slipware pot Abbiati had shown us the previous summer, the impressions of the potter's fingertips still visible in the clay. An ecstatic expression had come over Kitty's face as she slotted her own fingertips into the dents. She was not as immune as she liked to pretend to that feeling of intimacy across the millennia, that visceral jolt of connection.

I suggested we break for lunch, and Kitty went back to the village to cook for Sogliano. Somewhat masochistically, I stayed behind in the House, ate my stale sandwich, and forced myself to take notes from an ancient text on Pompeii's architecture, which Kitty thought might contain some useful passages on wall-painting techniques or the use of color.

It was slow going with my head so thick and stuffy. I kept turning to the dust jacket to look at the illustration of the ancient author, who had the imperious profile so typical of the Romans; he had done many things in his interesting life, the biographical note said, including making catapults for Julius Caesar. There was also a photograph of the modern-day editor, whose task had been to make the text more accessible to contemporary readers. He looked unfortunately similar to his subject.

I took down some of the ancient architect's descriptions of ingredients used in paint pigments. White from lead oxide; black from charred resin; purple from vinegar added to yellow ochre, or from murex shells; good quality green from powdered malachite.

At the end of this section was a detailed footnote by the editor in which he discussed the confusing change of color in these pigments over time. Modern viewers, he said, looked at the extant wall paintings and found it perplexing that Pompeiian artists had decided to make the sea and sky so green. This had occurred to me too at first: had they in fact looked green to them? Or was it an artistic device to depict them as such? But, as with the donkey and the rosebushes, a clue had been mislaid. The editor explained that two blues had been used in Pompeii's wall paintings, a cheaper one made from copper sulfate, and true blue, made from powdered lapis lazuli. The cheaper pigment, over much time, turned green.

The other dominant color in the interiors of buildings, the footnote went on, was the scarlet so ubiquitous it's called Pompeiian red, and this was visible inside homes both humble and grand. Yet red pigment was rare in the ancient world, and very expensive, since it was made chiefly from cinnabar, a strange ore that produced mercury beads when struck with tools. Red's dominance was in fact due to the heat of the pyroclastic surge that buried Pompeii, which had turned yellow ochre pigments red. Yellow walls had been very popular, particularly in less well off parts of the town.

There had been another red pigment in use, the editor noted. Vermilion, even more rare and expensive than cinnabar, was applied only in the wealthiest homes, but these walls too now looked black, heat having played games also with vermilion.

Near the end of the book, I found one more shining bead for Kitty to string alongside her observations about the ever-changing eye of the beholder. The ancient author had a long rant about the new style of wall painting in Pompeii (he was not to know that it was also the city's final style), saying it strayed from the fundamental role of art, which he believed—following Aristotle—was to imitate nature, not indulge the imagination. He didn't like the beast-headed statues, the winged Psyches and Cupids that were cropping up everywhere, all the whimsical illustrations that so charm and intrigue us now.

That way depravity lay, he wrote. Art should consist of 'reliable images of definite things,' and only then could it have a positive moral effect on the people viewing it. What was good for the eyes was good for the soul; fantasy and the unbridled imagination were good for neither.

By the time Kitty returned I had a throbbing headache myself.

'Look what Ettore gave me,' she said, her hand at her throat.

It was a necklace with a cameo pendant, not one of the cheap tourist imitations, but the real thing, an antique. I had spent time in the shop within the Hotel Vittoria in Pompei, looking at the displays of cameo jewelry, considering buying one for Kitty. The owner had given me a poetic monologue about cameos being presented as a vow of love to travelers, and something about a Renaissance pope who didn't cover his hands all winter because he so admired his cameo rings, and died from a chill.

'It's carved from coral,' she was saying. 'Ettore says it was made before the bay was polluted and the coral disappeared.'

To see it against her chest made me spiteful. 'It looks nice on you,' I said. 'Rebecca has one quite similar.'

Wounding Kitty gave me a quick, disgusting rush. Doubt sows itself so effortlessly in the human heart.

A week after graduation, I took the Chinatown bus to New York, my worldly belongings culled to what I could carry. My bank account was fuller than it had ever been, thanks to the first instalment of the Lushington funds. A friend had arranged for me to house-sit his parents' apartment in downtown Manhattan while they were away for the summer. My only responsibility was to keep the pot plants alive.

My internship was at a small production outfit founded by a woman from a famous American family who was able to make whatever films she wanted because she had endless pots of money. This didn't bother me, there were much worse things to do with inherited wealth than make documentaries, though it was annoying she wasn't prepared to use any of that wealth to pay her interns.

My first day at work was inauspicious. I stupidly decided to walk from Washington Square to the office in Koreatown, and got caught in a summer downpour. When I arrived I was drenched. Roxanne, the founder, was unimpressed, and also unfriendly. She made it clear right away that she regarded hosting interns as on par with community service – something without any benefit to her company, since most of us were clueless – and she wouldn't have time to supervise me.

Another intern, Atul, was assigned to help me get settled, and by midmorning I was alone in front of a computer with nothing to do. I watched for an opportune moment to ask Roxanne for a task. She and her senior producer, who were about the same age, late forties, called back and forth to each other from their desks, planning where to go for lunch. Near noon, they stalked past me in heels and freshly applied lipstick.

At the door, Roxanne turned and said to Atul, 'Tell her to get to work on the right-wing radio thing.' Then she deigned to look at me directly. 'You can type fast, I hope?'

'Yes,' I said.

'Good.' And she and her producer left for the day.

Atul came over to my computer. 'She wants you to take transcriptions of right-wing talk radio in real time,' he said. 'You can stream some of the stations over the internet.'

I didn't want to reveal the depth of my ignorance of American media and politics, so I nodded as if I knew what he meant and he went back to his desk.

I waited until he'd gone out to get lunch, then called a friend who was doing an internship at a news magazine. I related my assignment and she gave me some names to look up: Sean Hannity, Rush Limbaugh, Laura Ingraham, Ann Coulter. I'd never heard of any of them. Online, I managed to find one or two places to stream live radio, and eventually found a cache of audio files of Rush Limbaugh's recent broadcasts.

The sound was tinny and the levels were unreliable – his voice, in a permanent state of outrage, sometimes dropped low. I'd turn up the volume on my headphones and suddenly he'd be shouting into my ear, as if he were sitting beside me. But this was the task I'd been given and I wanted to do it well. I sat in front of my computer for the rest of the afternoon, typing out his vitriol about illegal immigrants, the treachery of liberal peaceniks who didn't support the war in Iraq, and the high treason of anybody who didn't think of Bush as America's saviour.

I left at the end of the day feeling dazed and filthy, as if I'd spent those hours inside a blister of hatred. I cancelled a dinner with friends and went back to the apartment in Washington Square. If I put my head out the kitchen window, I could see all the way up Fifth Avenue to the Empire State Building. I ate baked beans on toast and lay on the couch, surrounded by other people's things, listening to the sounds of the city revving up as darkness fell. I felt as if the words Limbaugh had spewed were lodged in my brain and trying to fornicate with my thoughts.

Before leaving the office I had printed out the day's transcription and left it on Roxanne's desk, but the next morning she showed no sign of having seen it, ignoring me several times on her way past, always toting a coffee cup before her like a charm to ward off evil.

I wasn't sure I could spend another day floundering in hatred. I was being pathetic, hiding away in the intern corner. I walked over to Roxanne's side of the office, where she and the senior producer were at their desks.

The two of them stared at me.

'I wanted to ask about the radio project,' I said.

'What do you want to know?' Roxanne said.

'Just what the film's angle is,' I said.

'I don't know yet,' she said.

'So the transcripts – you want me to take down what they're saying, that's all?'

'That's all.'

I was about to turn back to my workstation when she said, 'What's your interest in this business – camera, sound, editing, producing?'

I didn't think through my response. 'All of it. The process of putting it all together.'

She laughed. 'Spoken like a student filmmaker,' she said. 'In total control of the whole project, right?'

It was true that when I thought of making films, I imagined doing every phase of the creative process myself. Not out of some need for domination, but because I liked how every stage demanded something different from me, and together they seemed to form a perfectly calibrated artistic enterprise. Timothy Doring had managed to do it all – surely it couldn't be *that* hard.

But if I had to separate them, which would I pick? Producer? And sit in an office all day, sending other people out to do the image-making, the sound collecting? Editor? And work on somebody else's footage, with no say over the pace and style in which it was filmed? Camera person? And be given a list of shots to capture by somebody else? Sound? And be stuck holding a boom, forever at the edge of the frame? Each on its own seemed thin, unsatisfying, technical.

Off I went back to my private purgatory and continued taking down, word by horrible word, everything Ann Coulter had to say about the left's manipulation of the news media, including her regret that Timothy McVeigh hadn't chosen to bomb the building housing *The New York Times*, and her belief that Joe McCarthy was the ultimate American patriot. By the end of that day, and every day after it, the tendons in my wrists ached from typing, my eyes were red from staring at the screen, my ears rang with the voices of the peddlers of hate.

Transcribing those talk shows began to feel like a punishment designed specifically for me, for not paying more attention to what was happening around me, for only glancing at the head-lines. How had I made it through four years in America without learning anything substantial about its political system and processes? Alongside my core subjects, I'd taken electives in astronomy and literature and postwar Italian film, but not once had I made any real attempt to understand American history, not even after 9/11 – which, devastating as it had been, also felt slightly unreal, and the subsequent declaration of war a foregone conclusion, something that would happen no matter how much evidence was marshalled against it.

One of the talk show cycles I transcribed was a series of diatribes by Sean Hannity about liberal lower court judicial nominees who were, in his words, 'left-wing sleeper cells'. I didn't know that American judges in those courts were nominated for their positions, that even at those levels it was a political process of election.

And beyond that, how *did* the court system work in America? How was the government itself structured? What was Congress, really? What was Capitol Hill? This was stuff that most Americans had imbibed with their mother's milk, or at least had drummed into them throughout school. I was supposed to be clever, I had just graduated from an elite university, but that summer I felt as if I were being shamed into admitting I was in fact an imbecile.

Then the more uncomfortable reckoning began. I found it difficult to criticise America. How could I square my experience of American generosity – four years of free education, a liberal arts system designed to turn out creative thinkers; friends I loved, whose families had welcomed me into their homes – with this other sordid aspect of the place, the rage that was coursing through some of its citizens? Why did I feel similarly incapable of criticising Australia, with its own shameful history of annihilation and racism, its growing intolerance of foreigners of certain kinds and colours? Why did I feel incapable of criticising any country but the apartheid South Africa of my childhood, its sins now supposedly wiped away by the astonishing moral feats of 1994?

It reminded me of the strict boundaries my father had imposed on his empathy. The poor of Australia left him unmoved, but South Africa's poor gave him actual physical pain, a bleeding hole in his chest. I too seemed to have compartmentalised the world, into those I could censure and those I could not.

And so as the weeks passed, I began to feel glad for the absurd task I'd been given by Roxanne. It forced me into a political education of a sort, in negative, extremist, exaggerated terms, so that I had to guess at the actual nature of the events behind these distorted views. But still, an American education in some ways more real than the one from which I had just emerged.

Drinking out on the town with friends helped dissipate the sense I had when I left the office that my vision had been ripped in two. Like every other fresh college graduate, I pretended the city was mine, taking at face value Joan Didion's words about New York being a place for the very rich, the very poor, and the very young.

After one night of revelry, I decided to walk home in the early hours of the morning, enjoying my freedom. I knew that in Cape Town walking anywhere alone at night would come with risks. I avoided the well-lit avenues, and down a side street came upon a trailer with searchlights attached to it, grinding in erratic circles on their bases. The four beams were so concentrated they made circles on the dark sky. I'd seen spotlights on other nights, promising glamour somewhere in the city, but finding the source was like coming across the pot of gold at the end of a rainbow. It was a sign. My decision to go back to South Africa was about returning to the source. Only there would I have some control over the erratic circles I was making in my life.

But on other nights, I had nightmares about something happening to me in Cape Town. I would be startled awake, heart pounding, on the brink of being murdered. For three nights in a row I dreamed that a miniature Rush Limbaugh had found his way into my stomach, like a furious fetus, kicking and punching my flesh from the inside.

Your email arrived midsummer, saying you'd be in the city for work, and might I do you the great kindness of meeting. I never replied.

One morning soon after, on my way to the office, I stopped at the dog park on my corner to watch the making and breaking of canine alliances. I began to feel watched myself, but shook off the feeling.

I met a man in a crowded rooftop bar one evening and I woke to see the sun streaming through the window of his West Village apartment, onto the reddish hair growing thickly on his back. The next time I woke in his bed, his back was smooth and hairless, which was strangely disappointing.

He was the type of New York bachelor used to paying other people to make his life run well. He took taxis everywhere, never got on the subway. He ate out for every meal. He had a cleaner, and a woman who collected his dirty laundry and brought it back washed and ironed. His apartment was themed like a modern safari lodge, but when I asked about his coffee table book of wildlife photography he looked at me blankly. He'd never opened it – his decorator had placed it there.

One morning, when he'd left early for work, I dawdled in his apartment. In a bowl on his desk were slips of paper, past instructions he'd left for his cleaner. One read: *Please change the bedsheets. My girlfriend had her period.* This had not been me, but I didn't like him enough to care if he was sleeping with somebody else. What did intrigue me was the note's weird mix of registers: instructions to an employee, the laying of blame. I imagined him waking in the morning beside this woman to discover the stain, his disgust. I didn't see him again.

A blackout happened; power was out across the Northeast for a couple of days while I was home sick, running a fever. I didn't venture out of the apartment, lived off instant noodles made with cold water. My body was slow to respond to the Advil and I lay sweating on the couch. I found myself reliving in a feverish way an incident from my past, while outside the skyline remained eerily extinguished.

I was a young teenager. Mandela was newly elected. Spirits were high, but so too was the threat of terrorism. At a play with my parents, part of an arts festival celebrating the new South Africa, the theatre lights went out.

Anxiety rippled through the audience. Somebody announced, by the glow of a cigarette lighter, that the town's power was out, no signs of foul play, and the feeling in the room shifted. In the dark, the black actors onstage started singing the new national anthem. Most of the audience joined in; the festival had attracted a diverse, arty crowd. I could hear my parents singing beside me but I could not sing because I didn't yet know the Xhosa words – we were still learning them at school. My father gripped my hand.

My fever broke the same day the power came back on in Manhattan, and life went back to normal.

I went for brunch with friends, and the man in the booth next to us was South African – white, middle-aged, shorter than he probably wished to be. He made it known he was wealthy. I told him about my imminent return to our country, my filmmaking plans. I hadn't learned nothing from my encounter with Timothy Doring: aspiring artists like me were supposed to be open to any opportunity dropped in our paths, to advocate for ourselves at all times. So when this man invited me to his loft in Tribeca for dinner a few days later, I said yes.

In his kitchen, while he rubbed chilli oil on a plump steak, a tall and very striking woman was making herself a salad. He didn't bother introducing us. She was a model, that much was clear. It was also clear that she despised this man but was somehow dependent on him. She was living in his apartment, 'just for a while', she eventually told me, after I'd made repeated attempts to engage her in conversation. She was from Slovenia. Another girl turned up and proceeded also to make herself a salad in the kitchen, without a glance at me or any communication with the others. I began to feel uncomfortable.

He served me the grilled steak in the living room, and while we were eating he dialled up a famous film director he knew, saying he had a young woman with him who wanted to get into film. He handed the phone to me. 'Hi,' I said lamely. The director said he had to go and hung up. The steak began to taste like sawdust in my mouth. There were no more sounds from the kitchen; the models had gone out. We were alone.

He looked at me across the table, assessing me. 'Put your hair up,' he said, interrupting as I was telling him about my wine farm film.

It was an order. I tied up my hair with the elastic band on my wrist.

'What happened to your neck?' he said.

I froze. He moved out of his chair, stood above me and traced a finger low across my chest. 'This line,' he said. 'It looks like a scar, but it's a wrinkle.'

I had fixated on the steak knife beside my plate. Part of me, the docile part, was convinced things would be okay. That it would be rude for me to run out of there.

In my trance of inaction I ended up next to him on the sofa, where he put his bare feet on my lap and said I should massage them.

'You think your passion will protect you,' he said. 'You think that's all you need to remain interesting to men.'

I was touching a stranger's feet, smooth everywhere, the nails trimmed and filed, the feet of a rich man.

Through my fear I understood that he was voicing the misogynistic version of what the tutor in my feminism class had warned us about. I thought of you then, Royce – I maybe even missed you for a moment, in spite of everything that had passed between us. But you are not so very different from a man like that. You pay us to stay greedy, to keep dreaming big, only until we hit our thirties, all the while making us wonder, Does my female body hide my talent or host it? Then the bonuses stop, and we are on our own at the point where we might have needed you most.

He lay back against the cushions and I saw his erection straining against his pants, which was the shock I needed to find the will to act. I don't remember what I said or how I left his apartment, whether he tried to convince me to stay or let me go without protest. Outside, the air in my lungs was sweeter than ever before. I ran shaking and laughing all the way to the subway, feeling like Bluebeard's final, cleverest wife. A second lucky escape. Or stupid captivity? The models I abandoned to their fate.

As I was entering my last few weeks in America, Roxanne called me into her office one morning and said she was sending me to Capitol Hill to interview members of Congress about new media ownership legislation, as background for the right-wing radio project.

My face must have gone completely white, or yellow; I certainly felt as if I might faint. I had become used to sitting in my cocoon in front of the computer. In a flash I saw myself wandering around corridors, looking as inexperienced as I was, while all around me politicians and their staff power-walked to their next meetings. How would I get there? Did one say to a cab driver in DC, 'I'd like to go to Capitol Hill'? Was it a place, or a building, or a figure of speech? Was it really built on a hill?

Roxanne gave a shout of laughter. 'I'm kidding. You wouldn't survive five minutes!'

During my lunchbreak I went for a long walk, and happened upon fifteen elephants walking trunk-in-tail down Eighth Avenue, near Madison Square Garden. Traffic had stopped.

A woman watching the elephants, made chatty by the excitement, told me she was a bomb defuser for the Postal Service. She said they found bombs in the mail almost every week. Her brother, she went on, had recently returned from Iraq. He was depressed, and now he was being redeployed. I told her about my internship, made a critical comment about Rush Limbaugh.

'I love his show!' she exclaimed. 'That man has his head on straight.'

And I was once more glad to be leaving.

Soon after the cameo incident Kitty told me she had arranged, through Sogliano, for me to spend a day with Rebecca, ostensibly to learn something of her methods. I understood without Kitty having to say it what her real purpose was. My plan was coming together.

This wasn't as cruel as it might sound. I had Kitty's best interests at heart. I would nurture her suspicions that Sogliano was being unfaithful, and once their relationship had fallen apart I would create a large research fund for Kitty to use at her discretion. A fund big enough to guarantee her independence and influence on-site, without any need of Sogliano.

Since the start of the summer, to stoke Kitty's jealousies, I'd been encouraging her to spend time with Rebecca, to form an alliance, ask her advice on the politics of the site, to no avail. Rebecca had welcomed us back warmly, even offering to collaborate with Kitty on a piece of research on the skeletons, but Kitty had turned her down.

I had never seen Kitty intimidated by another woman, but then I'd never seen her in love before either. There was a lot about Rebecca to cause concern, from Kitty's perspective. Sogliano was her mentor; they'd known each other for years. Rebecca was a respectable thirty-four, already a professor at an established

British institution with links to the major museums, and research privileges that allowed her to live in Pompeii most of the year. She had two books under her belt and her academic star was still in the ascendant. In the monograph she'd published earlier that year, Rebecca had debunked beliefs about class and human bodies. She wrote that people from higher social classes in the past sometimes had the bad health and hygiene that only the poorest of the poor would have to endure in modern times.

Nutrition wasn't foolproof as a gauge of status either. Rebecca cited the English upper classes after the Industrial Revolution, who were often relatively malnourished, since the social mores of the time dictated that the rich eat refined foods like white bread and white sugar. Even dental care was sometimes worse among the rich. Emperor Augustus's teeth, she noted, had been described as 'small, few and decayed' at a time when the huge amounts of fiber in the diets of poor Romans meant their teeth were usually in good condition.

Her forensic analysis of Pompeii's skeletons was overturning assumptions that had once been used to bolster the theory that the city was half deserted at the time of the eruption. She had also refuted the long-held belief that the people who died in Pompeii's final natural disaster were predominantly female, infuriating a prominent male Italian researcher who had for years asserted that more women than men would have stayed behind in the city because of their natural attachment to their jewelry.

Though Kitty didn't put it to me in these terms, I think she found Rebecca's interest in dead bodies morbid. In her view, there was something refined about digging in the ground for artifacts and artworks, or slowly uncovering the painted boundary wall of an ancient garden, guessing at what had been planted in its beds. To look for hard evidence of human death unnerved her.

But while their approaches were different, Kitty and Rebecca shared a suspicion of stories about the past not backed up by evidence.

I went to visit Rebecca later that week, as arranged, at her workshop in the workers' village. She offered me espresso and we drank it in the garden, which had a view of Vesuvius.

'Are you planning to study archaeology yourself?' she asked, tying her red hair into a ponytail. She was no doubt unsure why I wanted to spend the day with her.

'Yes,' I lied.

'But at the moment you're here to help Katherine?'

I told her what I assumed she already knew, that Kitty's injury still had some lingering effects, and as her research assistant I wanted to learn more about Rebecca's techniques in case there was something I could be doing more efficiently for Kitty.

'She's lucky to have you,' she said.

'She's lucky to have Ettore.'

She raised her eyebrows. 'Oh yes. Him too.'

'Have you known him a long time?' I asked. I noticed the freckles across her nose.

'More than a decade. He took me under his wing when I arrived here. I was green as anything. He helped me cope with the fallout when I discovered the body cavities.'

'How old is he, if you don't mind me asking?'

She smiled, her gray-green eyes lighting up. 'I believe he turns forty-five this year, but don't tell anybody or he'll have you killed.'

'This is the first time he's considered marriage?'

'As far as I know. He jokes about being prepared to get married now only because it's recently become legal to divorce in Italy.' She paused. 'Is she planning the wedding?'

'No,' I said truthfully. 'Kitty wants to focus on her research.

There will be plenty of time for all that later.'

I sensed her relief at this news. She took the cups inside to rinse them, leaving me to sit in the sunlight.

Rebecca had clearly guessed at my feelings for Kitty, yet I didn't feel judged by her. To the contrary, I felt a connection between us. We both knew the sadness of loving somebody without much hope of ever making them our own.

I hung around for much of the day, watching as Rebecca worked. She didn't seem to mind. She was a gentle person, a natural teacher, explaining what she was doing without me having to ask. That morning, she was documenting a box of bone hinges. On each hinge she painted a number in India ink, according to her classification system. In the early days, she said, she'd experimented with a liquid solution of lampblack to preserve the bones, but now she waterproofed them with acrylic resin.

Inside the box, the hollow bones gleamed white, as if a beast had sucked them dry of marrow. Decades earlier, she told me, it had been considered a good idea to take femurs from the piles of human skeletons stored in the Sarno Baths and cut them into short pieces, to be used as replacements for damaged horse-bone hinges in excavated furniture.

'I had to get permission to take this box out of the baths,' she said. 'The rest of the bones are still there, in sorted piles. Skulls, mandibles, sacra, pelvic bones.'

'How many people helped you do the sorting when you first started?' I asked.

'My university sent a few students to help over the summers, but usually I was on my own.' She read my mind. 'I'm sorry I can't take you there. The baths are locked. The custodian goes on holiday in summer and he still doesn't trust me enough to give me my own key. He usually locks me in there while I'm working so tourists can't wander in. And so I can't leave without him knowing.'

I asked what it was like, down in those underground baths.

'Well, there's no natural light. The ancients preferred their baths to be dimly lit, they thought one felt warmer in the dark. There are rats. They eat the bags of pasta I use to balance the skulls while taking measurements. It was a war between me and the rodents before I could even get going on the bones.'

She worked on the hinges in silence for a while, as if she'd said too much. Instinctively I knew that not one of her male colleagues would have been prepared to do that work, that they must have sniggered behind her back at her willingness to endure captivity in that dank place with a pile of ancient, seemingly useless bones.

For though her research was by then gaining respect, when she'd first started out the skeletons in Pompeii were thought to have no archaeological worth. For centuries, she told me, excavated skeletons were robbed of their valuables and dumped in the baths. A few that were intact—sometimes composites of the bones of several different humans—were kept on hand in the eighteenth century in case of an important visitor. The workers would then be instructed to invent a memorable, if macabre, scene to make the dignitary feel his visit had been worthwhile. A room would be excavated, as if for the first time, to unearth a skeleton clutching a bag of coins, or reaching with bony fingers for the handle of a door, or hunched over a cradle.

I imagined how unnatural it would feel, to shovel lapilli and soil over an invented scene, covering history's tracks. Though I could also imagine the appeal of participating in the high drama of the reveal. It could be a solution to the contemporary dilemma of whether to dig or not to dig, I thought—just re-excavate the same house over and over for the tourists and everybody would go away satisfied.

Later in the day, I asked Rebecca to tell me more about the

superintendent in charge of Pompeii when she discovered the thirteen body cavities, the man who'd given them the false narratives she resisted.

She told me he had fashioned himself as chief magician of Pompeii. Early in his tenure, he encouraged the holding of séances on-site; Naples had been a hotbed of spiritualism for a while. He loved telling visitors made-up stories about the eruption: the guard who died loyally outside his sentry box, the priests interrupted mid-meal in the Temple of Isis, and the woman—a prostitute? a star-crossed lover?—caught mid-tryst with a soldier in the Gladiators' Barracks.

His approach was understandable, she said, given the years of his tenure. During the Second World War, he had begged the German troops, and later the Allies, to keep away from Pompeii, unsuccessfully in both cases. The Allies thought the Germans might be hiding within the ruins and in 1943 dropped hundreds of bombs on the site, just as Vesuvius was beginning to spew smoke, the precursor to its explosion early the following year when it showered Pompeii with a fine layer of ash, as if in retribution for the petty fighting of mortals. How else could the superintendent convince a country, a whole world reeling from the war, to take an interest in Pompeii again if not by invoking magic, and the promise of untold splendors waiting to be found?

'We have death itself molded and cast,' he'd said with great feeling on first witnessing Rebecca's casts. That was when the alarm bells went off in her mind.

I felt for Rebecca, for Kitty, for their predicament as female researchers in a male-dominated field. They constantly had to prove their seriousness, keeping as far away from magical thinking as possible. That day with Rebecca, I realized that only the male researchers could afford to get starry-eyed and make such mushy declarations as 'the great aim of archaeology is to restore the warmth and truth of life to dead objects.' The women had to be coldly objective just to stay in the game.

As I was leaving, close to evening, Rebecca told me she was trying to raise funds for a new research project, searching for the dead of Herculaneum.

It was a mystery to her why that city had yielded so few human skeletons, she said. Only about a dozen, compared to the thousands found in Pompeii. Granted, the site was less accessible to excavators, because on the day of the eruption the wind had been blowing to the southwest. Instead of being covered with ash and pumice like Pompeii, Herculaneum was destroyed by the first pyroclastic surge and flow, and buried under hard, tufa-like mud lava, difficult to remove.

There were various theories about the lack of bodies. The people had escaped. Earlier excavators had removed the skeletons. The groundwater had risen above the dead, destroying the bones. None of the theories were convincing to Rebecca, not least because people in Herculaneum hadn't had nearly as much time to leave as the citizens of Pompeii. Her own hunch was that a beach was now buried somewhere below Herculaneum's Porta Marina—the town was built on a high bluff—where people may have gone in the hope of being rescued by boat. It would require a major excavation to test this idea.

For a while after taking my leave I stood unseen in the garden outside her workshop, watching her at work. Vesuvius loomed above me. It often seemed to jump perspectives at dusk, moving closer or further away. It had lost its pennacchio, its constant plume of smoke, after the eruption of 1944, which made it seem harmless, as if it had retired from service. Not once did it occur to me that it might erupt while I was living in its shadow, though it was overdue for an explosion. Everybody said this was what lit the locals from within, gave them their manic energy.

I thought of waiting on the sea's edge with hundreds of people, caring only whether one of them was saved. Kitty. Human allegiances become so clear, are whittled down so very primitively, in the midst of a disaster.

More than a decade after that day with Rebecca, I read in the Boston papers about a researcher who'd made a sensational discovery in Herculaneum. The ancient skeletons of a hundred and thirty-nine people, huddled together in chambers formed by stone foundations along the waterfront, waiting to be rescued.

It was Rebecca of course, who was by then Rebecca Sogliano.

We had fallen out of touch, for obvious reasons. Regardless, I wrote her with my congratulations, on her discovery and on her marriage. I didn't expect to hear back from her: Ettore would have poisoned her view of me, I felt sure. Yet her response was surprisingly friendly. She said how thankful she was to have received the first Lushington Fellowship, which let her get started on the Herculaneum excavation, and the bonuses that had sustained her for many of the years since, while she searched—in vain, many had believed—for the dead of Herculaneum.

In her letter, she told me she had found the skeletons in tightly packed groups, covering their faces, all near the backs of the chambers where people had tried to escape the oozing flow. Rebecca thought thousands more skeletons might lie unexcavated along the shoreline.

She did not mention Ettore. But she did write that every year, on the anniversary of Kitty's death, she carried a bouquet of red valerian flowers up to the top of Vesuvius and threw it into the core.

My cousin Kevin collected me at the airport in Cape Town. I hadn't seen him in almost ten years. He was older than me and had lost all his hair, though he still had a young man's body, a surfer's tan. He had dropped out of high school but was now on his way to becoming a property magnate, flipping Atlantic seaboard properties to rich Europeans.

He drove fast, past the squatter camps on the N2 into the city, due at a business meeting and eager to drop me off at the furnished rental flat I'd found online, in a suburb called Oranjezicht. He was now divorced, he told me – his wife had wanted to emigrate to Australia.

'That's why you divorced?' I tried not to overreact. My parents had mentioned that Kevin was involved in some white supremacist stuff when younger, but had now embraced black economic empowerment and staffed his company entirely with non-whites, which gave him access to all sorts of government perks.

'Pretty much. I love this country more than I loved her,' he said.

Devil's Peak rose above us at the end of the highway. The road curved around its base, towards the sea-gazing face of Table Mountain.

Kevin took an exit at the very bottom of the mountain, whose famously flat top was broken only by the tiny hump of the cable car station. He drove up the slope, to just before the start of the stone pine forests, their broccoli-floret canopies blown into unlikely shapes by the wind.

I could see the City Bowl laid out beneath me, the CBD's buildings nestled in the curve of the mountain's arms, Devil's Peak on one side, Lion's Head on the other. These natural landmarks, familiar from childhood visits, now had an Alice in Wonderland quality to me, enormous and the wrong way round.

Kevin stopped outside my apartment block and I buzzed at the security gate. The landlord had left the keys with my next-door neighbour, Else, a Dutch girl with a big-toothed smile who came down and let me in.

My cousin carried my suitcase up to the third-floor flat and left, saying he'd be in touch.

The flat was a little shabby but had a wonderful view of the sea from the bedroom, and a balcony flooded with sunlight. I unpacked my suitcase, then sat on the balcony for hours, gazing at the rounded stone top and long green flank of Lion's Head, remembering a long-ago hike up it with my parents one summer holiday.

My American friends had understood my move to Cape Town to be a return home, and I'd stopped trying to explain that it wasn't exactly like that. My parents had moved often in South Africa when I was young – peripatetic as always – but apart from a year in Cape Town when I was a baby, we'd mostly lived in small university towns in the Eastern Cape. I had chosen Cape Town now not because I had friends there or knew my way around, but because those holidays with my parents were some of the happiest times of my life. The city was the most beautiful I'd ever seen – it still is.

My parents' history there, meeting and falling in love at university, gave it a special glow. They had given me their blessing to try to make a life for myself in Cape Town – it was safer than other parts of the country, an added benefit, and had a reputation for being a creative hub – though it meant showing up their own decision to leave, in a sense.

As the light faded, I wished I'd asked my neighbour some practical questions, such as whether it was wise to walk to the shopping centre at the bottom of the steep road carrying my passport and a wad of traveller's cheques, and on the way home a stack of cash.

I ate salvaged plane snacks for supper, watched the sun set behind Lion's Head.

In the morning, Else stopped by and offered to pick up some groceries for me since I didn't have transport; I gratefully accepted. It became apparent I would need to spend some of my Lushington money on a car – it was difficult to get around Cape Town without one, she said.

I called Kevin, and a few days later he took me to pick up a dented second-hand Mazda, which suited me just fine. I trailed him back from the dealer, so closely I almost rear-ended his BMW at one point, not wanting to lose him in the traffic.

He dismissed my fears. 'How can you get lost in Cape Town? Just follow the mountain home!'

The next day, alone, I forced myself to get in the car, and let my adrenaline carry me through the city. I very nearly did get lost – I could see the mountain, I just couldn't figure out how to get back to it.

My first two weeks were spent on tasks both mindless and complicated. I waded around various bureaucratic and logistical obstacles: an internet contract, a mobile phone, a private health insurance plan, an application to renew my South African passport. I had no idea where to buy sheets, let alone a fan or a fresh shower curtain. Even going to the shopping centre was an adventure, and I realised I was freaking other shoppers out by smiling and making eye contact, as if I needed to charm strangers in order to survive. I went on random drives, took the wrong off-ramps, got stuck in Cape Town's sluggish weekday traffic.

So many memories of childhood idyll crowded forward, as if my subconscious were encouraging me to map myself back onto the place. It should have been easy to open up to the magic of the city, the chart of youthful delights – the shops of the Waterfront, the twisting drive out to Cape Point, the colourful changing shacks of Muizenberg, the docks at Hout Bay. But right behind those memories would come a wave of disavowal, and then the nausea of disjuncture. Now that I was actually living there, feeling nostalgic about that time seemed suddenly wrong, forbidden – not so very different from somebody remembering picking mush-rooms gaily as a child in Polish woods during the bloodiest years of the Shoah.

I felt lonely, a little at sea. The part-time internship I'd set up before I arrived, at a film festival showcasing local films, was not due to start for a month. So when Else invited me to join her and some friends for drinks at Clifton Beach, I went along.

Not many of us swam that evening, the Atlantic's water was always too cold, but the sand was as white as it was in my memory and the sunset sublime. At our backs the silverleaf trees on Lion's Head glinted as if made from real metal. The mountain's green and grey folds were visible all the way to the end of the peninsula.

Else's group was welcoming, interested in what I was doing in Cape Town, but gradually they fell into their own comfortable conversations. I felt emptied out by the effort of building new rela-tionships from scratch. I missed my American friends.

I looked around at the youthful crowd on the beach, their iceboxes full of spritzers and cider, making the most of the start of spring. It was a picture postcard of racial harmony, among the middle and upper classes at least. These people were around my age, our short life histories bifurcated – the first half an experience of segregation, the second of integration. But unlike me, they were not fascinated by this scene. It had been their reality since the early 1990s, racially mixed primary schools, high schools and, later, university campuses. Now they were working side by side, young professionals in law firms and auditing companies and advertising agencies.

It occurred to me that I had left the country at the worst possible age, neither child nor woman, still tentative in my new friendships with the black girls at my recently desegregated school, caught up in the wave of pride in becoming poster children of tolerance and amity, but without time to normalise those relationships, to get beyond the symbolism.

In places where I had no deep claim to belonging, Australia, America, I'd been able to justify the sensation of being outside looking in. Now I was in the country of my birth and earliest memories, yet still I felt like an outsider, a gawker, no better than a political tourist. It was as if my citizenship had expired and nobody could explain to me how to reactivate it. I was fiercely envious of these South Africans of my generation who'd stayed, who had become authentically part of the Rainbow Nation.

I thought of Kevin – even him I envied. He was a survivor, sure, looking after his own interests first and foremost, but he'd found his place in the new disposition, had allowed the changes around him to manifest themselves in him. He was dating a young woman called Melanie and spent Saturday afternoons with her relatives out on the Cape Flats, drinking beer and watching sport on TV at the local pub.

I'd gone with him the previous weekend, glad I'd had some

practice with my Afrikaans on the wine farm the year before, and there too had felt set apart by my fascination with the way people of all races were gathered in the small pub without awkwardness. In fact my fascination made me the awkward one. The beer, the being together in that way, filled me with a warm fuzzy feeling I knew was out of kilter with the times. This was just urban life in South Africa in late 2003, but I couldn't get over how remarkable it was that in the space of a decade a communal reality could be so transformed.

Kevin must have noticed, because on the way home, driving drunk as was the city's culture, he made fun of me. 'Your jaw was down to the floor,' he said. 'What's the problem, don't you have any black friends in Australia?'

I said nothing.

'This is the new normal!' he laughed. And he swerved, almost hitting a cow that was crossing the N2.

Over the course of the next week, Kitty seemed increasingly restless in the House of the Golden Peacock. Partly this was my doing. I had told her Rebecca's relationship with Sogliano was very close, that I suspected something was going on between them. For good measure, I also said that Rebecca believed her forensic methods gave her the right to play God.

Kitty began to disappear during the day, leaving me to do the grunt work, saying she was going to look for a particular plant growing somewhere on the site, or mumbling about needing a different set of tools.

One morning, I followed her at a distance when she left the House. She was walking fast, with purpose, and I almost lost her when a group of tourists crossed the avenue between us. But when I caught up to her again, I could see where she was heading.

She didn't enter the Garden of the Fugitives through the gate leading into the back of the plot, but went through the rebuilt entrance of the small house at the front. I had to wait a while before I could safely spy on her through the slats of the gate.

It was clear she wasn't there to see the body casts; she hardly glanced at the shed. She paced the inside perimeter of the stone wall enclosing the garden, inspecting the ground. Every now and then she knelt and poked in the soil with a stick.

I wasn't sure what she was doing but I felt uneasy. It was not what I had intended, to spur Kitty to encroach on Rebecca's territory. For a week or two I said nothing about her absences.

When I next followed her, I was surprised to find a small team of workmen in the Garden of the Fugitives. Under her supervision, they were pouring plaster into holes in the ground along the edges of the wall.

It was time to intervene.

'I'm sorry,' she said when she saw me, not looking sorry at all. 'I was going to tell you soon, now that I've been given permission to use my grant money on this project instead of the wall painting.'

She scanned my face. 'I'm not looking for *bodies*,' she said. 'We're making casts of the root cavities of plants growing here at the time of the eruption. Ettore knows a paleobotanist in Naples who might be able to help me identify them.'

'But why this garden?' I said.

'I want to know what kind of garden the fugitives died in,' she said. 'It seems wrong the excavators hadn't thought to ask that question.'

I looked around at the men. 'Ettore arranged all this?'

'It took some persuading.' She smiled. 'He's happy I might be losing interest in the garden wall paintings. This is more tangible, at least, and he accepts that.'

'And Rebecca?'

Kitty's expression changed at my implication that she was trespassing.

'Never mind,' I said. 'Show me everything.'

She took me on a little tour, greeting the workmen by name. I watched as one of them poured liquid plaster into a hole that had been emptied of lapilli and reinforced with heavy wire. Another was digging out the already hardened cast of a root ball near the shed. It looked like a large stone octopus. Just as human remains had decayed within their crusts of volcanic debris, so too had the roots of plants, though nobody had seen the point of making casts of them before.

'Perhaps this is how it's meant to happen,' Kitty said. 'You start out blind and slowly you begin to see.'

There was some damage to the ancient soil layer, she told me, caused by trucks during the initial excavation decades earlier, but she was hopeful that beneath the more recent buildup a pattern of furrows might still be visible, another clue to what had grown there. There was also a small section, near the eastern wall, that was still at its original, unexcavated level, and the men's next task was to remove the layers of lapilli and ash from it, to see what was underneath.

She laid a palm on my forearm. 'Ettore only wants what's best for me. I have to stop this worrying about Rebecca. Help me be strong. Can you do that?'

I responded by hugging her. She was very thin. Through her shirt I could feel her vertebrae. She felt fragile, as though she would snap if I squeezed too hard. I hadn't been taking good enough care of her.

You start out blind. And then you begin to see.

The streets of Cape Town began to take on substance, a couple of routes became routine. I said yes to everything: pizza with Kevin and Melanie and their motorbike-fanatic friends; tagging along with Else on outings with her circle of friends, who treated the city as a giant playground. They kayaked amidst the sea kelp, jogged past the Twelve Apostles, bicycled along the peninsula. I borrowed their gear and tried to keep up. Their enthusiasm was infectious, to a point. They found me strange, I'm sure, someone with a South African accent, retained by choice over the years, but no local smarts.

I went to buy a steering wheel lock and the shop attendant recommended all sorts of other self-defence gadgets. Mace spray to go on my key ring, and a gel I could inject into my tyres if I got a puncture so that I wouldn't be stranded on the highway, a sitting duck for a hijacking. But if I was going to make a permanent life in that city, I could not be constantly hamstrung by fear. I didn't take the extra items.

To further test my resolve I drove in the midafternoon to Newlands Forest, where evening fell early once the sun disappeared behind Devil's Peak. The mountain created different pockets of light and weather. On certain days it could be raining in the southern suburbs and sunny in Camps Bay, or mist would roll over into the City Bowl but leave the ivy-covered buildings of the university on the other side of the mountain untouched.

I parked in the empty lot below the forest and followed the track up the mountain.

The path was deserted. As I hiked I refused to look over my shoulder. I knew if I let myself be ruled by paranoia, I would come to hate the allure of the mountain, with all its shady places, its faces of grey stone. It would taunt me by being close but cordoned off by an invisible field of my own fear.

I hiked for over an hour, until it was almost dark. Driving home I passed a small church, set back from the road. It looked familiar. On a whim, I did a U-turn and went inside.

It was the church where my parents had married; we'd visited it one holiday. In the candlelit nave I could feel their presence strongly. It was there they'd said their vows, my mother in a dress she'd made herself, my father with a handlebar moustache. Their parents had watched from the pews, shy with their counterparts. Two such different family cultures forced to merge.

I knew well the stories of their campus romance. Their first encounter at the Fresher's Hop dance, my father's visits to my mother's university residence, the orchids he gave her, at the time an extravagant flower. Their political awakening had come later.

For the first time, in that church, I understood what it had cost them to leave. 'I don't want to die in Australia,' my father said to me once, on a walk through Sydney's Centennial Park. His words had seemed wilfully gloomy in that setting, beneath the wide canopies of Moreton Bay figs, a feeling of peace all around. He didn't believe in an afterlife, or in souls of any kind, so why did it matter where he died? But of course it mattered: his death would determine his life.

The morning after my hike, I took my brand-new video camera

out of its bag, charged the batteries, put in a new tape, dusted the lens. I wasn't concerned about having something to show for myself when it came time to report back to the Foundation on how I'd spent the funds, but I knew I needed to find a way to make a film, as a matter of adaptation if nothing else, to ease the feeling of being foreign. On the face of it, nothing had been stopping me from filming everything I saw, yet in all the time I'd been driving around, not once had I taken the camera out of the boot.

I told myself the right topic would present itself if I remained vigilant. Days later, the timecode on the fresh tape was still set at zero.

My remaining Lushington funds were enough to cover most of my living expenses, but the good life in Cape Town was pricey. At the private girls' school up the road from my flat, I offered my services as an English tutor and soon had a bunch of pupils. Mostly the richest of the rich, elite black Angolan or Mozambican girls whose parents were paying through the nose for them to study in South Africa, and a few white locals who lived in opulent Camps Bay houses.

Finally the start date of my internship arrived. I set off with the rest of the working city that morning, glad for once to have a real destination, a place I had to be.

The festival was run from the bottom floor of a building in a scruffier area of Sea Point, beside the ocean promenade. The founder, Abiodun, was Nigerian, and we got on well from the beginning, but he was mostly out of the office, travelling around the country to source films and meet with filmmakers. I'd initially hoped that my role might involve accompanying him on these trips but the festival's budget was too small. There were two permanent staff, a white South African man and a black Zimbabwean woman, both of whom were frazzled from overwork but seemed reluctant to give me any duties that might let me shine. They talked me out of submitting my wine farm film for the next year's festival – it was the wrong length, they said – and sequestered me in the screening room, where my task was to watch advance copies of films and write synopses for the program.

Still, it was an opportunity, I counselled myself in that windowless room, to see what local filmmakers were doing, to watch films good, bad and ugly, the ones that would eventually be shown in public and the ones that wouldn't.

Many were harrowing portrayals of difficult subjects – rape in AIDS-ravaged communities, gangster culture in the townships, xenophobic violence against people from other African countries in the squatter camps. I was impressed by the political engagement and critiques of these films.

But what really blew me away was a film about the Sea Point public swimming pool. It was a purely observational piece, with no narration: the whites who came early in the morning to swim laps, the families of all colours who came in the afternoons to picnic on the grass, the black schoolchildren who couldn't swim but still jumped confidently into the shallow end of the pool, the sunburned tourists baking themselves on the walls. The filmmaker had found the elusive balance between saying something and saying nothing at all. The film was a quiet commentary on the fact that the pool could now be shared, that everybody could immerse themselves in the same rectangle of water after having been so long kept apart by the law.

Yet when I made a case to the others for this film to be shown in the festival, they said it sounded boring, and on discovering the filmmaker was in fact French, they rejected it. 'But he's lived here for twenty years!' I said. They appraised me coolly. Their decision, they said, was final.

In the long days I spent alone in the screening room, I began to realise that on the farms I'd been able to think of myself as an interpreter of some small aspect of South African life for Americans, conscious that whatever I filmed would be, at the very least, different enough from their own lives to justify my gaze on it. But living in Cape Town I could no longer be an interpreter. If I made a wrong move, picked the wrong topic like the French filmmaker, a local audience would see right through it, or, worse, take offence, and I would be exposed as an interloper. I was afraid I might make a spectacle of something that people who lived there considered unremarkable.

So my camera remained untouched. I resisted the urge to turn it yet again onto animals. I did not film the solo zebra and herd of wildebeest living wild in Groote Schuur Estate, at the base of Devil's Peak, nor the donkeys pulling carts on the shoulders of the highway. I toyed briefly with the idea of making a film about the ancient cycads in the botanical gardens at Kirstenbosch, a plant species that had made it through three mass extinction events and were protected as living fossils. Dozens had been stolen from the gardens, dug up overnight and trafficked on the lucrative black market.

But when I mentioned the idea to Abiodun, as he was on his way out of the office to catch another flight, he was dismissive.

'Who's going to care about the theft of a few spiky plants?' he said. 'We have much bigger problems.'

I was tempted, unhappily, by vineyards again, this time the ones within the city itself, in the leafy suburb of Constantia, where the Dutch governor of the Cape of Good Hope had built his estate in the seventeenth century. It was a relatively quick drive out there from the city centre, outside the impasse of rush hour.

I went there often, walked along the avenue to the old residence in the shade of huge European oaks. A bronze plaque nailed into one of the trunks explained that the trees had been planted to shield the vines from the Cape Doctor, which blows seasonally and brings with it a cloth of cloud. The belief was, if the wind blew the hair up from your head, the cloud was full of water and it would soon rain.

It was so very quiet on that wide path. From there, I could see across the surrounding neighbourhoods to the blue waters of False Bay.

There was a small museum in one of the outbuildings, holding a random collection of objects. A wine barrel made from the oak trees outside, a practice soon abandoned because the oaks grew so quickly in the Cape climate that the wood was too porous. An original bottle of the dessert wine Vin de Constance, for which the estate had once been famous, and which had been Napoleon's favourite while he was living in exile on St Helena – until phylloxera set in and ruined the vines. A wooden pipe with such a long stem that the governor needed the assistance of a slave to smoke it.

I wished I could find a way to make an interesting film about those objects or about the oak trees themselves, the only living witnesses to what had happened in that place of beauty and sadness. But the inspiration wouldn't come.

When Abiodun returned from his trip, he took me to an early lunch at a cafe in the nicer part of Sea Point. He was in a good mood and ordered a jug of Bloody Mary to share.

Over the meal, I asked dozens of questions about his background, his taste in film, his travels. He told me that he too had studied in America as an undergraduate, and had intended to return to Nigeria to make a film after graduating but was offered the festival directorship in Cape Town.

'This was in 1995,' he said, cleaning his spectacles with a napkin.

He was only ten years older than me but had a statesman's demeanour, a way of gazing into the distance that made him seem middle-aged. 'How could I say no? So here I am, almost a decade later, still circulating other people's films instead of making my own.'

'If you were to make a film now, what would it be about?' I asked.

'My family history, of course.' He gave me a quizzical look. 'I don't see why you won't just do the same.'

I didn't know him that well but the vodka had eased my inhibitions. 'Because you're black and I'm white. I'm on the wrong side of history for autobiography.'

'So what?' he said. 'I'm sick of whites making films about the suffering of blacks. I want to see whites deal with their *own* shit instead of trying to claim a moral free pass because they're so fucking interested in other people's suffering. So tell me, where would you start? What's ground zero for your family?'

'Swellendam,' I said with a certainty that surprised me. 'The Landdrost's house at Swellendam.'

'Quick, let's go, before I change my mind,' he said, motioning for the bill.

He must have noticed my glance at the empty jug.

'Oh please,' he said. 'I'm stone cold sober.'

Abiodun promised we'd be back in Cape Town by sunset. It was late November, a typically windy Cape day, and his car strained against the gale up the hairpin bends of Sir Lowry's Pass. On the other side of the steep pass, the wind dropped as we passed the orchards of Elgin.

I told him I was nine when my parents took me to Swellendam. On my mother's side of the family was an ancestor who'd been the town's magistrate in the days when it was a trading outpost for the Dutch East India Company, so she'd always wanted to visit.

We had gone there in midsummer, during the death throes of

apartheid. Outside the white-gabled residence there were volunteers welcoming the stream of visitors. Inside, while my parents paged through a ledger, I found a bedroom with a four-poster bed and a blue enamel chamber-pot beneath it. I climbed under the rope and onto the bed and laid my cheek against the pillow. It was rough, and smelt of lemons.

Abiodun was looking sleepy as we approached the long blue ridge of the mountain range above the settlement of Swellendam, and I wondered if he was regretting this impulsive daytrip. There was no signpost to the Landdrost's house, but we eventually found it, beside an informal rubbish tip.

The front gates were locked and spiked, the parking lot empty. When I buzzed the intercom, an elderly white woman emerged from the main building and peered at us.

'I'm afraid I may not be helping your cause here,' Abiodun said to me, waving at her.

Slowly the electronic gate creaked open.

In the lobby of the house, the woman gave us a visitors' brochure and asked for a donation. When I mentioned the magistrate, she began to speak in a torrent of Afrikaans, gripping my arm and pulling me over to a wooden scroll on the wall. My ancestor's name was embossed in gold beside the seventeen years of his service: 1760–1777.

She made us follow her on a tour of the house. Down the corridor was an empty room with a cobbled floor made of peach pits. In the kitchen, old copper implements hung from the ceiling. There was no fire in the hearth, only the desolate ashy remains of other fires on other days. I was certain that the place would not exist for much longer, that it would soon be bulldozed. Was this as it should be? Or was it better to leave it to its own slow public decomposition?

Magistrate. A glorified term for a town administrator, a civil servant. A functionary of the colonial state. Somebody whose days involved pedantic accountings of raw materials and goods, incoming bags of grain, outgoing vats of sheep fat. And in between, dealing with complaints from other masters about the behaviour of their slaves, making rulings on punishment, on when floggings were necessary. Somebody who was woken each morning by a brass band staffed by slaves playing in the garden outside his bedroom window, the alarm clock of white privilege.

When we left, the woman said goodbye to us with tears in her eyes, as if we were the last visitors she would ever see. And maybe we were.

I dozed most of the trip home. Outside my apartment block, there was a moment when I almost invited Abiodun up, though I doubt that had been his intention. He ended our expedition on a note of mentorship, snuffing out any erotic spark.

'I see your dilemma,' he said as the engine idled. 'But art is nothing but a catalogue of human experience. It has no intrinsic morality.'

Off he drove down the steep road towards the city, where he was meeting his wife and children for gourmet burgers on Long Street.

Upstairs in my flat, I checked my diary, hoping I had something to do the next morning. It was blank except for my own question from the past: *Are you happy?*

I was reminded this afternoon, watching a canoeist edge his boat into the Charles River, of a summer trip I took several years ago to Chicago, to celebrate one of my Fellows making partner at her law firm.

On the Sunday morning after the party, she invited me and a few others to take canoes out on the river. I fell behind the pod, struggling along between the silent skyscrapers rising up on either side of me, a gleaming canyon of metal and glass. Next thing, a coconut bumped into the side of my boat. I stared at it floating there in the greenish-brown water, husk and all, wondering if I'd had a touch too much sun. I scooped it out: it was real.

That surprise coconut brings to mind how I never quite knew what to expect when I was with Kitty, what she would find next or where we would end up. It felt good to be swept up in her passions, a piece of flotsam willingly carried along in her wake.

Her plant detective work meant I no longer had her to myself in our workspace in the House, but this was an adaptation necessary to her success. The Garden became a hive of activity, with Kitty at its center. Other researchers and archaeologists I'd never seen before began to stop by to take a look. Sogliano, who was seldom at our previous site, became a semipermanent presence, joking with the team of local laborers, plotting next steps with

Kitty, and giving anybody who visited a detailed explanation of what she was doing. Rebecca began to visit too, seemingly supportive of the project, and I could see that Kitty was making an effort to be friendly to her in return.

I stayed mostly in the background, watching as Kitty grew in confidence, building her networks, becoming unafraid to ask for favors or assistance when needed. For the time being, I put my plan on ice. Kitty had asked me to help her stay focused on her work, and I would do that until she was in a stronger position on-site.

Sogliano's paleobotanist, a bald little man who seemed confused as to why his work was suddenly of interest to his much more glamorous colleague, came out from Naples for the day to collect several large plaster root balls and a piece of carbonized stem for analysis back at his laboratory. He inspected the site closely and told Kitty that an aerial photograph of the Garden, showing the ancient soil contours, would be of great help in identifying what had grown there.

On hearing this, Rebecca offered Kitty the use of an expensive hydrogen-balloon photography unit she had borrowed for the summer from a research partner, a gesture that led to a suddenly genuine bond between the women.

Our team gathered at five a.m. on the day of the shoot. The photographs had to be taken before the sea wind began to blow midmorning. Rebecca and several of the workers attached the three Hasselblad cameras to the large, egg-shaped hydrogen balloon, and very carefully released it from a platform into the sky above the Garden. Stationary, low-altitude photographs were taken by radio control.

At lunch, cooked by the wife of Antonio, one of the workers, and served to our group in the garden of their home in the village, those gathered were high-spirited. I could see how pleased Kitty was to be properly part of this community, beside her future husband and with a new friend and colleague in Rebecca.

I thought she'd forgotten about me, but during the meal she pulled me aside. 'Have you seen their back plot?' she said. 'The one behind the orchard? Go take a look.'

An orchard of apricot trees was directly behind the house. According to Antonio's wife, the roots were so deep the trees never needed watering. Beyond the orchard, through a gate, was another walled plot, a small rose garden. The roses had large, loose crimson petals arranged around an open-faced yellow center, quite different to the roses I was used to, with their compact layers of petals hiding the filaments within. These rosebushes were trained onto stakes to grow in evenly spaced rows, and around each thick anchor root was a circular furrow. Even with my untrained eye I could see why the rose garden had attracted Kitty's attention. The spacing between the anchor roots was similar to that in the Garden of the Fugitives, and the water furrows here would explain the round depressions preserved in parts of the Garden's ancient soil layer.

The wind was up by then, and I could no longer hear the lunch party. The flowers bobbed to and fro, and I imagined their scent being transported over the wall and through the village, out into the empty stone buildings of the excavated city. Had the fugitives died in a rose garden like this one? A quiet and fragrant place?

I learned later from Kitty that those flowers were modern versions of *Rosa gallica*, the Campanian rose famous through-out the ancient world for its heady scent. Pliny had advised rose growers to pour warm water around the roots to make the eagerly awaited flowers bloom more quickly. The past is not so alien after all, I couldn't resist saying then to Kitty, who was gracious about my teasing.

The rose had always held great symbolic power for the ancient world, she told me. All roses were white, one legend went, until Aphrodite, Greek goddess of love, pricked her finger on a thorn while trying to revive Adonis, god of desire, god of beauty, as he lay dying. Her blood turned the flower red. I preferred the legend that the first rose grew from wounds inflicted on Cupid while he was tortured in the underworld by women furious at being disappointed in love.

The rush of energy I'd used to try to establish myself in Cape Town ran out early in the new year. A torpor settled over me. I called in sick to the film festival, day after day. My video camera remained in its bag. It was the long summer school holidays, so I had no tutoring responsibilities.

I stayed home watching the sun inch its way across the floor until evening, when people in the flats around me, back from work, turned on their televisions, took showers, banged pots. At night, the wind whooshed down the face of Table Mountain so ferociously that something in the building's roof came loose and began to lift and thud, lift and thud.

It alarmed me how quickly my store of confidence had been emptied. I'd assumed it was like an organ embedded in me, but it was more like a gourd that I carried outside my body, which needed regular refilling by other people. Affirmation is a drug like any other: the more you get, the more you need.

I paged through novels left by previous tenants. One was *London Fields*. The character Nicola Six haunted me, the way she knowingly embraced her own murder. My decision to return to South Africa began to feel fatalistic. My tooth enamel was chipping like hers, I too left skidmarks in the unwashed toilet; all the signs of my mortality could no longer be ignored. A conviction overtook me that I had returned in order to die. Not just any death, but a punishing Kafkaesque death, being drowned, or stabbed by a million needles, or sliced into paper-thin pieces with a butcher's knife.

Melanie surprised me by regularly phoning to see how I was, though each time I declined her invitation to join her and Kevin for dinner. One day she buzzed me from the intercom outside, asking if she could come in. It was past noon and I was still in my pyjamas, but she pretended not to notice.

She stayed for hours, telling me about their New Year's Eve party (I hadn't gone, had stayed home and watched the fireworks rising in bursts above the City Bowl), and the motorbike tour they were planning to the Klein Karoo in winter. I was raised out of myself by her presence, her stream of talk. She was wearing a leather jacket and boots, in spite of the heat. Her weave had an auburn tinge in the sunlight. We figured out as we talked that we were the same age, both born in 1980.

'Kevin and I are from different generations but we have the same simple background. That's one of the things I like about him,' she said, after telling me she took supper to her mother every evening, a platter of crustless sandwiches from high tea at the Mount Nelson Hotel where Melanie waitressed. Her mother lived in a basic maisonette in Manenberg, on the Flats. 'Our families are very similar.'

I was speechless. What had my cousin told her about his family, his parents who had stockpiled tins of bully beef during the '94 election and locked themselves indoors for days, convinced a black Armageddon was upon them? They had since moved to Mozambique because they thought the blacks there were less belligerent, and were now making piles of money running a game-fishing concession for rich white South Africans. It was true my

father's family had been poor, but they were also *white*. I'd sometimes felt pity mixed with something else – derision, or scorn – for
my paternal grandparents, for managing to be poor whites during
the years when whites in general had absolutely everything going
for them.

Melanie laughed. 'I know what you're thinking,' she said. 'Kevin
warned me your side of the family have the opposite of a chip on
their shoulder. He says it's more like you've got a big vulture sitting
there, pecking you every time you forget to apologise for your skin
colour.'

'Has Kevin told you what he got up to in his twenties?' I felt
like hurting him for talking about my parents, about me, behind
our backs.

'Yes,' she said. 'He told me everything. You have to understand – my brother had a motorbike accident a year ago. The tank
exploded. He looks like Freddy Krueger now, but he's alive. Kevin
was riding with him when it happened. He risked his life to drag
him out of the fire. So I don't care about Kevin's past. What I care
about is how he treats me now.' She patted my knee, like an old
friend. 'You're too hung up on these things.'

I was embarrassed to realise I was about to cry.

'What is it?' she said.

I chose the least complicated answer. 'I think I might be
depressed.'

'I got depressed when I moved to Durban. I only lasted half a
year there before I moved back. It's normal, when you don't know
anybody.'

'I think it's more than that,' I said. But I didn't know how to put
it into words, the sinking feeling I had when I looked out at the
city around me, filled with strangers thriving, or not thriving.

For a few days after Melanie's visit, I considered making a film about her and her brother, my literal counterparts: a portrait of a family who had lived on the other side of my experience.

But Abiodun's words of caution kept ringing in my ears. Was this really the type of film that modern South Africa needed, another well-crafted documentary about black suffering made by a white girl? Besides, I could see it all too clearly, as if I'd made it already. It would start with archival footage of forced removals of communities from thriving neighbourhoods close to Table Mountain out to the wastelands of the Flats, with its rows of soulless korre buildings. I would interview Melanie's mother about the valiant attempts of the community to rebuild a sense of civic pride in spite of their loss, about her late husband's activism in opposing rent increases, her work in the youth centre.

There would be baby photos of Melanie and her younger brother, and stories of their time at school, where her much older brother was recruited by a teacher to resist apartheid using any means necessary, including violence. The family's heartbreak when this son died in exile in Angola, only a year before Mandela was released. The joy of the 1994 elections, followed by the slow devastation of Melanie's younger brother as he joined the Americans gang and got into drugs, while she put herself through a hospitality course at the Technikon. Their father's death from AIDS-related tuberculosis. Her brother's sudden conversion to Christianity, the beginning of a new life, and then the motorbike accident that left him disfigured, dependent once again on his mother.

The film would end, of course, with a sequence showing Melanie putting on her leather jacket, climbing on the back of Kevin's motorbike, closing the visor on her helmet and zooming off along Route 62 in a cloud of red dust.

Maybe such a film would have been adequate in the early '90s, when those suppressed stories needed anybody at all to be a witness to them. But ten years on I had no idea what sort of film was appropriate, except that it probably wasn't a film made by somebody like me.

My depression deepened. I felt I'd sunk below the low-water mark, from where it might be impossible to pull myself back up. On the phone to my parents I pretended to be upbeat, and they didn't seem to suspect anything was wrong. The new school year started; I did my tutoring sessions on autopilot.

On the days I had no work, I began to go back out alone into the wild spaces of the city, no longer feeling defiant, but driven by more disquieting emotions. I wanted somebody to hurt me so badly that I would have a reason to leave South Africa forever, could blame my departure on trauma instead of my own failure to connect. Or I would be murdered. A human sacrifice to appease the gods. If I couldn't live there, at least I could die there. A perversion of my father's desire to die in the country in which he felt most alive.

Each morning on her way to work, Else left her copy of the *Cape Times* outside my door, and I scanned it for news of violence in isolated parts of the city. A report of a stabbing near Noordhoek Beach sent me for a run along the sand there, alone except for a few horseriders trotting in the shallows. A mugging outside a cave in Silvermine Nature Reserve gave me reason to go hiking there. On these expeditions, I resisted the overwhelming natural beauty, left the scales over my eyes.

A month passed, two. Abiodun had long since sent me a blunt email saying he had found a replacement intern, as clearly I was no longer interested. Else invited me out less often on the weekends. Even Melanie stopped calling.

Then two things happened to drag me briefly out of the pit I'd dug for myself. The first was an email from an ex-boyfriend at college. We'd lost touch since my freshman year but I still felt tenderly towards him. His name in my inbox brought back a vivid memory of lying in his arms and watching the first snow I'd ever seen fall outside his bedroom window.

'It's been a while since we were in contact,' his email began. 'Lately I've come to the realization that I need to change the way I'm living. I have decided to apologize to everybody I've caused pain or hurt at any stage in my adult life. Only by doing this will I be able to become a better person. While we were together I cheated on you five times.' I stared at the screen and started to laugh. 'I didn't tell you about it then because I thought it would hurt you, but now I can see that this was selfish. I hope you can find a way to forgive me.'

Relief flooded through me: I was not alone! The scales were slightly different, but our impulse towards moral reckoning was the same. We were both trying to figure out how to live. I sensed he was under instructions from some kooky personal-development program, or going through a religious conversion, but his regret seemed genuine. I wrote back a lighthearted email saying a few stolen screws as an eighteen-year-old did not matter, but if he needed me to forgive him, I did.

The second thing that happened was Table Mountain caught on fire. It had been hideously hot for a few days, an Indian summer, with the dry berg wind blowing incessantly. I woke early one morning smelling smoke, and from the bathroom window saw that a fire had crept so far down the mountain's face that the forests of stone pine, the last natural barrier before the rows of mansions began, were alight.

Else knocked on my door in her nightie. On the radio they were saying our area was to be evacuated. She asked if I wanted to come with her to work until it was safe to return.

She drove us to Bellville, where she worked as a designer for one of the last textile factories left in the country; Chinese workshops had begun to obliterate the local industry. She was wearing a skirt made from fabric of her own design, and bead jewellery. Her white-blond hair was neatly blowdried. I was disappointed in myself, basking in her kindness after months of avoiding her.

In the factory's studio, she and her colleagues of all ages and races chatted over coffee and koeksisters. I felt a painful admiration for Else. She had been in Cape Town for only two years but had made a life for herself that was rich and satisfying. Why couldn't I see my time there as an adventure too? Why did the stakes have to be so high? Why had I told everybody that I was moving to South Africa permanently, backing myself into a corner, making this not an experiment but a moral quest? I was so sick of myself, of every edition of myself.

Else gave me a quick tour of the factory. Suddenly, my filmmaker's eye opened wide. The factory floor was stocked with weaving machines made up of thousands of needles moving so fast they were invisible. Else slowed one of them down and I watched the two thread-pullers meeting in the middle of the machine then running back to their respective holes like mice. Beside the machines, black women waited, their only task for all the hours of the day to thread and rethread the needles. Nearby, rolls of material were pressed, a layer at a time, through a chemical bath in which the dyes were set, and next to that was a 'rubbing' machine that simulated on samples the effect of years of human bodies sitting on upholstery.

In the tearoom, I turned on the TV and tried to still my beating heart. I was excited by the thought of filming those machines, the way they made one thing into another, just like the wine bottling plant in Worcester. A visual symbol of transformation.

I could even dripfeed a bit of autobiography into it, make glancing mention of my paternal grandmother starting work at age fourteen as a weaver in a textile mill. Or my grandfather's early working life in a mattress factory, stuffing coconut fibre between metal springs by hand, at a time when poor whites like him lived and worked alongside poor blacks. I could show that it had been part of the point of apartheid to 'decontaminate' through segregation the sort of mixed neighbourhood in which my grandparents had grown up, how different my father's reality had been as a result. For after the National Party came to power when he was a baby, his parents benefited from subsidised housing for whites, which let them buy their own home in a little cluster of racially unmixed families. Start with some economic stratification to break down bonds of social trust, then legislate some hardcore segregation, and eventually you have the perfect recipe for fostering feelings of racial superiority.

A white guy about my own age walked into the room and put on the kettle, introducing himself as Deon. He was shorter than me but muscular in a way that suggested daily, rigorous exercise. We made small talk for a while, and I asked what he was doing at the factory.

He told me he was trying to convince management of the benefits of using recycled water to rinse the fabric after the chemical soaking. He was doing a postgrad in geographical science, working on harvesting the water of the artesian springs that flowed from Table Mountain. These springs fed a network of underground canals beneath the City Bowl, built by the earliest European settlers. Not many people knew about them, he said. His mother had been among the first to rediscover them, back in her university days.

By the time I returned home that evening, the fire now under control, I had abandoned my idea for a film about the textile factory. Instead I could make one about the city's hidden waters.

Deon had told me his mother sometimes took select groups down into the canals and I'd given him my number, saying I would love to come along. People like them didn't sit around worrying uselessly about complicity and consequence, they took their skills and put them to practical use, got to work fixing one thing at a time.

I went to bed feeling that my loneliness had lifted ever so slightly.

In the morning, the air smelled charred and the blackened lower slopes of Table Mountain were a nightmarish vision of hell, but there was no sign of the fire having resurrected itself overnight. I googled the water canals and discovered that somebody had beaten me to it – a documentary film had already been made about them by a social geographer from England.

I had become an inspiration slut. Always too quick to abandon one idea for another. I feared that this would keep happening until I found solid ground within myself, a foundation from which to say something good and true.

A teacher had once said of me to my parents, a veiled insult which they interpreted as a compliment, 'Clearly, she has a lot on her mind.'

While Kitty waited for the balloon photographs to be developed and for the paleobotanist to give his verdict, she began to excavate the only part of the Garden of the Fugitives that had never been dug up, the section against the eastern wall.

Every day, when I arrived at the Garden thinking I was early, I would find Antonio and the other laborers already sweating in the morning heat. They were experienced in methods of excavation, but still Kitty preferred to be there while they worked. She came earlier and earlier each morning herself and stayed later in the evenings. And I made sure to stay with her, so that she could never doubt my devotion.

Their first find, in the top layer of the volcanic ash, was a trapeta, a wedge press used to extract oil from young green olives, which many ancient authors had noted was the preferred base for perfumes.

With your love of visual processes, you would have enjoyed watching the men remove layer after layer of compacted ash and soil, until there before us was a trapeta, an everyday object that, through its good fortune of being trapped beneath volcanic material for so long, now seemed as significant as a radio signal from another solar system.

This was followed, a few days later, by the discovery of a large stone kennel, built against the wall. Given its size, Kitty believed it was designed for a watchdog, which meant that the crop grown in the Garden would have been considered valuable, and at risk of theft. There were many mosaics around Pompeii depicting watch-dogs, the creatures all black as soot so that a thief would not see them at night. Canine body cavities had been found elsewhere in the city, most famously of a dog still chained to its post, but in the Garden we did not find the animal itself.

Near the kennel, high on the wall, the men later uncovered a votive niche. In it was a cracked but intact statuette of Mercury, wearing sandals and a winged hat and carrying a staff around which wound a serpent, and beside him a statuette of the goddess Maia, mother of Mercury.

I was there with Kitty as the niche and statuettes were revealed. She said nothing to me as she inspected, tagged, and photo-graphed them. I knew her well enough to know this was not the time to ask questions.

She disappeared for the rest of that day. When I knocked on Sogliano's door early the next morning, he said she was at the research archive in Pompei, and later on he was taking her to the Naples National Archaeological Museum, to look for the notes from the Garden's original excavation.

'She'll be exhausted,' I warned him. 'All that reading on her own, searching the archive, with not enough sleep.'

'Rebecca went with her,' he said. 'She knows the archive better than anybody. And today I will be accompanying her. She can nap in the car.'

I lingered, hoping for an invitation to join them in Naples.

'You're in charge of excavations,' he said as he prepared to close the door on me. 'Don't find anything important!'

All day, I worked hard alongside Antonio and the other men.

Most of what we found in our sieves was modern debris, so we worked fast, shifting larger and larger volumes. Only as we approached the ancient soil level did we slow down and work more cautiously.

Though it was still light, one of the men trained a spotlight on the soil surface. I copied them, getting down on my hands and knees to search for fragments. We began to find pieces of things that even I could recognize. Clamshells, filbert shells, and several bigger spiky shells, which I knew were from a snail that had once been used to make purple dye, and was also sometimes eaten by Pompeii's poor. Antonio found a carbonized date seed with a piece of fruit still attached to it, a snack abandoned half eaten. I knew from Kitty's research on plant species that dates would have been imported from elsewhere; for some reason, the palms that had grown in Pompeii did not bear fruit.

The men identified a few shards of bones from larger animals – cow and pig – which had evidence of cleaver marks, proof that they were the remains of a meal. My contribution was to discover a single grape glinting beneath the spotlight, its sugar caramelized to glass in the extreme heat of the pyroclastic flow.

Nearby, the laborers had earlier in the week found evidence of stakes for a pergola, and the root cavities of the vines that had been trained on them for shade, so we all knew what lay beneath the remaining mound: the triclinium, a set of three stone couches surrounding a low table where summer meals would have been eaten.

It was too late to start on it. I told the men in my basic Italian to stop for the day, to go home and eat with their families. They turned off the spotlight and left me alone in the Garden.

In the twilight, the whitish pieces of bone and shell stood out against the dark background of the tarpaulin on which they'd been laid. They made me think of a picture Kitty had shown me in one of her books, of a floor mosaic excavated from the dining room of a villa on the Aventine in Rome. The mosaic was in a decorative style, popular at the time, known as 'unswept floor.' It was filled with images of discarded shells and bones, seeds and pits, fishbones, lobster claws, wishbones—designed to look like the real-life debris of a feast thrown to the ground around a triclinium, as was the ancient custom.

The scraps we had unearthed would, I hoped, please Kitty on her return. They were probably the accumulated debris from many meals, but I liked to imagine they were the remains of the last supper of the people whose body casts lay in the corner of the Garden. The final meal of the fugitives.

Elsewhere in Pompeii, evidence had been found of other last meals being prepared on that clear morning: a cheesecake covered in poppy seeds, a medallion of ham flavored with bay leaves and fig slices left baking in an oven. What if *this* were the moment of calamity, Vita, right now, as you read this email in your cottage in Mudgee? The remains of your breakfast—the oatmeal burned at the bottom of the pot, the eggshells in the trash can, the tea bag in the sink—preserved forever. Just one of your thousands of meals, rescued from domestic oblivion and given the power to speak for you across millennia.

I wondered if Kitty would also visit the paleobotanist while she was in Naples, and receive confirmation of her theory. For I knew she must be right, that the root cavities in the Garden were those of *Rosa gallica*, and the plot was what she believed it to be, a market garden.

Roses were in great demand in those times, I'd been learning, and not only for perfume. The petals were strewn on the floor at festive banquets, or dropped from hidden panels in the ceiling to rain upon guests—so many that there were exaggerated stories of people being suffocated by them. Garlands of rose petals, hand stitched by slaves, were believed to stave off drunkenness, and were draped over bodies at funerary rituals as a sign of affection. The rich liked to float petals in their wine. The rose bookended the cycle of Roman living, for all life began with romantic love of a kind and ended with a body covered in red petals.

That roses had been grown for commercial use in the Garden was, I knew, an elegant and useful discovery for Kitty to make. Not many market gardens within the ancient city had been properly excavated or cataloged at that point, another blind spot of archaeologists. Yet this was not enough to explain her secretive behavior of late. I suspected there was more to it, that she had a few more ideas up her sleeve.

Deon did not call. May passed in a wet blur. I tutored my pupils, occasionally went out with Else. Kevin and Melanie left on their motorbike tour of the Karoo. My loneliness intensified. But I tried not to succumb to the need, which rose and fell in me like a tide, to go alone into isolated parts of the city, seeking punishment.

Until one cool morning when the mountain's siren call sounded too loud and clear to resist, and I was once more lured up its slopes.

It was a weekday, the best time for something to go wrong, with fewer people hiking in the wilder stretches. In the empty botanical gardens the fynbos had a pungent smell, like body odour.

From the moment I began to climb the steps through the gully at the start of Skeleton Gorge, I had the feeling of being watched. No, it was stronger than that. The fire had not touched that side of the mountain. Mist had collected in the ferny wetness of the gorge, and for some reason I thought of an account I'd once read of a woman who survived an attack by a crocodile. She described sensing the presence of evil as soon as she submerged herself in the still water. But that was an innocent animal's malice, and the wild predators were long gone from Table Mountain. This was something else.

I stopped to rest after an hour, at the point where the path emerged from the dense cover. I looked at the city below, feeling nothing, then kept climbing over low boulders until the packed earth gave way to pristine white sand. On the very top of the mountain was a beach, a thousand metres above the sea, at the edge of a natural reservoir the colour of tea.

In the elation of summitting I kicked off my sneakers, ran through the sand and splashed up to my thighs in the freezing water, ignoring the signs forbidding bathing.

Afterwards, I lay on the sand feeling a fierce itchiness in my toes as they thawed in the sunlight. When I reached for my shoes I saw the figure of a man standing on the opposite, rocky edge of the reservoir. He was wearing long pants and a cap but otherwise was too far away to reveal much of his identity: black or white, old or young, I couldn't say. From his stance, I knew he was watching me.

I put my shoes on quickly.

But instead of going towards the man waiting to enact upon me what I had claimed to desire, I fled in the opposite direction. I ran to the path leading down Nursery Ravine. It was more exposed than the gorge, which meant less cover for me, but also for anyone following. I moved fast, looking over my shoulder to see the empty rock steps mocking my fear.

I put my head down and pushed through the heart pain of the rapid descent, Camus' retelling of the myth of Sisyphus beating through my brain, reminding me of my cowardice. The endless punishment by the gods for his sins, pushing a stone uphill in agony then watching it roll back down, pushing it back up again, over and over. On his return downhill to the same rock at the base of the mountain, Sisyphus is aware that he is sealing his fate, his death. Yet he goes to it, accepts it.

I tripped, landing badly, and smacked my head on something.

An hour was lost to me. By the time I got up and kept going, the sun was on its own downward loop, heading into the Atlantic for its nightly drowning. The figure I'd seen at the top of the mountain seemed as distant as a dream.

I reached the wooden stairs at the bottom of the trail, then the grassy hill and the paths of the botanical gardens, and finally the car park, where mine was the only car.

The last rays of light caught the clouds above Devil's Peak as I hurtled along the highway. I had proven myself incapable of facing my punishment. My head was hurting, my thoughts were tangled. I tried to remember what Camus had actually written of Sisyphus – something about atoms of stone, the mineral flakes of a mountain forming a whole world. I cast about for another way to understand what I was doing in Cape Town, and alighted on the idea of an exorcism of my old identity, a ghost needing to be chased out of me before I could move on.

But this seemed too harsh an interpretation: I loved that country. What if, instead, I could think of myself as a pilgrim on a quest for enlightenment – since to be a pilgrim is to be always passing through, a wayfarer, moving by foot up the mountain and down the other side, repenting by recording every detail of the journey to share with other sinners. What if the essence of a place, the *genius loci*, were apparent only to those on the move, those who come to observe for a while and then leave, or those who are banished and can never return?

Back at my flat I found a Lushington gazette and a pair of gold earrings in a pouch in my mailbox, in blatant disregard of the city's epidemic of theft.

It had been you on the mountain, only you. You had robbed me of my brush with fate.

I threw the earrings off my balcony, into the grass growing at the side of the abandoned lot next door, and fell asleep on my bed before it was dark.

I awoke confused, my head throbbing, my mobile phone buzzing in the pocket of my windcheater. It was Deon, saying his mother was giving a tour of the underground canals the next day and I was welcome to come along.

I said yes quickly, no games. His voice sounded to me like salvation. I could maybe cling to him for a while. A weak move, but better than the degrading path I'd been on, inviting somebody to make a violent decision for me, on me.

Later that evening, Else stopped by with a curry she'd made, and a black eye. Laughing, she told me she'd been mugged on her way to the post office by the gang of kids who lived under the overpass, punched in the face by the same ten-year-old she'd once taken to Nando's for a meal.

I'd long wanted to visit South Africa, and I had a wonderful time in your birthplace when the opportunity presented itself. But I did not climb Table Mountain, much as I would have liked to see the white sand of the secret beach you describe at the summit. The cable car took me up and back down an entirely different section of the mountain, from which I had a stupendous view of the sea in all directions, but also tourists everywhere, eating fast food from the café at the top. It was never within my power to rob you of your moment of reckoning.

Kitty returned from Naples with the good news I had been expecting—roses had indeed been grown in the Garden of the Fugitives, according to the paleobotanist. She did not tell me much about what she'd found in the Naples museum, except to say she had hoped to find more than she did.

Within a few days, she had completed the final phase of the excavation, uncovering the triclinium and its low table. On the last day the work team was there, Kitty presented a large-format aerial photograph of the site to Antonio, and, to my great delight, another to me, singling us out for our contributions. That photograph still holds pride of place on my bedroom wall, as you may remember. It's the last thing I see before I fall asleep, the first sight to greet me each morning.

Everybody pored over the black-and-white photographs, seeking the new perspective they allowed of the place in which we'd spent so many weeks. Seen from above, the Garden was a neat gray rectangle splattered with white from the plaster in the root cavities, which looked star-shaped against the dark ground. The water and soil furrows made patterns of circles and lines, as if somebody had written a message in the dirt. It felt to me that I was looking at the surface of the moon. The shed's roof was tiny from that height, tucked against the wall. It was clear that growing space for the rosebushes had been maximized—the foundations of the house took up less than a third of the plot.

With the excavation over, I was eager to assist Kitty in writing up her research for publication; I had missed our communion of minds. Yet once again she seemed reluctant to accept my help, saying her energy levels were good and she felt it would be more productive to work in the archives alone. I wondered if Soggy had been whispering in her ear.

Insultingly, Kitty asked me instead to help her plan a birthday party for Sogliano. For my usual selfish reasons I dissuaded her, repeating what Rebecca had told me, that he was sensitive about his age. She agreed to abandon the idea.

But a week later, an envelope was put under the door of my cottage. Inside was an invitation to a surprise birthday party for Sogliano, starting at four p.m. the coming Saturday. The venue was the Villa of the Mysteries, one of the most extensively excavated rural residences outside the old city walls.

I felt terrible. Not only had Kitty gone behind my back to plan this stupid party, but she'd wasted time that she could have spent on her work. She had told me she was going to the archives when in fact she must have been making preparations. That very morning, she'd said she was returning to Naples with Sogliano for several days, to meet again with the museum curator; perhaps this too had been a lie.

On the day of the party, I forced myself to take special care with my ablutions, and put on the one good suit and tie I'd brought from home. I left early in the afternoon, giving myself plenty of time to walk along the path around the city walls. I passed the Herculaneum Gate and went out along the Via dei Sepolcri.

Like all main roads to ancient Roman towns, this street was lined for miles with tombs. While they had been given a prominent place, there was a reason these tombs were built outside the walls of the city. Not all Romans believed in an afterlife, not in the way we would now understand it, but they still had a healthy respect for the harm the spirits of the deceased could do if not appeased.

I had walked that road before but never taken the trouble to look closely at the inscriptions on the tombs, mostly names and titles, dry grandstanding. But there was one that seemed unusual, a fragment of a dispute between two men. It took me a while to translate with my schoolboy Latin, but I made out enough to understand that the man buried there wanted to tell all future generations that he had been falsely accused of a crime of some sort. *Stranger, delay for a while,* it began. *This man whom I thought was my friend produced informers against me.*

The Via dei Sepolcri was denuded of vegetation and the sun beat down on the cobbled roadway. This tomb had a shaded bench built into it, designed to encourage passersby to stop and consider the man buried inside. A lure to guarantee immortality, to make the living think on the dead and their grievances, and it was still working thousands of years later.

I sat on the bench to rest and thought about what I would want written on my own tombstone. It would have to be something that made Kitty feel bad forevermore for not loving me back, the plaintive curse of the neglected. And then I tried to imagine a life without her, and couldn't. Without Kitty, I would hardly exist.

The excavated tombs stopped not far from the Herculaneum Gate—there had never been much political will to continue excavating outside the city walls. I passed the entrance to the Villa of Cicero, an ancient country residence discovered by accident by modern farmers working their land. The road split. The left fork led to the Villa of Diomedes, and eventually, all the way along the coastal road hugging the Bay of Naples, to Herculaneum. The other road led to the Villa of the Mysteries.

I hadn't been to this villa before; it had been closed for restoration for two summers. Kitty must have pulled all sorts of strings to host the party there. It was huge, I'd heard, ninety rooms in all, and prized for its sumptuous decorations and spectacularly preserved wall paintings, left in situ, not removed to the museum like most others.

The villa was built on a sharp slope and the walk up to its entrance left me winded. A few guests were milling about on the terrace when I arrived, nobody I recognized. Most of them were admiring the hanging gardens planted on either side of the portico, another remnant of the glory days of the villa.

The view was breathtaking. The Vesuvian slopes were a familiar bright green leading down to the sea's blue line. Beside the villa was a vineyard, and I saw an old couple sitting outside the farmhouse there, scowling at the party guests. They'd most likely been children when the villa was discovered beneath their farmlands.

A waiter appeared beside me with a tray of drinks. I took one and drank it fast, thirsty after the walk.

I spotted Rebecca. She was wearing a short black dress, her hair swept up into a French roll. She waved at me but made no attempt to come over. I took another drink and sipped it more slowly.

It was past four and waves of guests were arriving, all in formal wear. The air filled with mingled perfumes and aftershaves. I felt self-conscious in my suit and tie and wished I'd gone to the trouble of renting a tuxedo for the night.

A cheer suddenly went up, and applause, and I saw that Kitty and Sogliano were walking up the road from the line of parked cars, holding hands. For somebody sensitive about his age, Sogliano looked extremely happy, but Kitty's smile was tight at the edges. I knew instantly that she hadn't been part of the planning, that she was as surprised as he was. She was wearing a demure blue evening dress, and next to Sogliano she looked very young and unworldly, more like his daughter than his future wife.

I glanced at Rebecca, who was giving instructions to a group of waiters. She had outmaneuvered Kitty.

My fortunes were improving.

Kitty came over to me as soon as she could get away from the knot of people around Sogliano. 'What's going on?' she said.

'I have no idea.'

'We got back from Naples at lunchtime and there was a note from Rebecca saying to put on our best clothes and come out to the villa.' She swiped a glass from a passing tray.

Sogliano was exclaiming excitedly as each friend came forward to greet him. At his side stood Rebecca.

Kitty looked me in the eye. 'You said he didn't like birthdays.'

'*Rebecca* said that,' I reminded her.

Kitty composed her features to greet somebody she knew, exchanged a few words in Italian, then turned back to me, her face slack. 'I know,' she said. 'It's got nothing to do with you. I'm sorry.'

For as long as we could, she and I loitered on the terrace, avoiding the others, until we were all summoned by the waiters to enter the villa for dinner.

The doors led directly into a large peristyle court. Though the peristyle was not the usual place for a feast, its floor had been covered with rugs, and low couches were set up in groups of threes—contemporary triclinia. Torches burned in the corners, throwing light and shadows across the room.

Sogliano came over to find Kitty, and led her to a couch in the center of the courtyard. He lay theatrically down along its length, gesturing for her to sit next to him.

All around me, the guests seemed to understand some rule I didn't, and were lying on the couches amid much hilarity. My stomach twisted.

Kitty called to me. 'This one's yours,' she said, indicating the couch next to hers. Rebecca was already sitting on the third couch of the triplet, a handsome Italian man beside her.

I lay down and listened to the hum of voices. I'd had a lot to drink on an empty stomach.

'You're not actually allowed to lie down,' Sogliano was teasing Kitty. 'Only the men can recline at feasts.'

On the table between us was a platter of boiled eggs, olives, and lettuce. The waiters poured out a very sweet honey wine. I drank mine and tried to catch Kitty's eye, to see if she was still angry, but Sogliano was working his charm, fussing over her, feeding her morsels, and soon they were giggling and whispering to each other.

I raised my glass whenever the waiter came near me, drinking the wine like water. Another course was brought out, roast meat and seafood. Sogliano ate with gusto, licking his fingers.

'This fish sauce is made to the ancient recipe,' I heard Rebecca say to her companion, 'with blood taken from a mackerel while it's still alive.'

I picked at the food, lay back on the couch, and wished for the night to be over.

'And now, according to custom, the women will get up and move a couch to the left,' Sogliano announced to the room, to laughter and protests.

'That's got nothing to do with custom,' Kitty said, moving to my couch. And then she saw what had been engineered. Rebecca was now next to Sogliano.

We both ignored the dessert plate of cheese and fruit, pickles and oysters. With our heads on the armrest, we watched Sogliano and Rebecca talking and joking.

'Is this really happening, this open flirting between them?' Kitty said.

I looked around the room. Everywhere, men and women were flirting with one another, moved on from their spouses. We were clearly not the only ones who'd been drinking too much; the food was salty and no water had been offered, only wine. From eggs to apples, a complete Roman meal was supposed to go, but I had eaten neither.

I felt content to be beside Kitty. I tilted my head and studied the painted wall beyond the columns, and could just make out the image of a skeleton holding two wine jugs. The flip side of feasting is death. The ancients had always understood that. A banquet is life in miniature. You arrive hungry, eat and drink your fill, make merry, then go to sleep. All feasts, all lives, must come to an end. *Death, tugging your ear, says: Live, I am coming.*

Kitty sat up and said she needed to get some air. I went with her, picking my way across the peristyle between the reclining diners. Sogliano and Rebecca didn't seem to notice us leaving.

As soon as we were out of the room, Kitty ran off down the corridor. It was dark. The corridor and the adjoining rooms it led to were lit only by the occasional torch. I struggled to keep up with her, feeling my way drunk and blind. I staggered through two rooms, my eyes adjusting slowly, and out into a larger room, its walls red in the torchlight. I knew we were in the Hall of the Mysteries.

Through her tears, Kitty was peering at a wall showing a large figure of a woman bent over another woman's knees, accepting care after punishment or torture, a bright red wound across her naked back. This was one of a series of paintings thought to depict an initiation into a secretive female Dionysian cult, the passage from girlhood to womanhood.

Kitty started to ramble. 'Pompeii, when you first see it, suggests a life of grace. A life so enchanting you ache to live it yourself. But do you know what the first excavators found beneath this room? The skeleton of a boy chained by both legs to the wall.'

I was taken aback. Kitty had not spoken much of slavery before; scholars of Pompeii usually skimmed over it, treating it as another commonplace practice of the ancient world.

In a gesture of unthinkable confidence I drew her toward me, and to my surprise she didn't resist. She opened her mouth against mine. I tugged at her dress. We were horizontal all of a sudden, against the hard floor. My fingers were on her skin, her breasts in my hands. Fabric and flesh all mixed up.

I lifted the hem of her blue dress, touched her thigh, and she froze. For a moment too long I pretended not to notice, and moved instead to cover her body with mine.

She struggled to her feet, her dress rustling as she put it back into place, and left without a word.

I lay there in the flickering torchlight, thinking horrible thoughts about murdering Sogliano and hiding his body among the skeletons in the Sarno Baths. I wished that the volcano above us would no longer restrain itself. That it would send down its slopes an incandescent avalanche of rock and ash suspended in white-hot gas, each pyroclastic surge and flow reaching further and further, smothering everything in its wake, blacking out the moon with clouds of ash and pumice, darkening the world.

Cities and towns, modern and ancient, would be erased forever from maps. Thick forests of poplars would grow over the ashes once more. And thousands of years into the future, somebody would discover my distended body and guess at why I'd been alone in that room, partially unclothed, and why the young woman in the long dress had collapsed in the corridor outside. They would come up with theories as to why we were the only two people not at the communal feast on the night deadly Vesuvius erupted once more. History, I suspected, would not judge me kindly.

Deon became my guide, the person who could get me to the place I'd been unable to reach on my own, a companion for the short days and long nights of the Cape Town winter. Though that's not exactly true. It was his family who guided me, who folded me into their clan.

Soon after we started dating, he invited me to dinner at his parents' home. It was in a street of houses I'd often ogled when driving past, a giant glass box perched above the kelp fields and boulders of Bakoven. I soon discovered, on subsequent visits, that I was only one among many guests regularly welcomed there. The Jouberts' relaxed style of togetherness was at odds with the post-modern lines of their home: they mistreated the house and every-thing in it, encouraging people to eat on their laps on the white sofas in the lounge, not minding if wine was spilled on the carpet.

At first I thought this was just the behavioural luxury of very wealthy people. They could buy another sofa, get the maid to deal with the carpet stains. But in fact – and this was a rarity for any white South African family, rich or poor – they had no maid. At the end of each meal, everybody chipped in to pack the dish-washer, sweep the floor. Deon's mother, Bibi, was no pampered trophy wife. Her lined face was always free of make-up, and she did all the cooking and most of the cleaning herself. His father,

John, took care of the garden and the pool; the younger brother, who still lived at home, was responsible for doing the laundry.

People came and went constantly, flowing through the house, sleeping overnight in the multiple spare rooms, turning up for breakfast beside us the times Deon and I slept there. I was accepted without question by his parents and brother and cousins and family friends, made to feel I belonged as much as a blood relation.

It became clear to me that the reason Deon wasn't curious about people was because his parents were so curious about *everybody*. People's life stories unspooled at every meal. His parents were always ahead of the rest of the table, not even I could get in a prober before they did. This was the only thing they seemed to ask in return from their many guests – to be interesting, to participate in the conversations around the huge wooden dinner table that John had made himself.

The characters rotated, but there were regulars. A Pakistani astrophysicist. An elderly Zimbabwean grande dame who had in her heyday pioneered a type of genetically engineered seed. A Croatian Iron Man champion who told tales about deep-diving in cave pools. Multiple cousins, uncles and aunts who all seemed to be doing things they were passionate about. One uncle was the media manager for the Democratic Alliance. Well before the days of apps, a cousin was developing a mobile phone notification system to help people with AIDS reorder their medications.

Bibi and John loved to have their guests give a talk or show photos after dinner. They said it reminded them of the olden days, when they and their friends used to project their holiday slides on a wall, heckling whoever was managing the rate at which the slides changed if they got boring. 'There is absolutely nothing more excruciating,' John liked to say, 'than looking at somebody else's pictures of wildlife. Bush. Bush. Bush with speck of warthog. Bush with ear of elephant.'

One evening, the astrophysicist tried to explain his research to the assembled group. We were drinking John's home-brewed brandy, made from buchu herb picked in Silvermine; it smelled of blackcurrant but tasted like petrol. Mayhem descended when the astrophysicist started talking about what he called the Zone of Avoidance, which had something to do with things hidden behind the Milky Way. There were fart jokes, Bibi shouting from the kitchen about never hiking behind John. Eventually the astrophysicist gave up trying to explain anything and let us ooh and aah at the pictures of the universe on his laptop.

On other nights I was there, the interest in these presentations was more serious. A black friend of Deon's, who had grown up in a township in the Eastern Cape and gone to a private school on scholarship, gave a slideshow about his university chemistry thesis. He was working on a way to detoxify glue, which street kids sniffed for a high, so that it wouldn't harm the nervous system. After that night, whenever I saw the street kids under the overpass – the ones who'd mugged Else – instead of feeling swamped by guilt I felt a glimmer of hope.

I still wasn't sure how I felt about Deon himself. We didn't have a lot to talk about when it was just the two of us. But I decided to ignore this in order to keep spending as much time as I could with his family, soaking it all up, taking note of every detail of their lives, hoping I could learn from them. They didn't lock their front door, for example, and they had no burglar alarm, nor any bars on the windows. This wasn't something they bragged about, it was just how they chose to live.

Deon didn't lock his car either, a new Citi Golf his parents had bought for him. He left a window down permanently so that anybody looking for valuables wouldn't need to break in, and also so a bergie who lived in the park near his house could sleep on the back seat on especially cold nights.

It irritated me that he took the car for granted, accustomed to his parents' largesse, but it impressed me that he didn't mind sharing it in that way. I often found myself moving between those two poles of feeling when I was with him. I'd have 'gotcha!' moments, when I thought I'd pinpointed what it was that didn't sit quite right with me about his family's approach (paternalism? unconscious entitlement?), and once made the snarky comment to him that only people fortune has smiled on could have such endless trust in others. He let it go, as he let many things go.

And then I would hear of some new detail that nobody in their right mind could deny was a sign of goodness. His parents had founded an orphanage in Gugulethu; Deon was personally sponsoring township kids at the private high school he'd attended; the family had set up an incubator for social entrepreneurship.

I later learnt from Bibi that she had been tied up in the house many years ago, held at gunpoint while burglars systematically stripped the place of everything worth taking. She told me this while we were cooking chicken breyani together in her kitchen.

'It was after that,' she said, 'that we stopped locking the house.'

I was silent, fighting the desire to tell her about my solitary hikes earlier in the year. I had never told anybody about them, not even when Deon took me back up Skeleton Gorge, past the reservoir, to sleep in the Mountain Club's hut. Just the two of us eating tinned mussels by candlelight, watched by a century of white mountaineers in photographs on the walls.

'You see,' Bibi went on, putting a pinch of chopped onion on top of her short brown hair (she believed this stopped her eyes watering), 'that's when I stopped living according to the law of paranoia, believing that forces were conspiring to make my life painful. Instead I embraced the law of *pronoia*. The belief that the universe is conspiring to shower me with blessings.'

I kept trying to get a proper read on her and John, but the two of them had somehow slipped free of labels. At first I'd assumed they must have been hippies in their youth, classic liberals marching and protesting against inequities through the worst of the apartheid years. But that wasn't the case. John was a lawyer, had met Mandela and represented some ANC activists back in the day, but he had also done work for an asbestos company, supporting the owners in their refusal to give workers proper compensation when they got sick. 'For valid legal reasons,' he said, taking the rap from the rest of the table when they called him out on this. And the photos on the walls of Bibi in the '70s and '80s showed her enjoying the fruits of apartheid in white enclaves with nary a black face to be seen: Kruger Park campsites, fun runs, pools, beaches.

They weren't bleeding hearts – my parents would not identify with them, or even like them much, I realised early on – but they had found another way to exist in that country, through all its ups and downs. John and Bibi hid nothing, but they also ceded nothing. They considered themselves African, and couldn't fathom the thought of living anywhere else on earth, but their inherited fortune (Bibi's ancestors had founded a diamond mine) was kept in overseas bank accounts. They lived well, they gave generously. I admired their lack of self-consciousness, their refusal to buy into the guilt complex, their way of turning away from petty concerns about the state of their souls and looking out into their country with the conviction that they deserved to be there, that they could do good there *and* live well.

'Why should we not want to live well?' John said one evening at the dinner table. He still had a head of thick black hair and it made him look much younger than his sixty years. 'That's what we want for all people, is it not? We want the poor to live better lives, to have comfortable homes and close families, eat good food. So what use is it for us to deny ourselves such a life? I would say it's a moral obligation for us to enjoy our luck, to share what we have, but to enjoy it too. Otherwise what we're asking other people to work towards means nothing, if when they get there they have to feel guilty about what they have.'

In many ways I aspired to live like John and Bibi. Sometimes I fantasised about marrying Deon and taking a permanent place at their table. But my creative paralysis did not lift.

Occasionally when I was with the family, I felt my class consciousness flare up like a rash, and could not resist taking the victim's cloak for myself. I would exaggerate the deprivations of my father's childhood. 'He didn't even have shoes until he was fourteen,' I said to them once, but how could that be even vaguely true?

The Jouberts loved to hear about my delinquent ancestors. My great-grandfather who had lived in old age as a homeless drunk in an itinerant black community, which seemed to tolerate his presence because he could buy booze at the whites-only bottle shop. The cures my grandmother peddled, traditional Afrikaner folk remedies – ginger for colds, Epsom salts for any ailment, cloves for toothache, solid camphor sewn into a bag for my father to wear around his neck during polio outbreaks.

'Your father is a peasant,' my mother liked to say whenever presented with proof of his backwardness, his abiding suspicion of credit cards, doctors, wristwatches and mobile phones. (But she said it with great love in her voice. They were so bonded, so co-dependent – they rubbed balm into each other's elbows in winter, shared a single coffee at cafes.) When I told stories about my father's family for the Jouberts, it was with an ugly nugget of resentment that I did not have what Deon's family had, the power and freedom that great wealth had given them, even if they did use it in the service of good.

'The Khoisan's name for this region around Table Bay was Camissa, which means the place of sweet waters,' Bibi had told our tour group on the day I first met her. She was wearing pink gumboots, which were just visible in the dark as we sloshed through the tunnels beneath the City Bowl. Stalactites hung from the old brick, illuminated by our torches.

I did not feel that the water was sweet. It smelled foul, and I'd avoided looking at the walls of the tunnel too closely for fear of what I might see. Yet it was tranquil down there, with the traffic muffled above our heads.

'The Dutch made Cape Town a shipping stopover because of this fresh water from the streams and springs,' Bibi said to us. 'The water was eventually used for everything from irrigation to hydropower. It used to flow in open canals through the city, until the British decided to cover them for sanitary reasons. Most of this water now flows directly out to the Atlantic and is wasted.'

Her grand plan was for the recycled water to be used in the stadium that would be built for the 2010 Soccer World Cup, if South Africa won its bid to host the competition. And indeed, she made this happen, as I learned from a television broadcast years later: the pitch at Green Point was irrigated using the city's sweet waters.

I almost sent an email to congratulate her then, and to ask whether she would now begin work on her secret dream, something she'd once told me in confidence, knowing Deon would frown upon any water use not of practical benefit. One day, she hoped, the canals would be opened up again and a section of the

City Bowl could be traversed, just as in Venice, by gondola.

But too much time had passed since I'd abandoned without proper farewell her beloved city and her son, and the family into which she'd welcomed me, and I left the note unfinished in my drafts folder.

I did not apologize to Kitty after what happened in the Hall of the Mysteries.

Instead I went into the town of Pompei the day after the party and placed a call to my financial advisor from the hotel. He agreed to set up a research fund for Kitty, and to courier the paperwork so that she could access the money as soon as possible. He must have heard something a bit frantic in my voice, for he engaged me in fatherly conversation about my plans once summer was over. He recommended business school, in small part as continued protection against the draft (though by then the risk of this was low), but mostly because that's what someone from a family like mine does when at a loose end.

You see, Vita, talented people like you and Kitty have always needed people like me, benefactors of one kind or another. We all know that. But what you might not know is that we have always needed you too. Status is linked to art and intellect, that's part of it. If I can't be creative or talented myself then the next best thing is to give my money to somebody who is, so that I might by proxy dip my toe in those salubrious waters. But I think it's more about the raw need part of the equation, need that has to radiate from both parties.

The contract arrived a couple days later. In it I bestowed on

Kitty a grant generous enough to cover all her living and research costs, to be paid every two years for the next decade.

I took it to Sogliano's cottage midmorning, when I knew he would be working elsewhere on the site. Kitty was sitting at a desk in the courtyard, surrounded by manuscripts.

It was there, on that warm August day, that she asked me to leave Pompeii, to leave her in peace. She said that the night of the party had confirmed what she'd long suspected. I was an unhealthy influence on her. I was trying to destroy her relationship with a man she loved and a female colleague she respected. She tore my contract in two and said I should never return, that she did not want to see or hear from me again.

It was a Joubert family tradition to gather the fittest of the extended clan once a year and swim almost eight kilometres in the permanently freezing Atlantic sea, from Robben Island to the beach at Bloubergstrand.

Each participant, from Deon's thirteen-year-old cousin to Bibi's elderly but still strapping father, had to raise a certain amount of money, and the proceeds that year were to go to a project, run by John's sister, to mitigate the contamination of the river flowing through the informal settlement outside Hout Bay.

Deon and I were officially a couple by then. It wasn't a grand amour, but an alliance that suited us both. He liked, I think, that I was an outsider looking to clip into the richness of his life without him having to do the same in return, my network in Cape Town being non-existent.

It felt like Deon had the keys to the city, though he jangled them lightly, as if he were its caretaker. He took me to one hidden gem after another: a friend's holiday house in the remotest part of Cape Point, owned from the time before it became a national park, a professor's beach shack at Smitswinkel, a great-aunt's cottage in the Cederberg.

The rest of his time, when he wasn't studying or volunteering, Deon spent doing extreme exercise with his many friends. I had never seen humans so fit. I kept trying to figure out what was really driving them, but Bibi had my number, and she teased me that I probably had a theory about physical exhaustion being the only state in which the modern white South African feels exempt from responsibility for the past, the only time the accusatory voices in their heads go quiet.

I knew they all thought me humourless at times. Bibi liked to say that the country's sense of humour was its strongest and most stable bridge across difference. But I wasn't South African enough to cross that bridge as easily as they did.

On the day of the swim, I waited on the sand at Bloubergstrand beside the stacks of towels and flasks of coffee. There were a few of us non-swimmers, and I found myself chatting to an attractive black woman about my age. Her boyfriend was a postgrad in the same department as Deon. We dug a little deeper, shared our names, and suddenly we recognised each other.

Magdalene. We had gone to school together for several years as children. She had been one of the three black students admitted into our class of thirty white girls once certain government schools were allowed to desegregate, almost overnight. But we didn't talk about any of that. We traded stories, joked about our old needle-work teacher, Mrs Funnybone, whose reign of terror at our school had been no laughing matter to ten-year-olds.

I remembered, in the swerving way that forgotten knowledge returns, that her father and mine had briefly worked together on a multiracial sports project. They'd co-coached a rugby team made up of boys from both the rich white parts of town and the poor black townships. A recipe for disaster on paper, but our fathers had been enriched by the experience. I told Magdalene that my father used to come home from training on a high so palpable it filled the whole house with feel-good pheromones, and she said her father had too.

The swimmers began to appear just the other side of the breakers, and in the rush of activity to welcome them ashore, I lost sight of Magdalene. Deon staggered onto the sand wearing only wetsuit pants – on his chest, he had written a message for the sharks in black grease: I AM NOT A SEAL. He grabbed me and gave me a sloppy kiss, which was not at all like him. He was happy to be alive.

Later that night, around the Jouberts' dinner table, Magdalene was seated at the far end. As soon as the party moved into the living room for potluck dessert, I sat down on the sofa beside her and her boyfriend, Jürgen, though it was clear they were deep in conversation.

She gave me a bright smile, but he did not hide his displeasure at being interrupted. He was German, one of the department's superstars, according to Deon, so focused on his work he sometimes forgot to eat for days. He got up to refill his glass.

I thought of the scrunchie Magdalene had worn around her braids as a child, a gold-flecked one. I used to stare at that scrunchie, coveting it, as she sat in front of me in history class, the teacher droning on about the Battle of Blood River. Memories like this of our shared childhood had bombarded me all afternoon.

'You used to wear Impulse deodorant,' I said to her. 'The mauve one.'

'And you used to wear your hair slicked back like a china doll,' she said. We were eating melktert, a dessert I'd not had in a decade. 'No bubble fringe for you.'

We were just getting warmed up when John clapped his hands and asked everybody to gather around.

'I'm on,' Magdalene said to me.

'You've got slides to show?' I asked.

'No,' she said. 'You'll see.' She got up and conferred with John.

Wine was poured, jokes were made, and the room's energy shifted into anticipation. I examined Magdalene closely as she stood waiting to address us. She was tall, about my height, but curvy in ways I wasn't. She was wearing a cream wool top and beige pants and was barefoot – Bibi and John's salons had a shoes-off policy to encourage relaxation. Her short hair was neatly Alice-banded.

'For those of you who don't know me, my name is Magdalene Mbuso,' she said. 'I grew up here but trained as a psychotherapist in Germany, where I learned to incorporate alternative methods into my therapy, things like group sculpting, family constellations, enactment, narrative composition. I now specialise in working with white South Africans struggling with extreme feelings of guilt for what happened in this country.'

She paused to scan the room and calmly met my gaze.

I was stunned. Around me, the stillness of the room was confirmation that even in that mostly unburdened crowd, she had touched a nerve.

'For some of my clients,' Magdalene continued, 'the weight of their identity as white South Africans is so heavy it has crushed their ability to see themselves as anything else. It is a painful, painstaking process, but I believe it is possible to rebuild an identity that does not use shame as a crutch yet still acknowledges the shameful elements of one's past.

'Tonight I'd like to guide you through an experience-sharing session, followed by a group sculpt,' she said. 'So I need a volunteer. Preferably somebody from a generation older than my own, someone who experienced apartheid as an adult, not only as a child.'

John put up his hand and everybody laughed.

'Okay, John,' Magdalene said. 'Come over here.'

She tossed him a cushion and the two of them sat cross-legged on the floor, facing each other. She asked him to close his eyes and placed her hands on his knees.

'Forget about everyone else in this room,' she said. 'I want you to tell me about your very first experience of *sensing* racial difference. Not a conscious awareness, necessarily. Just a feeling of something being off. Something being awry.'

John opened his eyes. 'Would it be okay if I lie down?' he said.

'You can if you like,' Magdalene said, putting the cushion under John's head as he lay down on the carpet and closed his eyes again.

We all sat in silence. The currents of tension built and subsided. The wood in the fireplace sighed. Magdalene waited.

For a moment I thought John might have fallen asleep. But then he started talking.

'As a boy, I used to play with our maid's son, Bernard. We had morning tea together. We'd sit on the stoep and share a sandwich. I got my milk in a china mug, Bernard got his in a jam tin. He and his mom, Dinah, lived in a room off the garage.

'We weren't best friends, but he was part of my daily life. Until he disappeared. I asked my mother where he was and she said he'd gone to live in the township with his grandmother. It was only much later, when I was studying law, that I realised he must have been forced to leave. That was the year the law was passed stipulating that a maid's children couldn't live with her on a white property once they were older than four.

'One day, my mother thought Dinah had stolen her watch. Dinah was furious at being accused. My mother fired her soon afterwards. And then I found the watch, between the cushions of the couch. But I didn't tell anybody I'd found it.

'Years later, when I was home on a varsity break, I was at the butcher's when a black man my age tapped me on the shoulder.

"John," he said. "Is it you?" I had no idea who he was. "It's me, Bernard," he said.

'I don't know why, maybe because the other people in the shop were staring at us, but I pretended not to know him.

'All he bought there, I remember, was a single chop.' John's voice cracked. 'One lamb chop, wrapped in wax paper.'

From the corner of my eye, I was surprised to see Bibi looking stony-faced. Did she feel that John had been humiliated? Deon looked as if his mind were elsewhere. Jürgen appeared smug, which annoyed me. What did he know about any of this stuff? Then I caught myself. He was German. He would know more than most.

Magdalene made a gentle motion over John's body, as if clearing away cobwebs, and helped him up. He returned to his seat beside Bibi and blew his nose loudly, as if to show he had nothing to hide.

'Would anybody else like to share something?' Magdalene asked. 'Somebody of a different generation this time?'

A few of us put up our hands. I was convinced she would pick me. I had already decided I would tell the story of the burglary and the decapitated baby bird, had been rehearsing it in my head.

She chose the girl sitting next to me, Felicity, one of Deon's many cousins, who was a professional kayaker. I'd heard she had been given a chance to emigrate to Canada and train with a top coach, but had turned it down to stay in South Africa.

'Whatever you'd like to tell us,' Magdalene said.

Felicity lay back on the cushion, and after a while she began to talk. 'This isn't about my first experience of racism,' she said, 'it's about something I'm dealing with now. Many of you know I live alone in an old house in St James, above the railway tracks. I've lived there since I graduated. I love that house. I love being able to see the sea from every room in it. I like having no neighbours.

'But that's in the daytime. At night, the house terrifies me.

I think it may be haunted.' She paused, as if waiting for the room to laugh at the idea of ghosts. But nobody made a sound.

'A few months ago, I came home late from training,' she went on. 'It was already dark. When I unlocked the front door, the music box on the piano in the hallway was playing and the ballerina was turning, like somebody had wound it up. Like in a horror movie.

'I didn't want to be pathetic, so I marched up to the box and shut it. After a large glass of wine, I went back to the music box and opened it. The ballerina wouldn't turn. I wound it up but nothing happened, I couldn't get the thing to play again.

'Another night, I came home and found plates smashed to pieces on the kitchen floor. The doors and windows were locked, there was no sign of a break-in.

'The worst thing, though, is the footsteps. The house has wooden floors and they creak. It could be the boards warping as the temperature changes, I don't know. But it sounds like somebody pacing around my bed. I've started taking sleeping pills and they're affecting my performance, my times, but what can I do? People tell me there's a rational explanation for what's happening. Or worse, that it's all in my mind.'

Felicity's hands were clasped on her stomach. The fire had burned down to embers and the room was lit a dark red. The session had begun to feel like a full-blooded seance.

'I don't want to move out,' she said at last. 'I think the ghosts, if that's what they are, are trying to tell me something. Or warn me of something. What if the message they have is only for me? How can I leave without knowing what it is?'

Magdalene put her hands on Felicity's shoulders. 'Listen to me,' she said. 'The past asks different things of each of us. For some people, listening to what it seems to be saying is enough to clear a space to live with a clear conscience in the present. Others seek something less passive. They want to redesign the present so that the mistakes of the past cannot be made again, or use the lessons of the past to wrest control of the future.

'It may help to remind yourself how insignificant you are in the grand pageant of history. We each get to march along for a song or two before the procession of life winds its way down streets inaccessible to us. To be a good person you don't need to know the entire history of your country or family. But your relationship with the past must remain fluid, as should your relationship with yourself. You are always a work in progress.'

I felt suddenly dizzy – the wine, the rich dessert, and now this feeling of something clicking into place at the base of my spine, a feeling that I was exactly where I was supposed to be.

Magdalene blew briskly across Felicity's body.

After a while, Magdalene turned to the rest of us. She told us to split ourselves into two groups, letting the emotional resonance of what John and Felicity had said guide our choice. 'Whichever story echoes your own experiences more strongly,' she said, 'go to that person.'

We did as she said. There was no nervous laughter at the absurdity of the situation. Magdalene had somehow short-circuited our defence mechanisms.

For the next hour or two – time really did pass differently, as if we were in another dimension – each group re-created the stories we'd heard. I had gone to John, though most of the others of my generation went to Felicity's group. His story reminded me of things my father had experienced, and I was still more invested in my parents' memories of South Africa than in my own.

Everyone was assigned a role: somebody to play John, someone to play his mother, his father, Bernard, Dinah, the people in the queue at the butcher. Magdalene instructed John to arrange us in tableaux of the key moments in his story. We were to stay in the moment until we felt emotion of some kind, and at that point express it, verbally or with actions.

In the first tableau, I was given the role of John's younger sister, though he had not mentioned her in his story. She had been playing with her dolls on the floor when John discovered his mother's watch, had seen him find it.

In each new scene, there was always somebody who became animated. There were tears, shouts of anger. At one point Bibi, in the role of Dinah, writhed in pain on the white carpet, holding her stomach. I was surprised to see Deon, the ultimate positivist, looking extremely pale on the other side of the room, one of the ghosts walking around Felicity's bed.

The session ended as abruptly as it had begun, on Magdalene's command. Everybody, all of a sudden, wanted to talk to her. I overheard people telling her about dreams they'd had, dirty secrets, hidden prejudices, scarring memories, harmful thoughts.

She listened for a while, then expertly defused the weird feeling in the room by putting on one of John's old records at high volume and taking a bottle of red around, refilling people's glasses. Before I could speak to her myself, she and Jürgen left to go home.

I went to Rome after I left Pompeii. I'm not sure why. In a daze I wandered the cobbled streets around the Pantheon, washing the sweat from my face with the cold water that ran continuously from taps in the squares. The shining white plaza in front of St. Peter's blinded me. In a graveyard beneath another church was a room decorated with the bones of thousands of exhumed monks. The lamps were made of skulls. I stood before the Bocca della Verità, the ancient drain cover meant to swallow your hand if you don't tell the truth, and waited for it to swallow me whole.

I longed to die. But suicide was never an option, in spite of my father's example. I was young, and I believed that death was something that had to happen *to* you, that it could not be approached as an equal partner.

The more pressing challenge, then and now, was how to withstand the endless accompaniment of the voice in my head. Every waking minute of every day, I cannot escape it, except on those occasions when I can eavesdrop on somebody else's inner voice—through art, in other words. It is the only break from ourselves most of us ever get.

Those were difficult days. I thought at the time they would be the worst of my life. I did not know what was in store for me. The earthquake had happened, but the eruption was biding its time.

I have just put on a pot of rice for dinner. It's pretty much all I can eat now. Gone are my luxurious evenings at restaurants with velvet curtains. The palliative care nurse has said I should relent and leave my home to die elsewhere. But so far I've refused.

The steam is rising from the pot like a signal from a papal conclave: a choice has been made.

Soon after I had decided to start therapy with Magdalene, my parents visited. For the weeks they were in Cape Town I pretended to be settled. I told them I had hours of footage for a new film but wasn't yet ready to talk about it or show them a cut. They were distracted, anyway, by being back in the captivating city where they'd first met, so much so that sometimes I wondered if they were imagining a final homecoming for themselves.

As I'd predicted, they didn't much like Deon's parents. They turned down an invitation to a communal dinner – John had asked my father to speak about his anti-apartheid activities afterwards, which made my father blanch. He muttered something later about not wanting to be a performing monkey for the local intelligentsia. I didn't bother explaining that it wasn't like that.

I was relieved to avoid the dinner, for if Magdalene had been there, I wouldn't have been able to keep her secret from my parents any longer. They would have remembered her, asked about her parents, re-established a family friendship. They would have found out about her work, and my father, astute psychologist that he was, may have seen what was going on and tried to talk me out of it. He didn't believe in therapy, even of the non-experimental, traditional kind. His take was that you couldn't fix a person without engaging with their wider context, which was why his own work focused on education and social policy. I knew he would find the idea of white people going to see a black therapist to have their white guilt assuaged ludicrous. And in his view, white guilt was not something that should or could be 'cured' at an individual level. Whites would only be free of it once the underlying enablers of their domination had been dismantled.

But he did not know how desperate my situation had become.

Magdalene did our introductory session over the phone from her office, before my parents arrived. This was her custom, she said, when starting with a new client, setting out the terms and conditions and discussing therapy styles without the intensity of being in a room together, which she said some people found intimidating at first. She made her position clear from the start: we may have known each other as children, but we could not now be friends.

I was more than happy for her to set the tone. What, in any case, could I have asked to deep-vein us into the real stuff: What did it feel like to walk into that classroom and see the white shining faces of the children of your tormentors? When the whole school held hands in a circle in the playground, observing a nationwide minute of silence for peace, do you recall that you and I were side by side? What did you think of me crying while 'Bridge Over Troubled Water' played at the end of that minute, getting a kick out of a display of emotion to which I had no real claim? Is that why you stayed resolutely dry-eyed?

Magdalene was right. We could not be friends.

She had studied, she told me during that phone call, under the psychotherapist Diederich Fischer in Germany. Normally he only took graduate students, but he'd agreed to train Magdalene as an undergraduate because he had a special interest in South Africa, having been a missionary there in the 1950s. On his return to Germany, he'd left the Church and become a psychotherapist. Over the years, he'd developed his own idiosyncratic therapies while working mainly with members of the Tätergeneration – the 'perpetrator generation', those who were adults during the Second World War – to help them process feelings of guilt and shame. It was he who'd suggested she might find it interesting to work with the agents and beneficiaries of apartheid when she moved back to South Africa.

Magdalene's own methods were similarly wideranging. Many were considered unconventional, even outlandish, by other psychotherapists, but she disliked the one-size-fits-all approach, and felt that the rules dividing schools of thought and therapy were arbitrary, more about the egos of therapists than the needs of clients.

Furthermore, she said, if chaos wasn't embraced as a guiding principle of treatment, what hope was there of understanding the chaotic morass of the psyche, of luring the unconscious out into the open? One mode of therapy could never satisfy the demands of all the different selves contained in one person.

Among her treatment options was rage-reflection therapy, where she shouted racial abuse at clients, forcing them to hear the things they thought privately about others. Another was a Truth and Reconciliation Commission of one, with Magdalene as judge and jury, and the client in the witness box, slowly chalking up each shade of privilege, measuring to the tiniest degree their proximity to wrongdoing, a ledger of ethical accounting.

'But usually,' she said, 'for whites of your generation, I recommend something less punishing. The goal is to find a way back to compassion for yourself as a child. To claim your past, not disown it. You came of age at the same time this country came of age, so your past is split in two. The decade of your childhood was happy, yet those years have been written off as one of the worst periods in history. And then, like magic, things changed just as you became an adolescent. The world expected you to do an about turn, to be proud of a national identity that you'd been taught to think of as shameful. This is confusing to a child, even a teenager. You felt cut in half.'

Before we had really started, then, she'd put her finger right on the bruise, pressed it a little to see if it hurt, if this was the place where the work needed to be done. I'd always thought that only I understood my childhood in this way: more proof of the prideful nature of my pain.

There were two lines Magdalene would not cross. There'd be no physical punishment – apparently whites of a certain age often asked her to spank them, because it took them back to childhood memories of black nannies giving them hidings, and they craved that simplistic transactional circuit. And she refused to play the sangoma, the witchdoctor, another common request from white clients, those thinking they could access the true Africa through her, who wanted to see the throwing of bones and slicing of animals' necks, and visions in the spray of blood.

We settled on a combination of therapies, with a large dose of what Magdalene called reverse talking, where she would mostly talk to me rather than the other way around, to intervene in my thought patterns.

'Your conversations with yourself are not always constructive,' she said. 'They force me to engage with you on your terms. Therapy is really just about learning to have a different conversation with yourself. But before you can do that you need a new vocabulary. That's where I come in.'

On the afternoon of my parents' departure I drove them to the airport, and spent the evening grooming myself with greater care than I had since arriving in Cape Town. I scrubbed, exfoliated, flossed, bleached. I painted my toenails maroon, in imitation of the colour I'd spotted on Magdalene's toes at the Jouberts' house. That night, I lay in bed listening to the rain, sleepless with the anticipation of seeing her again.

I arrived too early at her consulting rooms, on the lower floor of a lemon-coloured terrace. It was in a fairly rough but rapidly gentrifying section of the Bo-Kaap, the historic Cape Malay slave neighbourhood nestled in the foothills of Signal Hill. The building was one of a row of Georgian houses painted bright colours and edged with white.

I'd parked nearby, in a section of De Waterkant I knew and felt comfortable in, with its cafes and shops. Magdalene's rooms were just the other side of the invisible boundary between the two neighbourhoods. I had to hand it to her – even this journey to see her would give most white Capetonians an ever so slight nudge out of their comfort zone.

In her rooms, a middle-aged white receptionist was on the phone, so I took a seat in the waiting area. Goldfish drifted in a bowl of water on the table.

Magdalene was, like me, so young, and yet her practice was already flourishing. At John and Bibi's house, she hadn't seemed young at all. She had been uncannily confident, in control.

I remembered one sports day at our school when some of the girls had made fun of Magdalene for not wearing a bra, the mounds of her breasts showing through the fabric of her top. The rest of us, still flat-chested, wore expensive sports bras regardless, coached by our mothers not to give the other girls an inch. I wondered if Magdalene had in fact been older than us, if she'd been placed in a lower year at the new white school because the teachers had assumed she wouldn't cope. I'd never asked her age.

Magdalene's office door opened and out came an over-weight white man in his fifties, not somebody I would ever have guessed went to therapy of any kind. He spoke to the reception-ist in Afrikaans, looking really happy – he had a beatific gleam about him.

I applied lip gloss.

Magdalene appeared at her door, beckoning me in with a smile. I'd been expecting to see her in the same conservative clothes she'd worn at the Jouberts', but she was wearing a polar-white dress with a dramatic ruffle at the neck and towering red heels. She looked spectacular.

Inside the room she asked my permission to tape our sessions, which she said was a useful way to track our progress. Then she had me take off my shoes, lie down on what looked like a massage table against one wall, and close my eyes.

She put a blanket over my legs and stood holding my feet through it at the end of the table. The moment she touched my feet a sleepy feeling spread through my brain, as if I'd been hypnotised.

When she spoke, it was in a low, lilting voice. 'I'd like you to consider the difference between guilt and shame,' she said. 'Guilt is feeling bad about something specific. Shame is feeling bad about yourself, without a clear reason why. One of the thinkers I respect on this topic puts it like this: guilt means you *did* something bad, shame means you *are* bad.

'We now know that guilt is relatively easy to get rid of, and not only that, it's an empathy-driven emotion. To feel guilty involves taking the perspective of the other, and it is therefore an adaptive emotion – it can lead to pro-social actions, like apologising or making reparations. It can be a way of holding yourself to a higher standard of behaviour.

'Shame, on the other hand, is a much trickier kettle of fish.

Shame invites punishment. It's a dirty, dark, secret emotion. It's isolating. It is much more closely linked to narcissism than to empathy. People who feel extreme shame are more aggressive to others, and less aware of the consequences of their actions. They often don't have the ability to feel guilt, for guilt involves looking outwards and taking another person into account, guessing at how that person might feel. Shame does not like company. Freud was intrigued by the connection between self-blame, or shame, and despair.

'But there is a third state – chronic guilt, which for all intents and purposes is indistinguishable from shame. This is guilt suffered over many years, often in silence, without it translating into any healthy coping mechanisms. It too presents as narcis-sistic, inward-looking, inactive. Chronic guilt results in the same punishment-seeking behaviour as shame. Self-harm, for example, or extreme risk-taking.'

She paused here, and let go of my feet. I wanted her to hold them again, to feel the warmth of her palms through the blanket. Her words were so comfortingly precise. I had never once thought of the exact difference between shame and guilt. That alone made me feel better, being able to hold those two words up to the light, to look at their glinting facets, turn them around and around like solid objects.

After a silence, she took hold of my feet again. I almost wriggled with joy.

'Another thing I'd like you to mull over,' she said. 'I sense you have connected this feeling – whatever you decide it is, guilt, shame, chronic guilt – to something external, a big-picture feeling about growing up here as a white. This may be so. Certainly it is for many people I see. But it might help to think of it as some-thing personal, applicable only to you. This feeling you have could come from the private dynamics of your family. It may be something that, as an only child, you are more attuned to. From an early age you were asked to see through your parents' eyes, and did not have a sibling with whom to share that obligation.

'It might be a combination of both, of course, the personal and the political – a perfect storm. An only child born to parents with a highly developed sense of ethical responsibility, who were themselves struggling to make sense of their lives. But it could be that it would not have mattered where you were born, that this feeling has nothing to do with South Africa. You may have felt it regardless of the social circumstances in which you were raised. You could even choose to think of it as genetic, or epigenetic; that is to say, you have a predisposition, an emotional inheritance, that makes you highly susceptible to feelings of guilt or shame. Unhooking the feeling from this country may let you see it more clearly.'

Magdalene then guided me through a long meditation, asking me to picture myself at the bottom of a deep pit. Who else was in there with me? How did I feel? If I tried to climb up the sides, did the soil crumble or hold?

When she blew over me to signal the end of the session, I could smell the cherry scent of her lipstick. I opened my eyes, feeling refreshed at a cellular level, as if I had been asleep for a thousand years.

The receptionist caught my eye as I paid afterwards. 'She's good, isn't she,' she said. I felt so choked up I couldn't respond.

I walked slowly back to my car in De Waterkant, appreciating each smooth rounded brick of the cobbled road. Magdalene was going to fill the psychic hole in me, one spoonful of sediment at a time.

That night I went with Kevin and Melanie to their favourite pizza place in Vredehoek. My cousin had hurt his back on their motorbike trip, pinched a nerve, and wasn't much interested in conversation. Over limoncello at the end of the meal, Melanie looked at me with a sly smile. 'You're in love,' she said. 'Is it Deon?'

I almost told her the truth, that what she was picking up on was somebody being allowed to fall in love, guiltlessly, with herself, or at least with the child she'd once been. Magdalene had warned me not to take my memories of childhood too seriously, that they weren't necessarily reliable, were possibly fantasies I was using in the service of my current preoccupations. But she also said it was crucial that I stop hating the child I had been, or what that child represented.

'Lavish love on your young self,' she'd said at some point during the guided meditation, and I had imagined wrapping my two-year-old self in reams of cottonwool. Humans, she told me, develop a sense of shame before we even have the ability to record our memories. Guilt only comes later, with memory. Already this had helped me reconsider my muteness about South Africa, the strange desire to have my tongue cut out so that I would never be tempted to say anything about it or my relationship with it. I had no language for my shame because I'd had no language when I first felt shame.

But I stopped myself from saying anything to Melanie at the last moment. She was right. I *was* in love.

Magdalene had specifically warned me of the danger of erotic transference, whereby I would pursue only her forgiveness, her acceptance, her love. The cliché of seeking atonement through romantic love, of thinking I could make up for all my perceived wrongs to a body of people on the body of one person.

My feelings for her will pass, I counselled myself that night. This is just the first stage of the process. But in truth I knew it was all over, that I was already incapable of considering a life without her.

I did as my financial advisor suggested and put in an application to do an MBA after I returned from Italy. He made a few calls, I made an extremely generous donation, and next thing I'd been accepted, though the start of the semester was only weeks away.

In retrospect, it was probably the worst possible place for me to be, given my state of mind. The business school was just across the river from the college. After the first few days of orientation, surrounded by men with perfect smiles and firm handshakes and a few brave women dressed as carefully as shop mannequins, I was drawn irresistibly back to the places Kitty and I had spent our time as undergraduates.

I haunted the dining hall of our dormitory, and smacked a squash ball against the wall in the basement court. I hung around in our entry hall. Nobody questioned my presence. None of the students from other years recognized me, which tells you just how little impact I had made.

I lived off-campus, unable to endure the competitive camaraderie of the business school's residences. Each get-together was a chance to expand your Rolodex, every class an opportunity to dazzle a professor who might hire you for his company.

There was a chapel near the campus, and within it a fountain and fishpond. At a certain time each day, later and later as the season changed, the sun shone at an angle on the water, turning the fish a luminous orange. Very few people came into the chapel, and it was there that I felt closest to Kitty.

I liked to lie beside the fountain and imagine I was in ancient Pompeii. The church flowers, arranged anew each day, perfumed the air; the water tinkled over mosaic tiles, the fish trailed their delicate tails. Some days, I pictured Kitty having her lustrous black hair braided by slaves beside the pond. Or having a sponge squeezed over her slender back, the water flowing down her skin. Most of the time I just lay there and cried.

I didn't intend to start spying on Magdalene. All stalkers probably say that afterwards, when they're caught in the act. It's true I was spending a lot of my free time in De Waterkant, hoping to catch a glimpse of her on her lunchbreaks. There was a Dutch cafe, its interior spotlessly white, which served moer koffie, and I gravitated to it each day after my morning tutoring sessions. I sat at a table with a view of Lion's Head and felt no desire to climb it, which in itself was progress.

One day, when the cafe was bustling with a lunching crowd, Magdalene and Jürgen arrived and took a table in the corner. They didn't see me. They were arguing, and there was a look in his eyes that suggested he was breaking up with her. She stopped eating halfway through her meal.

She left before he did, placing money on the table – a final grasp at dignity. I followed her, thinking I could pretend to bump into her and offer consolation in her moment of need.

But as I watched her go in and out of boutique clothing shops with wet eyes, I couldn't bring myself to approach. I wanted to keep gazing at her while her pain showed unmuted.

The next day, I parked outside her rooms in the late afternoon and marked spelling worksheets in my car. When she left work, I followed her Mini Cooper and discovered that she lived in a luxury security block not far from my own flat, further up the mountain, with a guard stationed permanently at the boom gate.

Soon I knew the rhythm of her weekends. She went to Sea Point for a spinning class on Saturday mornings, and met friends for brunch afterwards at a restaurant along the promenade. She liked watching matinées at the art-house cinema in Gardens, and on Saturday nights she preferred the bars and clubs on Long Street to those in Claremont, where the varsity students congregated.

Sometimes I would engineer an encounter with her at one of those clubs. Deon hated dancing, but if enough of his friends were going he'd tag along. On the dance floor I would feign surprise at seeing Magdalene and we'd make exaggerated hand motions to communicate over the noise of the music. She always seemed relaxed about seeing me. Cape Town is a small place, really, and she must have been accustomed to running into her clients. Her response, I knew, was also a way of being discreet, of keeping the fact that I was a client of hers confidential.

At the end of one of those nights, as the DJ shut down his console and the crowd grumbled about having to leave, Magdalene and I were swept up in a plan hatched by an overlapping group of friends to go skinny-dipping.

We took a maxi-taxi from Long Street, which dropped us at the edge of Newlands Forest. The reservoir in the woods there was much lower down Table Mountain than the one I'd hiked to alone, at the summit. There was a gibbous moon, and everybody's breath was coming out in visible clouds – it was the last month of winter. Keeping Magdalene's silhouette always in view, I followed the others along the track. She and I, it turned out, were the only women in the group, and were both struggling in our heels.

We came to the fence surrounding the reservoir, which the boys were scaling in what looked like a zombie invasion; drunkenness had made them more nimble, or just immune to the fear of falling. Magdalene hitched her green dress into her undies, threw her shoes over the fence, and started to climb. I followed.

On the other side, the boys were stripping off in a pack, whooping as they dive-bombed into the black water. Magdalene slid her dress over her head. She stood facing me in her underwear, and shivered in a long shudder from her shoulders down. I stepped out of my jeans, pulled off my top. The boys had forgotten all about us, were already swimming to the other side. We turned away from each other as we took off our underwear.

I stepped gingerly to the edge of the reservoir. There was no ladder or steps, just sloping walls covered in plastic sheeting. The only way in, other than jumping, was down the plastic slope.

I jumped. On the far side the boys cheered. The water was gelid. As soon as I was in it I was desperate to get out, and like some sort of prehistoric amphibious creature, I threw my wet body against the wall, but I could get no purchase and slid back down. The situation was ridiculous yet I was on the verge of anxiety.

Magdalene was sitting naked and dry on the top of the wall. 'Grab my legs,' she said, lowering herself towards me.

I put my hands around her ankles and felt the hint of stubble on her lower calves. There was the sound of her flesh unsticking from dry plastic as she moved her bum back up the wall, and the wet sound of my flesh against the plastic as she dragged me up after her. We were undone by an attack of laughter, stuck there on the wall, unable to move.

Eventually we made it out. We dressed quickly, shaking with cold, each glance at the other setting us off on another laughing fit. But at the same time I took in *everything* – her breasts hanging underlit by moonlight, the depth of her bellybutton, the goosebumps across her stomach.

John arrived soon afterwards in the family van to pick us all up, in spite of the late hour. We dropped Magdalene off at her apartment, barefoot, freezing, her wet underwear showing through her dress as she did a morning-after tiptoe past the sleeping guard.

There was one more long week to wait after that night before my next session. Magdalene always recommended a gap of at least a month after the initial consultation, to allow the effect to settle. It seemed to me a shrewd business move too, for it showed her clients that she was genuine about their recovery, not merely interested in taking their money.

I arrived early again for my appointment. In the waiting area, the receptionist was arranging silky black and pink proteas in a vase.

When Magdalene's door opened, Bibi emerged. Our eyes met. She went straight to the desk to pay.

I hadn't told Deon I was seeing Magdalene, and as far as I knew, Bibi hadn't told her family she was either. It surprised me that the indefatigable, all-competent, pronoid Bibi was not immune to guilt, or shame, or chronic guilt, or whatever she was seeking to alleviate. Then I thought of her rolling on her white carpet before her family and friends, clutching her stomach in pain. Of course her stake in that country was unstable.

Magdalene was back in full therapist mode. On weekends she dressed down but for work she overdressed; perhaps it was a way of getting into character. That day, she was wearing high-heeled boots with tailored pants and a jacket, all in her signature burgundy. She'd had her hair braided (I knew where she went for this, a salon nearby staffed with local beauty school trainees). Her make-up was flawless, her lipstick reapplied between clients.

She made no reference to the night at the reservoir. She asked me to lie down on the treatment table, and my whole body began to anticipate her touch. But she didn't touch me at all during the session, and instead used what she called biofield therapy, hovering her hands above my body.

'I will do the talking again today,' she said. 'You told me you struggle with feelings of self-hatred. The twin of this emotion is self-love, if we follow a classically Freudian interpretation of the dual components of narcissism. Might it help to think of your desire for punishment, your fixation on your unspecified, endless guilt, as a form of self-involvement?'

I heard her belly rumble close to my ear.

'White guilt can be deeply pleasurable to experience,' she said, 'which is something that's not much spoken about. Pleasure and pain are close emotional cousins. The pain of feeling bad is followed quickly by the pleasure of considering oneself to be ethically enlightened enough to know punishment is deserved. But they are connected also at a biological level. Guilt stimulates dopamine receptors. It's not a leap to say that you can become, quite literally, addicted to it.

'One writer on the topic puts it like this. Our parents lived in a time when racism was enshrined in law. A time of white power, when blacks were punished for being black. Now we live in a time when racism is forbidden by law. It is the age of white guilt. As a black South African, I'm still a victim of racism, but I can no longer claim to be victimised by it. I am expected by whites to be a moral authority by dint of being black. Some cannot stand it if I behave in ways that offend them, if I squander what they see as my ethical advantage. And at the same time, all whites, no matter their personal belief system or history, are automatically stigmatised as racists, and must go to extraordinary lengths to prove they are not. For the masochists among you, there's much allure in this.'

Though my eyes were closed, I could sense that she was moving down the left-hand side of my body. Each nerve ending seemed to be inflamed.

'From what you've told me, it appears you haven't been much altered by your experience of living in America or Australia. It's as if you floated through them like a ghost. And in fact you *have* been a ghost. Researchers describe people who have suffered trauma as being in a trancelike state, unable to look away or contemplate anything but the traumatic event itself. It's a state of total absorption.

'You might have felt that nobody in those other two countries could understand the uniqueness of your guilt, that whites there cannot grasp what it means to be an oppressor of a non-white *majority*. South Africa's whites make up less than ten percent of the population, whereas America and Australia have populations that are overwhelmingly white. The guilt felt by a small portion of a large white majority can be indulged without much consequence; everybody knows that nothing is really going to threaten the status quo. Even if genuine, it is the guilt of the victorious – the battle was won a long time ago.

'White South Africans of our parents' generation experience guilt or shame that is straightforward, textbook. Their parents, your grandparents, invented a system to dominate a feared black majority, and they benefited from it for years.

'Your guilt has a twist to it. As children, your generation of whites saw that ancestral power being lost, handed over by your elders to that feared majority. So you had everything to lose, unlike white Americans, white Australians. In fact, you have lost almost everything, or you will soon – your power, your jobs, your money, the land you have owned. You've paid the price for letting the majority rule, as it should. Yet still you're regarded as the worst culprits of all the whites in the world.'

Magdalene's voice was both gravelly and sweet. For some reason a scene entered my mind – I don't know why, something I must have spied on as a young child – of my mother in the bath and my father kneeling beside the tub, moving a razor very gently through the soapy hollow of her armpit while she held her arm up, perfectly still.

'You may not know,' Magdalene said, 'that during the apartheid years, many white psychiatrists argued that black people could not experience depression since they were not able to feel guilt to the same degree as whites. Guilt, in the sense I'm discussing it, has always been a racialised emotion, a marker of supposedly higher feeling and moral intelligence.

'We can trace this further back, to the idea of original sin, and whites as the chosen people, who through their guilt about their sins maintain their superiority. If you choose to believe that everything is your fault, then the corollary is that only you are the world changer, the giver of everything good as well as bad, the only one with the ability to fix things. All others, all the victims, are like children, pawns you move around with impunity – or with punity and crippling guilt. Either way, it's a self-aggrandising project.

'Many of my clients like to point out that injustice and abuse of power exist everywhere in the world. Others say that every person alive today is descended from a tribe that has at some stage in its history been both victor and vanquished. So how far back do we take it? One generation? Two, three? Why not all the way back to the triumph of our species over other species of humans, whom some historians believe we may have systematically killed off? Perhaps the Genesis story in the Bible is in fact a parable about this genocide. We, *Homo sapiens*, took the ribs and bones of other human species we massacred to remake ourselves as the *only* humans.

'This line of thinking is useful for some white people. It enables them to face up to their own, more immediate wrongdoing. It expands their moral energy, can goad them into action.

'For other whites, however, this thinking is a curse. They are made defensive by trying and failing to comprehend the enormity of that continual human suffering, from the very beginning of our time on earth. So they spin their own wrongdoing in either relative or essentialist terms. At least we didn't do X, they think. Or, We aren't that bad compared to what the Y did to Z. Or, most common among your generation: It wasn't me, I shouldn't have to feel responsible for decisions I didn't make. This way of thinking can lead to the false conviction that the injustices of the present are similarly outside your influence, that things will remain the same regardless of what you do or don't do.'

Magdalene was standing at my feet by then, her hands above my ankles. 'The dictates of atonement shift all the time, and it's hard to keep up. Well-meaning whites are often very confused as a result. Should you speak up, share your shame, and in that way overcome it? Or should you shut up and let somebody who isn't white speak for a change? How much should you dwell on your own story, and how much on other people's? Is asking others to forgive you, to tell you you're a good person, a form of moral neediness?

'For people like you, Vita, who live in their heads, the danger is getting trapped in a state of frozen ethical awareness. Your insides have turned to ice. You're unable to create. You're aware that your ability to empathise, which you might secretly prize, isn't really enough to get you where you need to go. And you're right, it's not.

'This is what a colleague of mine calls the empathic fallacy: the belief that if you listen hard enough, and feel empathically enough, you can break down the barriers between people from very different backgrounds. But like negative change, most positive change in the world happens because people are forced kicking and screaming into it, against their will. Yet those same people, years later, will happily take the credit for the changes they once resisted so fiercely. It's not necessarily that the arc of the moral universe is long and bends towards justice, but that human memory is short and selective.'

I sensed Magdalene standing by my head again, her hands a few inches from my ears. I could hear a roaring sound, a seashell effect. She stood there for an eternity.

'A final thought,' she said. 'On the difference between bigotry and racism. I don't see a lot of bigots in my practice. To walk through my door you need to have a critical perspective on yourself that the majority of bigots lack. Most people who come to me are relieved when I tell them they're not themselves bigoted. But non-bigots can still be blind to certain forms of bigotry. And in a racist – a bigoted – society, this means everybody is implicated, whether they like it or not.'

The air around me went cold after a while. I opened my eyes.

She was at her desk. She watched as I put on my shoes, drumming her fingers on the table, her long nails clicking against the wood.

'Could you try something for me before our next session?' she said. 'Film yourself. Just sit and look directly into the camera, don't do anything else. Sit with the discomfort for as long as you can.' She switched off the tape recorder and began to make notes on her computer.

Later that afternoon, I dusted off my camera bag and took out the camera. I recharged the battery, slid it into place, unwrapped a MiniDV tape and slotted it into the shelf. On my balcony, I set up the tripod. The sun was behind Lion's Head but had not yet dropped into the unseen Atlantic on the other side. It was the blue hour, the light perfect for filming.

But I couldn't hold the mechanical gaze of the lens for longer than five minutes. The red recording bead looked hostile, like a weapon's laser. Unmanned, with no human presence behind it, the camera seemed to have a cold intelligence, sucking my image into itself.

Though the evening was cool I started to overheat, and my eye began to twitch. I thought of Magdalene and forced myself to stay still for another minute, counting out the seconds.

The words of the old man pruning rosebushes at the end of the rows of vines came back to me. I could finally understand what he'd meant. *With that thing, can you see through people?*

I survived my first year of business school and spent the summer in Vermont, in what had been the housekeeper's cottage on the family estate. I'd let Dorothy go after my father's death. The main house was looking unkempt, but I couldn't yet countenance selling it.

The solar storm in early August kept me glued to the television each night for updates on the alarming effects that the weather in space can have on earth. Auroras were seen from Colorado to Illinois, voltage surges shut down telephone lines, taxi drivers received mysterious fare requests from cities on the other side of the country. Pigeons flew in the wrong direction, confused by the disruption to the earth's magnetic field. I relished the chaos, the suggestion of end-times, as only somebody who is miserable can.

One more year of endurance and I could escape into an office job in a nondescript building in Boston, do something bland and repetitive every day at my desk. Then the world would let me be.

I hadn't heard from Kitty since leaving Pompeii, though I wrote her every month. I kept my tone chipper, saying nothing, really, on paper but everything in the subtext: Please forgive me, please leave the door open a chink. My feelings for her had not changed or cooled as I'd hoped they might. If anything, they were more vehement.

In the fall, after classes had commenced, my longing for her became unbearable. I considered flying back to Italy and taking a stealthy trip to Pompeii, just to see her from a distance. I finally had to acknowledge this was a bad idea, and settled instead on a trip to the old plantations down South, the territory of her childhood, over Halloween weekend.

I must warn you, Vita, that I am about to tell you something I have never shared with anybody. Sometimes I wonder if I dreamed it up, a nightmare that so appalled me it came to seem real. My only reason for sharing it now is that unless I admit to what I *have* done wrong, nobody will believe my protestations of innocence over other, worse, misdemeanors and crimes.

I flew first to Savannah, where Kitty had once told me she was born, shortly before her family moved to Charleston. The afternoon I arrived, the weather was balmy. At a bed-and-breakfast in the Historic District, the owner made me a mint julep in a chilled silver cup, to take on my stroll through the garden squares of the city.

The drooping Spanish moss caught the last of the sun's rays. The sky turned dark blue. A pack of children ran past me with blood around their mouths. 'I have no face,' one said from behind a Halloween mask.

The church bells rang in the dark, which felt wrong, as if they were being rung by the devil.

I picked a restaurant and ate alone at the window, watching ghouls pass by outside. After dinner, I trailed a group taking a ghost tour through a cemetery. The guide was telling tales of Union soldiers camping in the graveyard, causing mischief by recarving the dates on tombstones.

In the morning I drove to Tybee Island, thinking I'd have crab for brunch, but I was too early and most places were still closed.

I couldn't imagine Kitty eating in one of them anyway, with a bucket in the middle of the table for the heads and claws, paper tablecloths, jugs of sweet tea. A mirage of the South, of the good easy life that had never been hers.

I took the back routes to Charleston. By early afternoon I was in the thick of a row of plantations, caught in the romance of light through oak trees. At a roadside stop, the waitress gave me directions to Williams Place, the plantation where Kitty, according to her college application, had worked as a guide during summers.

I parked beside the garden maze at the estate. The next tour was due to start in an hour, according to the man handing out information leaflets. I glanced down at his clipboard, a staff schedule, and saw the name Zelda Lushington printed at the top.

He must have seen something in my reaction. 'You know Mrs. Lushington?' he asked.

'I do,' I said, trying to keep my voice from sounding strange. 'Could you ask her if she has time to speak with me before the tour?'

He said he'd try to find her, and recommended I take a stroll through the nearby Biblical Garden while I waited.

I followed the pebble path into the enclosed garden, where a long-dead mistress of the house had once experimented with growing plants mentioned in the Bible. Her interpretation, it seemed, had tended toward the literal. She'd planted lilies for 'lilies of the field,' roses for the 'Rose of Sharon,' and an apple tree for Eve, though the apple of sin is in fact thought to have been an apricot. The mistress was a devout woman, according to the leaflet, who read to her slaves from her Bible during the rice harvest. Every slave was needed in the fields then, to scare away the flocks of bobolink birds on their southern migration, and they could not go to church.

I left the garden and wandered into a forested area closer to the river, past a reflecting pool, and found myself in a cypress swamp. I was reading a placard about cypress knees—the knobbly roots that poke out of the water—being immune to lightning, when I heard footsteps behind me on the boardwalk.

I turned. An apparition from the past, a woman wearing colonial garb, her long dress brushing the boards. It was clear she had no idea who I was. Kitty must have received enough visitors in her hospital room for her mother not to recall me. She was lovely in that light, graceful in her old-world clothes. Her nose no longer had the reddish tint of an alcoholic and there was shape to her figure. Her blue eyes were bright, her hair dyed black. She looked much more like Kitty than I remembered.

'You've got cash?' she said, glancing over her shoulder. The woods were quiet. Not many visitors, it seemed, ventured away from the symmetrical beauty of the landscaped garden.

Time eddied. I nodded dumbly, and followed her to a cabin on the riverbank. The details I noted in that heightened, nervous state remain clear in my mind's eye. A statue of a wood nymph. Atamasco lilies growing at the water's edge. A sign, which I'd already read, about rice being shipped directly from the banks of the river to Britain, for even Ireland in the 1700s didn't yet have the potato, and everybody ate rice. Ireland without the potato, I thought, following Mrs. Lushington. You never know how things will come and go. A potato is brought from South America to Ireland, and next thing they can't live without it.

I can still see the yellowed newsprint papered over the wall of the cabin, the wall against which she pressed herself. The paper dated from 1926. There was a headline about the first woman to swim the English Channel, an advertisement for a tonic for tired mothers, a cartoon that made no sense.

I have no idea why I stayed on the plantation after what happened in that cabin. I must have been in a state of shock when I turned up at the tour Zelda was giving of the main residence. She met my gaze, showed no sign of embarrassment, stuck to her script about the house's many disasters, told us that it had been burned down by Union soldiers, leveled by an earthquake.

What I gradually began to notice was the glint in the eyes of some of the other men in the group, young and old, as they followed her around the house. I wondered whether they were in the know as to exactly what was possible on the plantation. They gazed for too long at the bed, pretending to admire the carving of rice grains on the bedposts, while Zelda told us that in summer— a dangerous time back then, due to malaria—the beds had been pushed into the middle of the room to get the breeze off the river.

History is always bound up with fantasy. While the women, with their dreamy, glazed looks, seemed content to fantasize, the men—if they were anything like me—wanted actual consummation in the physical present. They wanted to touch everything, the silk copy of the Declaration of Independence which one of the Williams ancestors had signed, the old crepey dollar bills, the slave tags, the locks of hair, the damp sand kept in buckets in the bedrooms in case of fire.

The plantation had tapped rather profitably into an unending pit of desire. The same desire that Pompeii conjured in most men who stepped within its walls, tempted by the lasciviousness of the art and the louche secret gardens and inner courtyards, all the shadowed spaces hidden from view. Why else is the Lupanar, a brothel with rooms as small as prison cells, the most visited site in all of Pompeii? We long to lift the skirts of history, to enter into the past, to make ourselves master of it.

Though in all honesty, when I was with Zelda in the slave cabin I was uncertain as to exactly which role I was playing. The slave doing whatever his mistress wished? The slave avenging himself on the wife of his master? Or the master having his way with a slave? The fantasy is all, of course, but she could not have known that for me it had nothing to do with the specters of that plantation.

Each gorgeous age is built around some core of rottenness.

Charleston, where I spent a night before returning to Boston, was filled with signs of death. Cemeteries stuffed with corpses from long-ago epidemics and wars, space set aside in each for out-of-towners with the bad luck to die on their travels. It was common in those days for people to be pronounced dead before they were really quite gone. Bells were installed inside crypts just in case, and stories abound of them ringing out on new-moon nights.

Strangely, I could smell apricots everywhere in that town, even at that time of year. It made my heart sore to think of the ripe apricots Kitty and I had eaten together in Antonio's orchard. And that I might never taste them again.

For our next session, Magdalene had set up her office with two chairs back to back. A couple of mirrors were angled in front of the chairs, in such a way that when we sat I was able to see only her reflection, and she mine. This was for a refraction exercise, she said, during which she would engage my double, my hidden self. We started by sitting in silence for a very long time, until with a sigh I stopped fidgeting and met her mirrored gaze.

'Did you film yourself as I suggested?' her reflection finally asked. She was wearing a grey wraparound dress, and silver earrings that tumbled to her shoulders.

'I tried. It didn't feel good.'

'Why not?'

'Because I don't make films about myself.'

In the mirror, I watched Magdalene crossing her legs in a combative manner.

'If you want to be able to create again, you may have to forfeit your identity as a guilt-ridden exemplar of moral awareness and righteousness. That's an identity you're heavily attached to, but it's boring. For everyone, but most of all for you.'

It was as if she had punched me in the solar plexus. Without my guilt, who would I be?

Her reflection was measuring the impact of these words. Then she said, 'The more interesting question you need to ask yourself is whether making art is sufficient, in terms of facing these issues. I can't answer that for you. But I sense that you feel uneasy with the way artists are generally considered to be moral arbiters, as if the work they do carries ethical weight – unlike the work done by a dentist or a shopkeeper, say. Is art just one kind of work to you, or is it ethics? Is it activism? What if it's just ego, a means of consolidating your own selfhood? And if it can be any and all of these things, which kind of artist do you want to be?

'There might be another way to get past your block,' her reflection continued. 'What would happen if, instead of silencing yourself as a representative of a class of oppressors, you asked yourself what kind of art somebody from that class could make?

'I think it might be interesting here to consider the work of psychohistorians, who approach countries as if they're people in need of therapy. It's fairly fringe stuff, and ignores the role of economics, the plundering of resources as a motive for national aggression – but let's throw the net wide. The rallying cry of psychohistorians is that history repeats itself because of the propulsive effects of humiliation. Until a country no longer believes itself to be humiliated, it is always in danger of re-enacting its humiliation on other nations.

'Unlike most social scientists, psychohistorians hold that the social life of nations is never brightly lit – it cannot be understood using rational yardsticks. They believe that the traumatised country, like the traumatised individual, has a psyche that is fractured. It has an unconscious. It buries painful memories. It indulges wishful fantasies through national myths. For the citizens of any country, it is a shock to realise that other countries are governed by pathological drives equal to their own. The only equality might be that we are all equally fucked up. Or, as a famous Freudian put it, the alien begins at home, wherever that may be.

'Of course, this view is a fairly hopeless one. For it means that social change is pointless, not worth fighting for, since it won't make the individual any happier, won't make our civilizations any less discontented. It suggests the best we can hope for, as individuals or countries, is to get a bit of relief from the endless sublimation of our darker drives by uncovering some of what we have repressed.'

I was intrigued by what Magdalene was saying and also grateful to have an excuse to drink in her reflection.

'It's not always helpful to draw too direct a line between Nazi Germany and apartheid South Africa,' she said. 'But the German example can be instructive in certain cases and I think may be in yours. The Germans have developed an entire vocabulary and classification system for the different kinds of guilt suffered by different generations. Many psychoanalysts in Germany, including my mentor, have devoted their working lives to this.

'There is what's called the inability to grieve – the retreat of German elders into denial or sanitised versions of their experiences, both as perpetrators and victims during the war. Then there's the phase of dealing with the past, which started in the sixties, once the prosecution of former SS officers made more details of the Holocaust public. Young adults who were children during the war years, the worst years of Nazism, began to accuse their parents of complicity.

'But by the eighties, these war children were presenting with the same psychological problems as their parents. Severe depression and anxiety, mostly. History had caught up with them. They had often been traumatised by their experiences during those years of violence, famine, displacement, but just like their parents, they had never been allowed to grieve. They were not victims, the world had told them over and over. They were the exact opposite.

'And then, most interesting of all, we come to the war grand-children, the generation born long after the end of Hitler's reign. This generation began to present as young adults with the very same symptoms as their parents and grandparents. My mentor called this transgenerational trauma. He believes that most middle-aged Germans alive today suffer from it. He thinks that shame and trauma might be transmitted, like a virus, across history, through social, epigenetic and biological mechanisms. Each gen-eration inherits them in turn.'

She stopped, cleared her throat. I watched as her reflection took a sip of water from the glass beside her.

'What if we take the view that your symptoms are similar to those of the German war grandchildren?' she said. 'You all lost something of childhood's innocence because of the place and time in which you were raised. You inherited the accumulated guilt of your elders. There is no single traumatic incident in your life to which you can trace your condition, which is why you struggle to comprehend it. In Germany, some people feel that the only way to break the cycle is to deny themselves any powers of creation or procreation. To choose emptiness, to leave things fallow, unmade. A few direct descendants of Nazi leaders, for example, when they realised as adults the magnitude of what their parents or grand-parents had done, had themselves sterilised. They erased their future in the hope that it might atone for their past.

'You, Vita, may not have an actual barbarian in your midst. You may not be related to any of the architects of apartheid. There's no Himmler in your family. You have to wade instead through the murky waters of denial, of distancing. Insignificant acts of oversight mixed up with conscious acts of cruelty. The framed photograph of Verwoerd that a grandmother hung on her wall. A great-uncle looking the other way when the Whites Only signs went up.

'And you know, it's not so odd that you turned your camera first onto plants and animals, onto landscapes. Look at Leni Riefenstahl. I'm not suggesting you're anything like her, but it is interesting to me that in her later years, her seventies, she got her scuba licence and made endless underwater films about fish. She claimed never to understand exactly what she was guilty of – I didn't drop any atomic bombs, she said, so where does my guilt lie? A disingenuous response, but in turning to the non-human world, I wonder if she was processing exactly that question.'

Magdalene's reflection glanced at her watch.

I was in a trance from listening to her as she leapt from thought to thought.

She poured me a glass of water and waited for me to surface beside her.

You are still young in years, Vita, yet I sense you feel much older. But then the boundaries separating young, middle, and old age are always shifting. The ancient authors kept changing their minds about when old age starts. Some said forty-two, some fifty-six, some seventy. Cicero, who so famously made old age, even death, seem like something to look forward to—seeing land, entering the harbor, resting after the long voyage—died at sixty-three. Younger than I am now. A tender thought.

All your talk of therapy has made me think of something I once read about people who are 'open to experience.' Apparently, in extreme cases, this trait can become a psychological liability. People with it are more likely than others to become paranoid. Being too open to experience can take you places others might not go, to where you no longer know whether the thing you are open to is experience or delusion.

I was a little thrown by your suggestion that my curiosity, my openness to experience, might be a cover for something else. I had to remind myself this is all a game in service of my own needs, a riddle that I alone can solve. Which means I *can* choose what to believe, and which experiences I stay open to.

By December, Magdalene had begun to act strangely. Not in our sessions – in those, she was unfailingly professional. But my observations of her from a distance left me anxious. It was as if she were preparing to leave the city. I had moved often enough myself to recognise the signs. She became hyper-social, then bought a stack of packing boxes and stopped going out altogether. When I made subtle inquiries among Deon's friends, nobody knew of any plans. I hoped she was just moving into a new apartment, but really I knew something bigger was afoot.

At our last session before the Christmas break she seemed distracted. I had to remind her to turn on the tape recorder. Her appearance was dishevelled; she had a toothpaste stain on her thin sweater. That's when it became clear something was very wrong.

The impressionist reproduction above her desk had been removed, leaving two nail holes in the wall, as if a snake had struck venom into the brick.

'Are you redecorating?' I asked.

Magdalene ignored my question and got up to close the blinds. She lit a single stick of incense. The room, previously flooded with sunlight, became moody and aromatic.

She beckoned me to a pair of chairs, where we sat opposite each other, so close our knees were touching. When she took my hands and held them my whole body relaxed. I closed my eyes.

We sat there for a long time, fifteen minutes, maybe longer. After a while, I began to feel something like an electric current passing from her hands, through my arms and back out again at my knees.

Finally Magdalene spoke. 'Do you remember me telling you about the trancelike state of people who have unprocessed trauma, of whatever kind, big or small, personal or political?' she said. 'The total, destructive absorption they have in the place, the site, of the event? Today I want to snap you out of your traumatic trance and put you instead into a therapeutic trance.'

Her hands were smooth and dry. I could feel the tips of her nails pressing gently into the underside of my palms.

'Whereas up to this point in our work together I have talked at you, while you've accepted your passivity, it's time now for you to express yourself. You have become blocked using a visual medium like film because you were using it as a means of self-effacement. So I want you to turn to writing, something you said you tried at college without success. I want you to feel the discomfort of making things explicit in the way that writing enforces. The self will be harder to efface, as you'll see.'

She went on to say that I was to make myself a character in my own life. But first I needed to pick a foil. An antagonist.

'This can be somebody real or imagined,' she said. 'Or you can take elements from different people, augment and distort them. As long as there's tension there, somebody with whom you can butt heads. Somebody who will challenge your ideas about yourself, even pose some kind of threat. The point of the antagonist is not to let you indulge a fantasy of victimhood but to provide the scaffolding for your narrative fictions about yourself, which will be too weak to stand alone. They need to be firmed up, and for that you need to be writing *against* something or someone.'

I had begun to notice a sort of ticking feeling in my knees, as if Magdalene's blood and my own were pulsing in unison. I was also aware of a rising panic at the thought of having to write about myself, in any form whatsoever. Who on earth could I use as a foil to keep me and my fictions at bay?

My hands were getting sweaty, but Magdalene stoically kept hold of them.

'In this way, you will re-author yourself,' she said. 'If it helps, think of it as splitting yourself in two. You will send these volleys of messages, from both sides, to me, but at no point will I respond. I'll be a silent observer. An outside witness.

'Over time, you will refine and shape this mass of material you generate about yourself. You must be merciless or you will not win the battle with what Horney calls the old self's pride system, the things it clings to for survival – the neuroses, self-hatreds, the idealised and despised notions of who you are, the constant search for glory. The critical eye required for this phase of crafting is what will allow you to excavate your new self.

'Some psychoanalysts, I must warn you, see narrative therapy of this nature as dangerous. They say it allows your own delusions to gain power, to appear legitimate while in fact being distorted through story. I believe, however, that until you have imprisoned the self's fictions in a form strong and stable enough to hold them, they will keep haunting you. Art's psychotherapeutic power comes from pouring cement into the well of your own past, letting it not destroy, but immobilise the darkest, dankest stuff down there. Once you can inspect your own history like an artifact, you're a step closer to liberating yourself from it.'

Magdalene fell silent.

I opened my eyes.

She did not tell me to close them again, but looked at me directly, her large brown eyes hardly blinking. Having our eyes open did not dilute the effect of there being some kind of unbroken connection through our hands – in fact, it made it stronger. It was as if we were growing a new limb between us. For me to separate myself from her now would mean instant death for us both. We would bleed out together on the floor.

'I will not sugarcoat it for you,' she said. 'Going ahead with this, you may feel like you're being possessed, over and over, by different spirits jumping in and out of your body, speaking through you, leaving you exhausted and bereft each time. But follow it where it takes you and you may finally be able to face your future. Wherever you choose to spend it.'

She loosened her grip. I watched her hands leave mine and steadied myself for the inevitable shock of pain, the sudden flow of blood at the stumps.

'Do you have any questions?' she said.

I said nothing. Our knees were still touching.

She waited a while, then in the warm room she pulled off her sweater, sparks of static electricity exploding around her body. I had an urge to cover her, as if she were on fire and only I could put out the flames. Instead I excused myself to go to the bathroom, where I splashed cold water on my face.

When I returned to her office, the spell had been broken. The blinds were open, the incense burned down to a sad stub.

'Vita, before you go, I have something to tell you,' Magdalene said. Her voice had shifted out of the low timbre she used in our sessions. 'Please don't share this with Deon, I need to inform all my clients first.'

She was leaning against her desk, inspecting her cuticles. Her fingers looked strange with the long nails removed.

'I'm emigrating to Australia,' she said. 'You might know the town. Mudgee? A few hours from Sydney, I believe. I've been offered a job as in-house counsellor for a mining company. I thought they'd run a mile when I mentioned some of my methods, but they're desperate. Apparently nobody else wants the job.'

I couldn't speak, and she perhaps misinterpreted my silence as judgement.

'I know,' she said. 'Here I am helping all of you get over your white guilt so you can go on living here, and I'm taking off for a different promised land for whites. But I haven't been happy since coming home. I loved living in Germany. I liked relating to people on another level, without always being held to my own history. I feel I'm stuck in a moralising identity here, like a school prefect.'

She realised the tape recorder was still on and switched it off.

'I want to keep working with you remotely, if you agree,' she said. 'This exercise I've given you is when the biggest break-throughs can happen, and in fact it works better if I don't see the client during the process. It lets me truly be an imagined audience. It doesn't matter how long it takes you to finish it. I will be there until the end.'

I still was unable to speak. Very slowly, I lowered myself onto the chair opposite her desk.

She sighed and collapsed into her own chair, swivelling it around to face me. 'I have had, since I was a young girl, the same dream of wandering in a landscape that is being mined for something,' she said. 'Dug up. In my own therapy, my mentor identified it as the fear of being found out for who I really am. When I looked up images of this coalmine at Mudgee, it seemed already familiar to me. As a place that has haunted me. Looking at it, I was reminded that each and every one of us contains a whole world of suffering.'

I understood that in telling me this, she was sharing a more intimate part of herself. It made me feel brave. I needed to say something that would prompt a further intimacy.

'I'm glad you're leaving,' I said. 'It makes me see that I can give myself permission to leave South Africa too. Love is the one thing that can trump country, the one explanation people will accept for changing your mind, your nationality.'

She looked suddenly concerned. It was the look of a therapist who has for the first time picked up on a crucial warning sign in a patient, who is realising that she may have inadvertently put herself in harm's way.

'Your degree of acceptance of this next phase of our work together will determine its success,' she said warily, trying to get us back into neutral territory. 'Sometimes we process our neuroses as physical objects. Like a kidney stone being expelled from the body, causing great pain in its passage but giving relief once it's out.' She woke her computer, typed something into my file. 'The tapes, of course, are yours if you want them.'

I tried a different tack and told her I remembered her Xhosa name, the name by which she'd been introduced to all of us at school, before she changed it to Magdalene.

'Don't say it,' she said with a cautionary look. 'You will butcher it.'

I said it anyway.

Her mouth tightened. 'That's not my name,' she said. 'My parents really did call me Magdalene. On my mother's side there was a white grandmother and I was named for her. But that teacher insisted I must have an African name, so I made one up.'

'Magdalene,' I said softly, but she didn't hear me. Her phone was ringing. She was no longer with me, no longer mine.

As the weather warmed up, I interviewed for several jobs in Boston. I didn't need a salary. What I did need was the airlessness of a job, the diverting boredom that would drive any lesser man to despair. If I couldn't make meaning out of my life, I could at least make money. My coffers were full, but like a child building a sandcastle I wanted to keep squeezing new blobs onto the bulbous pile. It would be my only distraction from Kitty.

Eventually I was offered a management position at a firm that manufactured microelectronics. I suspect they gave me the job because during the interview I uncharacteristically regaled them with stories about Pompeii. They were staid corporate types who wished they were something else, and I played my hand. They hoovered it up, taking my candy for the morbidly curious. You say the word Pompeii and people go weak at the knees.

Leaving the building, I felt sick for cheapening my experience with Kitty, for trading on it, and I vowed not to speak of it again. A vow I kept until we began this correspondence.

After graduation, I bought the townhouse in which I still live, on the north slope of Beacon Hill. Change has never been my strong suit.

I started work at the firm, kept my head down.

I spent Saturdays in the library stacks on the college campus downriver, reading archaeology journals with an eye out for Kitty's name—in vain, for I found nothing.

But then I came upon evidence of her research somewhere I hadn't expected: in the university alumni magazine, to which I subscribed. In the June issue there was a profile of her work, and an accompanying photograph. It showed her excavating the votive niche on the wall of the Garden of the Fugitives, her arms wiry and tanned, her black hair in a braid. I recognized the picture. It was one I had taken, using her camera, only weeks before she asked me to leave.

The start of the article documented things I already knew, or which were not a giant leap for me to imagine, however painful. After a long engagement, Kitty and Sogliano were to be married later that summer in a small ceremony in the Garden of the Fugitives. She would not be carrying a bouquet; in keeping with ancient Roman tradition, they planned to give their guests rose garlands instead.

In the more in-depth sections on Kitty's research, however, I was finally let into the secret of the full significance of what she had discovered in the Garden. Not just that roses had been grown commercially in the market garden for use in perfumes and garlands, but *who* may have grown them.

Kitty described to the interviewer her hunch, after the discovery of the statuettes of Mercury and Maia, that the rose garden might have been owned or managed by a freedman, a slave who had been given or purchased his freedom. 'The cult of Mercury and Maia was one of the few religious cults in Pompeii to allow slaves to play a role in ceremonies,' she said in the article. 'Slaves could even act as office-bearers for this cult. This prepared certain slaves for a possible future life as freedmen, by letting them take part in the civic and religious life of the city.'

She went on to say that the small house built on the plot had puzzled previous excavators for seeming to contain two discrete dwellings. She had, from early on, suspected this was because one half of the house had been a perfume workshop, and the other the living quarters for the shop owner, but she didn't have the evidence to support her theory. The Naples National Archaeological Museum did not yield the missing pages of the original excavation report, and she had been about to give up her search for them when the museum's curator made a surprise visit to the site.

'It was raining that morning,' she told the interviewer. 'The curator and I took shelter in the shed built to protect the body casts from the elements, at the bottom of the garden. That's where he showed me a glass perfume bottle with a fluted neck. He said he'd found it stored in the collections with the excavation log from the plot next door. But there was nothing in that log mentioning a perfume bottle, which suggested to us both that it had been found on the fugitives' plot and wrongly cataloged.'

It was the raised seal on the base of this bottle that had given her a crucial clue to the possible identity of the fugitives, Kitty said. Inside the entrance to what she believed was once the perfume workshop was the remnant of an inscription, faded beyond legibility and not mentioned in the excavation notes. The seal on the perfume bottle matched what could still be seen on the wall, and it was fully legible: *Finest perfume from the workshop of the freedwoman Idaia.*

Beneath it was the rose symbol used by the wealthiest perfumer in the city, Gnaeus Alleius, to stamp all perfume vessels produced in his many workshops. This man, Kitty said, was known to have freed several of his slaves the year before the volcano's eruption, while thinking himself, wrongly, to be on his deathbed.

Some of these slaves, as freedmen, went on to run workshops

for him as part of his perfume empire. Once a slave attained his freedom, it was common practice for him to keep close business ties with his former master. For freedmen, it was often the only way to survive economically in a society bound by webs of patronage.

Yet as far as she knew, there was only one other documented case of a woman in this role: a freedwoman named Umbricia had run a workshop for her ex-master, the main producer of Pompeii's famous fish sauce.

'So for me it was an exciting discovery that a freedwoman had run the perfume workshop,' Kitty said in the article. 'It suggests freedwomen played a more active role in the city than has been believed, even though under Roman law, women were discouraged from making economic decisions without a male guardian's consent, whether they were freeborn, freedwomen or slaves—due to the belief that they had "lightness of mind."'

The shrine in the Garden wall, she went on, raised the possibility that freedwomen may also have played a role in the cult of Mercury and Maia, something that had not previously been considered. 'It makes sense,' she said, 'given that Maia, Mercury's mother, is the goddess of growth, the one who makes the flowers bloom.'

The interviewer asked Kitty if she believed the freedwoman Idaia might be among the bodies discovered in the Garden.

Kitty would not commit, saying it was currently impossible to prove this scientifically. She did, however, mention that one of the body casts looked to be wearing a pilleus, a conical hat worn by freedmen and occasionally by freedwomen for several years after being manumitted by their master. The figure wearing the hat was the one propped on its elbow at the edge of the group, surveying the destruction – always assumed to be a man.

'You're saying it might be Idaia?' the interviewer prompted.

Again Kitty would not be fully drawn. She spoke of her colleague Rebecca Birkin's determination not to let conjecture rob the bodies of their true identities.

But she went on to say she did think it likely that Idaia and her family would have stayed behind in the city to protect their rose garden and perfume workshop. When Vesuvius exploded, they would have sought shelter from the rain of pumice and lithics inside the workshop. As the lapilli accumulated, they would have been forced outside due to the threat of the roof collapsing. By then it would have been too late to leave.

Kitty pointed out that Idaia had been free for less than a year before the eruption. If the children in the group were hers, and if they were boys, they would have grown up to be full citizens, with the right to vote and stand for elected office. Given their ages, they would have been born while Idaia, still a slave, was unable to marry (though sometimes masters allowed their slaves to form de facto couples, in order to produce slave offspring). Freedwomen, however, *were* allowed to marry. One of the men in the group may have been Idaia's husband.

It was also possible, Kitty said, that the children were slaves themselves, purchased by Idaia to help run her new business. In those times, very rich estates owned thousands of slaves, the well-off owned hundreds, and even poor families owned a few.

There was one more twist to Kitty's findings. The Garden of the Fugitives had been named by Rebecca for those seeking to escape the devastation around them. Kitty said there might be an accidental irony in that choice, a possible double meaning to the name. She described the faint marks on the forehead of one of the casts, usually thought to have been created by headgear or jewelry pressed against the person's face at death. Kitty had begun to wonder if in fact this person might have been a slave runaway, recaptured and branded on the forehead by his master with the letters FUG, for *fugitivus*, another common practice. As a consequence, that slave may have been cheaper at resale, and a freedwoman just starting out on her own life after slavery could afford to buy him.

Looking at that article now, the paper as yellowed and thin as my own skin, I feel a terrible sorrow that it is one of the few remaining documents of Kitty's work. She was so focused, so certain she was onto something. She was making her very own declaration of independence.

We all metabolize the world and its injustices at a different rate. What was it that Magdalene said? We are all accountable to different phantoms from the past.

My parents were shocked at how easily I left South Africa behind. As easily as stepping out of a coat and letting it fall to the floor. I slipped the brutal ties and returned permanently to the second country of my childhood without warning, without a second thought, within days of my final session with Magdalene.

I was just in time for Christmas, and tried to persuade my parents we should spend it in Mudgee. They said no reluctantly, they had unbreakable plans. So I rented a car and went alone.

In their eyes, I think, the suddenness of my decision had undermined my previous attempt to engage with our old home-land, made it seem the passing fad of a person not sufficiently serious. I'd dropped film as a medium; now I'd dropped an entire country, a life history. Inauthenticity was a bugbear for them both, and no good art could come of it, my mother liked to say. Their own disappointment must have been part of it. By leaving I had also destroyed their fantasy of return.

Of course they didn't know that all I'd done was swap one obsession for another.

On a hot day in early January, anticipating Magdalene's arrival, I drove out to the open-cut mine where she had taken the job. I couldn't get in – all the entrance gates were locked – but from a nearby viewing point at the top of a hill, I could see across the landscape that had haunted her dreams.

It was a visual feast. The land was grey and black, from the undoing of the farm that had preceded it. Diggers moved erratically as if in a child's sandpit, falsely primitive in a virtual age. I watched as the overburden and the interburden were stripped away. The previously compact soil, packed over geological time into an airless layer, swelled on its spoil pile, expanding, breathing.

That night I, too, dreamed of ledges and paths winding down to pits filled with rainwater that reflected the sky. It was not a nightmare. It seemed right, a relief to be found out for who I really was.

I waited for Magdalene to arrive in Mudgee. She never did. She had vanished.

Years into my new life here, the elderly patriarch of the olive farm died. When the contents of his grand residence – the things the children and grandchildren didn't want – were auctioned off, I went along to stickybeak.

Among the antique furniture and ugly family heirlooms were boxes and boxes of flaked stone tools the old man had collected from all over his farm and the wider region. The only accompanying paperwork was a few receipts showing he had bought some of them from the coalmine's holding room, the place they put the things they found in the ground that they weren't sure what to do with, for a couple of dollars apiece.

Nobody bid on the stone tools. Outside the house, there was a queue for the sausage sizzle, and free sunscreen was offered from a giant dispenser, one white squirt at a time. I was back, it appeared, to where I'd started.

I have for a long while now been the head of the Thirle clan. A clan consisting only of me. The very end of the line. A whole dynasty whittled down to a single childless survivor.

By leaving you everything in my will, I do not mean to make our relations filial, to turn you into a reluctant daughter, unless that's what you want to be. You said in an early letter that you had watched me searching for Cordelia, the one who has not salted the meat. It made me smile at the time, and think that I had been right to make contact again.

An unexpected boon of our narrative connivance has been the chance to spend time with my younger self, to farewell him while also farewelling you. Before we started this correspondence, that heartbroken young man had felt to me like a stranger. I believe Magdalene was right about us being forsaken if we cannot find our way back to forgiveness of our earlier selves. A remarkable woman, was she not?

Out of the blue, soon after I'd seen the article about Kitty, an invitation to her wedding arrived for me in the mail. There was no accompanying note, just a thick-edged card inviting me, in English and Italian, to the rehearsal luncheon and the wedding ceremony itself.

The date was only six weeks away. It smacked of a last-minute invitation. Regardless, I sent an RSVP immediately, following her cue by including no note of thanks or personal inquiry as to her health and happiness.

The anxieties set in later. I worried about what I would do if her mother was there, and how I should approach Sogliano, what exactly he knew. Should I embrace Kitty on seeing her or shake her hand? Or neither? I agonized over what to wear, and had my hair cut in a new style that did not suit me. The final week before my flight went by as slowly as molasses.

The morning I arrived in Pompei was a feast day. From the Sanctuary of the Madonna of the Rosary came the sound of hundreds of people singing and praying together. Pilgrims come to ask for Our Lady of Pompeii's blessing, and a miracle or two, in the presence of the church's relics: a thorn from Jesus's crown, a section of the Holy Cross.

I had booked myself a room in a mediocre hotel, ignoring the classier suggestion printed on the back of the invitation.

For a couple of days and nights I lay low, not even venturing into the ruins for fear of seeing Kitty before I was ready. To survey the scene before anybody noticed I was there, I cautiously joined the locals for the passeggiata, the evening stroll, along Via Plinio, which followed the southern boundary of the excavations. Most of the wedding guests were staying at the Hotel Vittoria, and I observed the entrance from the café across the square. I recognized a few faces from college, friends of hers who had not known me well, and was heartened to see among them the skating partner who had dropped her on the ice. So Kitty *was* in the mood for exculpation.

I watched Professor Abbiati struggle on the stairs with his walking stick. He was an old man nearing the end of his purposeful time on earth, yet still I was envious of him. He would have been one of the first people Kitty thought to invite, in gratitude for his role in bringing her and Sogliano together.

During the quiet hours of the siesta, I inquired at the Vittoria's front desk for Mrs. Lushington, and was told that nobody of that name was staying there. I hoped—prayed—she was back in a heavy drinking phase and hadn't been invited.

The night before the rehearsal luncheon, I didn't sleep, not even for a minute. I lay awake watching the moon rise and fall outside the window, my heart like an insect rattling in my throat. In the morning, I shaved carefully at the basin in my room and put on my tuxedo. My head was thick with sleeplessness. My eyes were tinged red. I did not look my best.

On my way to the old city, I went into the Sanctuary and knelt before the shrine. Then I took the same path down toward the ruins that Kitty and I had taken together on our very first morning in Pompeii.

Everything green was moving back and forth in the wind, shrubs and bushes, vines and trees. I passed through the Porta Marina, and took my time at the entrance to the main Forum, balancing like a tourist on the flagstones built across its entrance so very long ago, to stop wagons from entering a square that had always been reserved for pedestrians.

To the north was the cone of Mount Vesuvius, the rim of Somma beside it. I blurred my vision, imagining what Vesuvius had looked like in ancient times when it was a single giant mountain, not yet diminished by its own eruptions.

At the Via Stabiana I took a right toward the Triangular Forum, a smaller public square perched dramatically atop the spur of the prehistoric lava flow on which the town had been built.

It was on the raised limestone base of the ruins of the Doric temple at the southern edge of the square that the luncheon was to be held. A show of Sogliano's power in part, for the temple was among the oldest buildings in the city, with spectacular views of the Bay of Naples and out over the plain to the Lattari Mountains. But the location also held private significance for the couple. I thought of the evening I had first seen them together in the nearby Theater complex. The bell tone of the phonolite. Kitty's wide-open eyes.

I arrived at the luncheon purposefully late. People were milling about on the lawn beside the rows of orphaned colonnades, some of them toppled by the earthquake of AD 62 and never properly rebuilt before the whole city was buried. Garlands of roses hung between the columns, just as they would have to celebrate a wedding thousands of years before. Tables had been set up under a marquee on the temple's base.

There were a lot of guests. Local workers and their families, functionaries of the Pompeii bureaucracy, Sogliano's colleagues, Kitty's friends. Perhaps the ceremony the following day would be smaller, for I wasn't sure all those people would fit into the Garden of the Fugitives. With a spike of consternation, I wondered if I'd been invited to the ceremony too or only the luncheon, one among many obligatory invitees. I could not think straight, nor recall what had been printed on the invitation.

Kitty and Sogliano were greeting people at the base of the steps leading up to the temple ruins. I kept moving around until I found the best place from which to observe, close enough to see her and hear what she was saying but out of her line of sight.

She looked different. It wasn't just the effect of her dress, a deep peach color that made her complexion glow. Nor was it the makeup she was wearing, unusually for her. Her face looked as if it were beginning to set, like a cake baked at just the right temperature. She had not aged since I'd last seen her, but she had matured. There was a confidence to her movements that had not been there before. She was becoming solid, a woman with something to say to the world, taking possession of what was rightfully hers, among them the man by her side. Even the red valerian flower tucked behind her ear was a sign not of girlishness, but of staking a claim.

Watching her, I missed the old Kitty, the one I'd helped mold and create, but I felt in awe of the new Katherine—I heard her introduce herself as such to one of Sogliano's family members. How would this accomplished, settled, married woman have space in her life for me? For weeks I had been plotting how to worm my way back into her confidence, but here before me was proof that she needed nobody, least of all me. All I had to bargain with were old loyalties, a smidgen of guilt, a pinch of indebtedness. It would have to do.

'He's started jogging,' she was saying to an American couple I didn't recognize, in response to their compliment on her fiancé's healthy appearance. Next to her, Sogliano was engaged in a conversation in Italian.

'It's a craze, it will soon pass,' she said. 'He thinks he's found the secret to eternal youth!' The couple asked if she jogged too. 'No, but I hike sometimes, while he's running up Vesuvius, all the way to the top and back,' she said. 'He's going later—I know, the day before the wedding. He says it will stop him getting cold feet about tomorrow.' They all laughed.

'So it *was* you,' somebody said behind me.

I turned slowly.

Zelda's alcoholic flush was back with a vengeance. She appeared to be several drinks deep already. 'You've got some nerve showing up. But then so do I. Wasn't invited, came anyway.' She glanced over at Kitty and Sogliano, surrounded by wellwishers.

'She knows everything,' Zelda said cryptically. She smiled, and her lips cracked.

I mumbled an excuse and lit out for the stone bench at the very edge of the bluff, which I knew was hidden from view. It was not too late to leave without Kitty knowing for sure I'd been there.

When I pushed through the brambles, a woman was already sitting on the bench, her upper body folded over her knees. She sat up on hearing me approach. It was Rebecca.

I had no choice but to take a seat beside her. We sat in silence, looking out at the flat ocean shading to topaz in the shallows of the bay.

'Kitty told me she'd decided to invite you,' she said eventually. 'The mystery is why you came.'

I see Rebecca now as she looks out at the sea from the brink of that steep cliff. She did not know what was still to come to her, that I would soon award her the first grant from the Kitty Lushington Foundation, having not yet formulated my age criterion. She did not know that there were hundreds of skeletons waiting for her in the caverns beside the beach at Herculaneum. Nor that one day she would become Sogliano's first and only wife, her reward for remaining loyally infatuated with him, regardless of the rumors, which he could never quite dispel, that he had been with Kitty on the volcano's summit the evening before they were to be married.

Rebecca shifted beside me on the bench. The past few years, she must have been hoping, like me, that the day of Kitty and Ettore's wedding might never arrive. She pinched her cheeks for color. 'Shall we head back?' she said. 'It's either that way or over the edge.'

I accompanied her to the throng of guests, but soon afterward I slunk away to my hotel.

I had not eaten a thing all day, and the drug of high hunger made my mind feel preternaturally clear. I asked the young man at the reception desk if I could borrow his scooter, said I'd pay him for the gas.

Off I sped into the traffic of the autostrada. I took the exit at the base of Vesuvius, then chugged up the winding road on its western flank until it was no longer paved, and then as far as the bike would take me on the dirt.

I continued to the top on foot. It was wild up there. Primal. The lava fields were covered with vegetation; even the red valerian had made it all the way up the slopes. I followed the thin track around the exposed rim of the crater. This was long before the authorities built a fence to keep people from getting too close. Rocks from my footfalls tumbled down into the chasm.

A bird called out, a whitethroat perhaps, marking its territory.

Two fumaroles puffed away within the gray center of the volcano, the steam white and pure.

Spartacus had led the slaves' revolt from his camp on the volcano's slopes, back when it was thickly wooded, a good place to hide. Now the great cone was nothing but a ruined ashy bowl within the semicircular ridge of Mount Somma, the collapsed outer caldera.

I found a good vantage point from which to survey the path. King of my domain, perched at the highest point of the mountain that the people of Pompeii had believed was home to Bacchus, god of wine and festivity, whose cults were orgiastic, destabilizing, designed to overthrow the social order, if only for a night or two.

The sun moved lower. I waited for Sogliano, unsure what exactly I would do when he appeared. He did not arrive. The wind dropped.

I will never forget the look on Kitty's face on hearing her name spoken at the summit by a man who loved her. The wrong man.

It was her faithless fear of me that made the ground fall away beneath her feet.

Fireworks rocketed into the sky above the shimmering metropolis far below, small pops reverberating in the air.

I am, my dear Vita, always yours,
Royce

In ancient times, was it not often the master who was illiterate, and the slave who could read and write? Who corresponded on his master's behalf, speaking not only of but for him?

If I am sorry for anything it's for making you into my plaything, the accessory of my recovery. But I don't think you would have wanted me to apologise, Royce. You would be proud of me, proud of my ruthlessness in getting what I want, glad to know I have created *something*, even if that creation has also destroyed you.

The radiator is hissing quietly in your Beacon Hill townhouse. Through the window of your bedroom, I can see the Christmas lights strung up between the old-fashioned black lampposts. The snow came early this year, and is falling heavily, smothering the sounds of the evening traffic. I took a long walk this afternoon across the white expanse of the Common, all the way to Frog Pond, where the summer spray pool is now frozen in place as an ice rink.

I have opened a bottle of Sauternes from your cellar. Yes, the '83. It is delicious. It tastes to me like ripe apricots, fruit of original sin. Or pearls dissolved in vinegar, which, you once told me, Caligula, the monster emperor of Rome, liked to drink before he threw his enemies off the cliffs at Capri.

On the wall opposite your bed is the black-and-white aerial photograph of the Garden of the Fugitives, the one Kitty gave to you all those years ago.

It is the first thing I see in the morning and the last thing I see at night, before laying my head on your soft pillow. I thought of taking it down, but I have found it gives me pleasantly barren, flat, guiltless dreams. So for now I will leave it there.

Yours,
Vita

Acknowledgements

Thank you to Simon Prosser for believing in this book from the beginning, and to Hermione Thompson, Anna Ridley, Hannah Ludbrook and Ellie Smith at Penguin Random House.

My deepest thanks to Sarah Chalfant, Charles Buchan and Jackie Ko at the Wylie Agency, and to Ben Ball and Meredith Rose for being by my side every step of the way through the hall of mirrors.

For friendship and moral support over the years, thank you to Jessica Berenbeim, Alex Massouras, Joanna Jeffery, Adrienne Minster, Hisham Matar, Diana Matar, Owen Sheers, Peter Hobbs, Sarah Hall, Gayle Rutherfoord, Sally Munro, Monalisa Sam, Catherine Black, Brenda Parker, Mike Swanson, Felicity Swanson, Mary Haw, Nadia Davids and Loula van der Westhuizen. Special thanks to Stephen Watson and Alison Lowry for setting me on this path.

My love and thanks to the Munting family and the Witthuhn family.

Thank you to Ken and Teresa Dovey, Lindiwe Dovey, Robert Mayes and Chiara Dovey-Mayes for unwavering support. For the joy they bring to my life, I thank my husband, Blake Munting, and our boys, Gethin and Arlen.

Sources

I have used artistic licence and taken many liberties with historical facts, details and geographies in my invented narrative. Aspects of the research done in Pompeii and Herculaneum by fictional characters in this book were inspired by the work of three extraordinary women: Wilhelmina Mary Feemster Jashemski, Sara C. Bisel and Estelle Lazer (who continues to do pioneering work on the human remains of Pompeii). I drew extensively on their articles and books in researching those sections of the novel, in particular: Sara C. Bisel, Jane Bisel, Shelley Tanaka, Paul

Dennis, *The Secrets of Vesuvius* (1990); Wilhelmina F. Jashemski, *The Gardens of Pompeii: Herculaneum and the Villas Destroyed by Vesuvius* (1979); Wilhelmina F. Jashemski, *A Pompeian Herbal: Ancient and Modern Medicinal Plants* (1999); Wilhelmina F. Jashemski & Frederick G. Meyer (eds.), *The Natural History of Pompeii* (2002); Estelle Lazer, *Resurrecting Pompeii* (2009).

I also drew on the following books about Pompeii for historical background and details: Joanne Berry, *The Complete Pompeii* (2007); Jean-Paul Descoeudres (ed.), *Pompeii Revisited: The Life and Death of a Roman Town* (1994); Matt Donovan, *A Cloud of Unusual Size and Shape: Meditations on Ruin and Redemption* (2016); Charles Pellegrino, *Ghosts of Vesuvius* (2004); Ingrid D. Rowland, *From Pompeii: The Afterlife of a Roman Town* (2014).

The sections on German vocabularies of guilt are drawn from aspects of the work of psychotherapists Helmut Radebold, Margarete Mitscherlich and Alexander Mitscherlich.

A number of sources provided me with food for thought in the process of creating my characters, though I do not necessarily endorse all viewpoints expressed in these works. I have occasionally alluded to, paraphrased or made mention of specific terms used by certain of these authors: Chimamanda Ngozi Adichie, *Americanah* (2013); Elif Batuman, *The Idiot* (2017); Burkhard Bilger, 'Ghost Stories', *The New Yorker* (12 September 2016); Brené Brown, *The Gifts of Imperfection* (2010); Pascal Bruckner (trans. Steven Rendall), *The Tyranny of Guilt: An Essay on Western Masochism* (2010); Inga Clendinnen, 'The History Question: Who Owns the Past?', *Quarterly Essay* (Issue 23: September 2006); Patricia Ticineto Clough & Jean Halley (eds.), *The Affective Turn: Theorizing the Social* (2007); J.M. Coetzee & Arabella Kurtz, *The Good Story: Exchanges on Truth, Fiction and Psychotherapy* (2015); Vincent Crapanzano, *Waiting: The Whites of South Africa* (1985); Richard Delgado & Jean Stefancic (eds.), *Critical Race Theory: The Cutting Edge* (1995); *The Economist*, 'What the Führer Means for Germans Today' (19 December 2015); Sigmund Freud, *Delusion and Dream* (trans. Helen Downey 1921); Avery F. Gordon, *Ghostly Matters: Haunting and the Sociological*

Imagination (2008); Elizabeth Gumport, 'Female Trouble', *n+1* (Issue 13: Winter 2012); Yuval Noah Harari, *Sapiens: A Brief History of Humankind* (2014); Hugh Haughton, 'Introduction', Sigmund Freud's *The Uncanny* (2003); Celia Hunt, *Therapeutic Dimensions of Autobiography in Creative Writing* (2000); Jeanne-Marie Jackson, 'The South African Novel of Ideas', *n+1* online (5 October 2015); David Lester & Rina Terry, 'The Use of Poetry Therapy', *The Arts in Psychotherapy* (Vol. 19, 1992); Hélène Opperman Lewis, *Apartheid: Britain's Bastard Child* (2016); Kim Mahood, 'Kartiya are Like Toyotas', *The Griffith Review* (Edition 36: April 2012); Kim Mahood, 'White Stigma', *The Monthly* (August 2015); Amedeo Maiuri, 'Last Moments of the Pompeians', *National Geographic* (November 1961); Ewald Mengel & Michela Borzaga (eds.), *Trauma, Memory, and Narrative in the Contemporary South African Novel: Essays* (2012); Claudia Roth Pierpont, 'Bombshells', *The New Yorker* (19 October 2015); Victoria Princewill, 'Hear Our Voice: Zadie Smith and the Problem of Her Single Story', *n+1* online (29 June 2017); Zadie Smith, 'Getting In and Out: Who Owns Black Pain?', *Harper's Magazine* (July 2017); Shelby Steele, 'The Age of White Guilt: And the Disappearance of the Black Individual', *Harper's Magazine* (November 2002); Chanoch Ze'evi (director), *Hitler's Children* (film, 2011).